THE

FAR DAWN

ALSO BY KEVIN EMERSON:

THE LOST CODE: BOOK ONE OF THE ATLANTEANS

THE DARK SHORE: BOOK TWO OF THE ATLANTEANS

EXILE

THE FELLOWSHIP FOR ALIEN DETECTION

THE
FAR DAWN

BOOK THREE OF THE ATLANTEANS

KEVIN EMERSON

KATHERINE TEGEN BOOKS
An Imprint of HarperCollins Publishers

Katherine Tegen Books is an imprint of HarperCollins Publishers.

The Far Dawn: Book Three of the Atlanteans

Library of Congress Cataloging-in-Publication Data
Emerson, Kevin.
  The far dawn : book three of The Atlanteans / Kevin Emerson.
    pages cm. — (The Atlanteans ; book 3)
  Summary: "Atlanteans Owen and Lilly navigate the frozen arctic hoping
to find the Paintbrush of the Gods—an Atlantean technology that can
reverse the course of climate change—before the evil Project Elysium
does"— Provided by publisher.
  ISBN 978-0-06-206286-4 (pbk.)
  [1. Science fiction. 2. Environmental degradation—Fiction. 3. Climatic
changes—Fiction. 4. Atlantis (Legendary place)—Fiction. 5. Arctic
regions—Fiction.] I. Title.
PZ7.E5853Far 2014   2014001879
[Fic]—dc23   CIP
                                                             AC

Typography by Torborg Davern
14 15 16 17 18   LP/RRDH   10 9 8 7 6 5 4 3 2 1
❖
First Edition

For Elliott

Before the beginning, there was an end
Three chosen to die

Three coffins on a gray beach.

To live in the service of the Qi-An
The balance of all things
Three guardians of the memory of the first people
They who thought themselves masters of all the
Terra

Simple boxes built from the wreckage piles.
The boards warped but still flecked with paint.
Three coffins at the edge of a cobalt sea.

Who went too far, and were lost
To the heaving earth
To the flood.

It has taken me two days to build them. Rusty nails pulled out with my teeth, hammered in with a rock now streaked with blister blood.

I don't know why I bothered.

I could have sunk them in the waves, like Leech,
In the smoke, like Elissa,
In the silence, like Anna,
In time, like my parents,
In the ice, like . . .

Three who will wait
Until long after memory fades.
And should the time come again—

But it won't.
This time, it is finally over.
This time, they are never coming back.
What's lost is lost.
Once, in a temple, beneath a lie, I said I wanted to be
true. I wanted to see truth.
I have been true.
But still I sit here, as gentle waves lick the coffin edges.
I have not set them afloat.
Because to do that, I'd have to see.
See the truth.
Of what is inside.
And I cannot face that alone.

PART I

[*GAMMA LINK CONNECTION LOADING* . . .
100%—welcome back to the Alliance Free Signal—*buff-
ering*—from the survivors in Heliad-7 of what we now
believe was an EdenCorp assault. They report that the
Three of Atlantean myth were actually in Desenna and
were seen escaping to the south. It is believed that Eden-
Corp is seeking the fabled Paintbrush of the Gods for
their secretive Project Elysium. There are whispers, too,
that some kind of exodus is about to take place from all
the Edens, that the domes are failing, and that the Eden
citizens will be traveling to somewhere called EdenHome.
There is still no word as to where this may be, but we've
heard ominous rumblings, because of the uranium stolen
from Cheyenne Depot and the rumor of the Ascending
Stars, that the rest of the planet may be in terrible danger.
We have tried to bring these reports to the Northern Federation, but so far, no one will listen. And so, we ask all of
you out there to stay vigilant, and, if you still believe in a
god, pray that the Three will succeed.]

"A JELLY BEAN CENTER!"

"Um . . ."

"Inside a cheese puff . . ." Lilly strained to hold the sail line as a gust smacked us sideways.

Above, the towering thunderhead loomed, blotting out the stars.

"Oh, right! And then dipped in chocolate!" I tugged my line while pressing the pedals in the floor of the craft. The swirling winds kept changing direction. I had to keep us aligned with them or we'd capsize.

"Yes! And called . . . ?"

"I know this! It's . . ." The craft responded slowly. The blue light of the vortex engine was dim. We'd flown almost two thousand kilometers since escaping from Desenna, over three days and nights. We needed a lightning charge to make it the rest of the way to the Andes. We had thought we'd be getting one from Heliad-7, except that Victoria had actually been planning to shoot us down all along.

"Here's a hint!" Lilly said through gritted teeth. "The song was: '*Once you get in the mix!*'"

Rain began to pelt us, fat monsoonal drops, drumming on the sails and becoming a deluge.

"I can't think of it!" I called over the driving water. "I'm not sure I ever had one. They sound so gross!"

Above, lightning spidered across the roiling cloud bellies. We were close, now. A bolt was bound to sniff us out soon. The big danger was if three bolts, or ten, found us at the same time and blew us into a million pieces. I arced in tight figure eights, trying to keep us a moving target.

Lilly brushed strands of wet hair from her face. Her sweatshirt and tank top and jeans were soaked. "They were! But not really! You just put the whole thing in your mouth and it tasted sort of like bubble gum."

"That's still gross!"

We'd been playing this game throughout the journey. Lilly and I knew, since Desenna, that we'd actually grown up during nearly the same years, and so we liked to quiz each other on candies and TV shows. It was all foggy from our time in cryo, but that made the game more challenging, and it gave us something to think about other than what we'd seen and where we were headed. There was only so much wondering and worrying we could do in a day. Lilly remembered more than me, probably because her memories hadn't been manipulated—

Elissa, Mom, cryo, Carey—

I shook my head, keeping the surge of painful thoughts away. There was so much, back there in the dark and fire. . . .

Elissa: my lost sister, rising out of her cryo tube.

Francine: not my mother, actually a technician in Paul's lab, where they'd manipulated my thoughts and hidden the fact that I'd been in cryo for twenty-five years.

Carey: shot for reasons we still didn't understand, his life escaping him on the balcony of the sunken hotel, Lilly and I giving him to the waves. Carey who'd been my enemy, then maybe my friend, but definitely the only one who cared about me, about the truth, even remotely as much as Lilly.

Lilly: who was all I had left.

The grief over Elissa, over Carey, came and went like tides; same for my bitter anger at Francine and Paul, and also violent thoughts of vengeance. I didn't share those with Lilly. It all combined to spin me in hopeless circles whenever we had a quiet moment. I let my guard down, either while flying through the dark or hiding from the sun.

Thinking about candy was much easier.

"Did it have the word *mix* in it?" I asked. "Oh, wait—" I felt a tingling on my arms, the hairs standing on end. I locked on Lilly's sky-blue eyes. "I think we've got one!" I looked up, trying to see where the invisible column of electricity was forming. We hadn't done this before. Would I even have time to dodge the bolt if it was too big, too strong—

But the sky exploded in white and it was on us before I could react. The bolt appeared fully formed between the mast and the clouds, a jagged wire of charge come to life. The craft vibrated and rocked. I held my breath, body clenched tight. It felt like, if I hadn't been blinded, I would have been able to see spaces between all the boards, the craft nearly bursting apart. Electricity buzzed around us, and my slow-healing rad burns tingled. The one on my scalp still ached almost all the time.

I heard the hiss of energy down the mast, then the reassuring whine of the mercury vortex. I opened my eyes to see it swirling at its brightest blue intensity, its magnetic propulsion at full effect.

"Okay!" I finally breathed. "Let's get out of here!" I repositioned my feet on the pedals, and maybe the relief of firing up the engine cleared my mind, because suddenly the name of the candy appeared. "Mixits!" I shouted, looking over—

Lilly was gone. The sail line she'd been holding flapped in the storm. "Lilly!" I grabbed the line and plunged the craft into a dive. I scanned the mists and water sheets and clouds, but there was only dark. Seconds, that was all we'd have before she'd hit the unseen ocean below. "LILLY!"

I pushed the pedals full to the floor, the newly charged vortex a miniature blue sun. Rain stung my face. The clouds whipped around me. The wind screamed.

I broke through and there was the oil-black sea, its debris-covered surface heaving with giant waves. Where was she? Was I too late? I leaned back, straining to level off, then banked in a wide circle. Could she have survived the fall? Even if she had, the water might have knocked her out. No, no, no, I couldn't lose her, not now, not after all we'd been through, after everyone we'd lost and not just like this, so random and stupid like none of the pain and suffering and effort had meant anything—

A light caught my eye, growing above me, like lightning, but . . .

Not.

I craned my neck and saw something illuminating the low layer of clouds, something turquoise. It brightened, and melted through.

Lilly appeared, bathed in blue light.

Not falling . . .

Flying.

The sight of her nearly made me scream or cry or both. Never mind how she was doing what she was doing. She was okay. That was all that mattered. The feeling made it hard to breathe. I couldn't even imagine surviving if she'd been gone.

A gust of wind knocked me sideways. I had to pay attention to flying or I'd end up in the water. I righted and made a slow circle, watching as Lilly lowered toward me. Her whole body was aglow, and when she got close enough, I could see that she was smiling in wonder.

"Are you okay?" I asked dumbly.

"Yeah!" she called. She spread her arms and did a somersault. It reminded me of the young girl I saw inside the Medium's skull with Rana. *We could play with gravity and space same as you might play with wind and water,* Rana had said. That girl had held something this same blue color in her palms and risen off the ground.

But Lilly's whole body was radiating, like that light was from inside her.

She swooped under the craft. I banked around and she darted up alongside. "Meet you back at the beach!" she shouted, laughing, and then arced up, out of sight in the rain and clouds.

I flew in the direction of shore, wiping sideways rain from my face. For a moment, there were only curtains of water and galloping fogbanks, and I wondered if I was even flying in the right direction, but then I saw the dark outline of a small abandoned town that had been half eaten by the sea. The fronts of the buildings along the water had all collapsed, leaving their rooms open to the air. Waves crashed against the rubble piles at their bases. Grasses and palm trees grew in the streets, on second floors. Vines wrapped through windows and over cock-eyed streetlights.

Lilly landed just south of town, on a high cliff with a thick canopy of trees that would protect us from the searing sun and prying eyes, while we tried to rest before another long night of flying.

I put the craft down and when I stepped out, Lilly, no longer glowing, met me with a hard embrace, the cold of our soaked clothes quickly warming between us. "Nice work," she said in my ear, and then we kissed. My body surged, a feeling that was the closest thing to joy I think I'd ever felt, a feeling I was amazingly getting used to over our days and nights together.

It also couldn't have been more different from the wells of sorrow I'd been sunk in at so many other times since we'd fled the death in Desenna. Dawn was always the worst. Lying in shadows trying to fall asleep after flying all night, with the faces of my lost family, of Carey, Seven, even little Colleen, waiting to greet me behind my eyes.

But between Lilly and me there was no more distance. No gills, no doubts, no differences even in our pasts. We were one against the world, and our kisses defied time. Holding each other now, our wet clothes stuck together, my hands rubbing her shoulders, her back, my lips exploring her chin, her neck, my body felt like it had a purpose so complete and obvious: no mystery, no technicians, no ancient DNA, just that I was meant to be here, now, like this, and our embrace seemed strong enough to keep the world at a distance.

"I love you, Lilly," I said for the sixth time since I'd uttered it inside EdenSouth.

"I love you, Owen," Lilly whispered back, her fifth time. Once I'd said it to her while she was sleeping.

And I felt so sure of it, so sure of us.

After a minute more of kissing, I said, "Mixits."

Lilly's smile glowed. "Ding!"

We arranged our blankets in the driest spot we could find. Rain hissed on the palm leaves. We lay down and tucked in and kissed more, and for a while I forgot all the dark and doubt and everything outside the warm space between us.

"So, what was that?" I asked a little while later. The rain had stopped, the leaves still dripping. Lonely birds called in the jungle behind us.

"Mmm," Lilly said sleepily. "You mean the flying?"

"Yeah." I squeezed her tighter. "I thought you were dead, I . . ." A shiver racked my body.

Lilly held me tighter. "The wind knocked me out of the craft, and I was falling and—I don't know—it was almost like instinct. I started to sing, the melody that calls the Terra, and as I sang it I felt this . . . understanding,

I guess. Like a connection to the air, to the ground, like I was part of all of it, not separate. And so then I just moved. With the wind, with gravity. It was such an amazing feeling." Lilly sighed. "I think we're seeing the world all wrong."

"How so?"

"I mean, not you and me. Everyone. Like, we're missing what it even means to be alive and part of something living. I felt connected to everything just now. Like we're all one being."

"That's amazing," I said, though in a way I felt jealous. When I wasn't feeling love for Lilly, all I felt was a lonely chill of loss and death. It was hard for me to believe that I was connected to anything in the world, other than her.

"I think the Atlanteans knew it," said Lilly. "I wonder if there's a way to give it back to the world. If we all felt like this . . . things might be different."

"Maybe we can," I said, and I was glad to hear this from Lilly. She'd wondered, days ago as we flew over Gambler's Falls, why we should save this world, with all its horrors. It was a feeling of pointlessness that I knew, like humanity wasn't worth it. But I felt like Lilly was— like we *were* worth it, and now she sounded like her old self, on a mission, and it made me love her even more.

"Ooh," said Lilly, "shooting star."

I looked up. "Missed it."

"Alien or trash?" Lilly asked.

"Mmmm . . ." We never knew. We just liked to guess together. "Three . . ." I counted down. "Two"—Seven never waited for one—"one . . ."

"Alien," we both said at the same time, and because we'd guessed the same, we kissed and then laughed, knowing how silly a game it was and yet not caring at all.

"Time to sleep." Lilly rolled over and I curled up behind her. "Another big day saving the world tomorrow."

"Right." I smiled. She sounded so content, finally getting to act on that fire she'd had in Eden. She'd yearned for this, to *do* something, to make a difference. I admired it, though I felt guilty inside that I'd never felt the same. Or maybe I had, too, before the cryo.

Soon I heard her breath slow. I tried closing my eyes, letting myself relax . . .

But there was Elissa.

Sinking in the ash . . . eyes popping open in her cryo tube . . . stumbling around the roof of the pyramid in Desenna, dead but alive.

I waited outside her classroom at the end of each school day.

I could see her now, in her favorite overalls, her hair in a braid.

Dad took us up to the high ledges that one night to

see a meteor shower that we'd heard about on the North-ern News Network. But the climb made his lungs bad. Elissa and I had to help him back down the carved rock steps, and Elissa started coughing, too.

In the dark night hours since Desenna, and during the lonely dawns, I'd pieced most of it back together. These memories, so many from the life I'd lived up until we'd gotten the black blood, a full life with a twenty-five-year pause between my near death from plague and when I arrived at Camp Eden. In between, my mind had been frozen in a trap of technicians and cryo dreams, just waiting to be sprung. Now, I was slowly putting each memory back into place.

Elissa always sat on the arm of the couch beside Dad for soccer games. That way she could jump off if there was a goal.

But even the good memories were like old puzzle pieces with frayed edges, and so when they were replaced, they didn't quite fit right:

Mom liked to make cookies during the game, to give her something to do because the competition stressed her out. We rooted for New Murmansk, because we liked their maroon and green uniforms, and Vivechkin, their star forward. Mom wasn't always happy, life would get her down . . . but she wouldn't have left.

Paul had tinkered with my memories, given me a mother who'd abandoned me.

She would never have left.

Removed my sister with a surgeon's precision, leaving only a strange cryo dream that had haunted me. Having Elissa back in my mind was a warm relief. . . .

We took that family trip in the winter one time, when the days were shorter and safer, to a set of hot springs a few hours north of Yellowstone that were gas free and safe to soak in. Elissa thought they smelled like eggs—

But it was never too long before the other memories would creep in.

Dead Elissa, her body lurching around the top of the pyramid in Desenna, lifeless and cold.

Mom and Dad. They're . . . probably dead.

The agony was always there, lurking since Desenna, threatening at any point to rise like a wave and drag me down from the high of being with Lilly to the murky depths where I didn't feel connected to anyone or anything. And when I sank beneath it, I felt more alone than a single star in the black above. Even the warmth from Lilly beside me wasn't enough.

I pulled away from Lilly and quietly got up. I knew when my feelings went this way that sleep wasn't coming.

I walked out past the craft and sat on the edge of the cliff, dangling my legs over the rough black rock. The stars were beginning to fade, the horizon a pale blue. The last few thunderstorms flickered to the north and south, floating far out over the ocean like giant jellyfish.

How was I ever going to get past this feeling? That there was just me, alone in the universe. And no matter how much Lilly felt like we had a mission or a purpose, I couldn't help feeling like what did this Atlantean quest even matter? Who was it for? I would die, too, soon enough. Even if I somehow survived all this, then in thirty or forty years—maybe before that, if there was another pandemic. So what was the point? Why even bother? I had no family to go home to.

It was like Seven had said, *these are just the anthills and we're the ants and anybody who tells you otherwise is a liar.* She'd felt meaningless because she was taken from her time. I'd tried to tell her that maybe this was her time. That maybe she was here now because of a design, a plan.

But I'd said all that before I'd known that I was like her. Taken out of time, used. I understood her so much more now, Leech, too, but what did it matter? They were both gone. Gone forever. How could there possibly be a point to all this random death?

The only answer I could find, that I kept coming back to like a beacon in the dark, was that I would do it for Lilly. That, and . . . what else was I supposed to do? Where else could we go? There was no third option, like Seven had wished for. Paul would hunt us down, wherever we went, and even if we escaped him, just ran off and hid somewhere, the world might be doomed if he found the Paintbrush of the Gods first.

We had to press on. I had to keep going, even if thoughts like these would haunt me forever.

Elissa liked ponies. All her life she wanted to see a live horse.

She never did.

She never will.

I sat there, watching the sky brighten and warm, watching the seagulls circle, and tried to be still as the storm swirled around me.

For a while.

Owen.

I'd been staring into the rainbow-oil shimmer of the sea. The horizon had grown white and the searing golden sun had just cleared the horizon.

I blinked, refocusing, and found her before me, shimmering in the air, my siren, who I now knew was the Terra. She appeared as she had before, with her waist-length black hair, the simple crimson dress with a copper and turquoise belt, the pendant of a great tiger around her neck. The new sun made her ancient lavender eyes glow.

"Hi," I said, and then thought that was a dumb thing to say to a vision of a sort of before-the-gods god, but my brain was too fuzzy, and I added, "You look brighter."

You are getting closer, she said, her burning gaze steady on me, *but so is your enemy.*

"Paul." I looked over my shoulder, but Lilly still appeared to be asleep. "Did she call you?"

No, but I did hear her singing before and felt her awareness of Qi and An growing.

"Yeah," I said, "she kinda flew."

Yes. But it will not be enough.

The Terra's words sent a chill through me. "What do you mean?"

You are nearing the lair of a Sentinel. You must find it. And then we can speak more in the white realm.

"A Sentinel. In the Andes?"

Yes. Time grows short, Owen. Before the beginning there is always an end.

"I've heard that." I found myself growing frustrated. "I'm a little tired for riddles."

The Terra almost seemed to frown at this. Her light flickered.

You must be wary of the Three.

"Wary?"

The Three is a lie. It has always been.

"What's that supposed to mean?" I asked, but I also remembered Paul's words when he spoke to us in the canyon back in North Dakota: *The Three is a myth,* he'd said. And then he made it sound like I was somehow different. And I was; I'd been able to go inside Lilly's skull even though I wasn't the Medium.

"How can the Three be a lie?" I asked. "I mean, we were selected, and there are the skulls, the maps."

The Three is very real. But the promise of the Three is a lie, because the Three will fail.

"Okay . . . but technically there isn't even a Three anymore," I said. "Paul killed Leech."

That is irrelevant.

"How can it be irrelevant?"

You will see.

"Fine, but . . ." This cryptic talk reminded me of what Lilly had read in the temple beneath EdenSouth. The end of the inscription, the part that Seven couldn't read, had said:

We must be wary of the Terra's patience. For if we fail her too often, she may make plans of her own.

I'd been turning this over and over: Lilly was the Medium, the one who was supposed to communicate with the Terra, Leech had been the Mariner, and I was the Aeronaut, the pilot.

Except then I was the only one the Terra actually spoke to. "Am I part of your plan?" I asked. "Of some different plan than just the Three?"

The Terra looked over my shoulder. I heard Lilly stirring.

Find the Sentinel, and I will show you.

"Owen?" Lilly called groggily from behind me.

I turned to her. "Over here."

When I looked back, the Terra was gone.

I blinked for a second. My brain was so tired. I wondered if she'd been a hallucination. Except her strange words echoed in my head.

The Three is a lie. The Three will fail.

What did she mean? How could she even know that?

I got up and returned to Lilly, crawling under the blanket beside her.

"You okay?" she asked softly.

"Yeah," I lied. "Sun's up. Keep sleeping."

"Okay."

I kissed her cheek and she rolled back over.

The thermal winds picked up, carrying the acrid scent of tar off the water. I put my hands behind my head and stared up into the palm leaves and diagonal slices of sunlight.

At some point, I must have fallen asleep, but for what seemed like hours, I just lay there, turning over the Terra's words and nursing a deep, cold fear. After all this, could we really be doomed to fail?

2

WITH THE RISE OF A WANING MOON HALFWAY through that night, we saw the first outline of the Andes in the distance. We'd left the ocean behind just after sunset, crossing jungle uplands that soon gave way to barren, dry hills. The monsoon wet was gone. We were back in the desert world. We passed dust-crusted towns, and cities as still as stone. At one point, we gave a wide berth to a trio of campfires with dancing shadows that were soaked in hellish screaming.

While Lilly flew, I sunk into my head and envisioned the maps, Leech's Mariner knowledge, and we set our course for the high mountain marker. Leech had oriented to an earlier version of the earth, before the Paintbrush of the Gods had caused the land to shift. The Atlanteans had literally remade the planet but had destroyed themselves in the process. Paul had said that he could perfect their science. I wondered how that could be possible.

We'd been flying silent for a while, and I could feel

all the dark thoughts starting to wake. Finally, I said, "Three layers of millet cookie . . . marshmallow in between two . . ."

"Ooh," said Lilly, snapping out of a trance. "Um . . ." She thought while adjusting the sails.

"Strawberry cream between the others."

"Oh! Me-O-Mys!"

"Yes."

"I would kill for one of those right now. Or a whole box."

"Me, too."

Silence fell over us again. The appearance of the mountains meant we were getting close, close to something that felt dangerous, and with the Terra's warning, all too uncertain.

It also meant the end of these days together, of Lilly and me, in between worlds.

"Look," she said. I followed her finger and saw a bony spine running along a ridge below, a crumbled wall. "Inca?"

"Probably," I said. The wall mimicked our course, arcing from one ridge to the next, almost as if the Inca had made this same journey.

"Do you think he'll be there?" Lilly asked quietly, even though we were far too high for any stray person on the ground to hear us talking.

"I don't know," I replied, just as quietly.

I knew she meant Paul. He had Leech's old maps, his sketchbook, and the radial sextant that had allowed Leech to plot the course to the Andes temple. They had Lilly's Medium skull, too. But he didn't have the maps in Leech's head, like I did, the maps the Terra had given me when Leech died. So did he know the exact location? Maybe he'd figured out how to use the sextant. Or maybe Leech had also sketched the route in his journal. I wished I could ask him.

Crack!

I heard the echoes of Francine's gunshot in the cryo facility again. Saw Leech spasming back . . . and later sinking in the waves . . . How could Paul have done that? Were we all that expendable?

The Three will fail. . . .

And I had another worry, one that had been gnawing at me along with everything else. "I hope we're not just leading him right to it again," I said. That feeling was back, like we were being toyed with. Where were Paul and his fleet of hover copters right now? There could only be two reasons why they hadn't come after us since Desenna: because they were ahead of us or trailing us, and either way I felt all too certain that they were lying in wait again.

"What else can we do?" Lilly wondered aloud.

"Keep bearing toward that orange star," I said, pointing to the south and west.

"Betelgeuse," said Lilly.

"Yeah."

"Orion's shoulder," Lilly added. "A red supergiant. Like, a hundred times the size of the sun. Wouldn't that be amazing? To see something like that."

"Yeah."

"After those Mars missions back when we were kids, I always thought for sure we'd get to go into space, travel to the stars, find new planets to colonize and all that sci-fi stuff. I would have given anything to do that."

"I know," I agreed, except that before I was an Aeronaut, even just the height of a tall staircase freaked me out, never mind the idea of flying up and out of the atmosphere.

The mention of stars reminded me of something less romantic. I got up and moved to the mast. I'd tied a small piece of rope near the top.

Victoria's finger dangled from the end.

Looking at it reminded me of the sound. The sound that Mica's sacrificial knife had made, like tearing soaked cloth. The resistance I'd felt as the knife met bone . . .

I'd been drying the finger out each night while we flew, and then wrapping it tight while we slept, to keep bugs off it. The skin had shriveled now and turned a dead gray. It felt hard and rubbery, and had long since stopped leaking blood.

I reached into Dr. Maria's backpack and pulled out

the white-handled knife that Leech had given me. There were flecks of dried blood by its hilt, from Eden soldiers back in the Rockies, and I tried not to think about how this trip was feeling all too similar to that one. . . .

I turned the blade away and pressed it into the skin of the finger. There was a moment of resistance, then a slice of the dried tissue curled free. I held the finger against the edge of the craft and kept whittling, removing grayish layers of skin and muscle, letting the flakes be carried away by the wind. Each stroke of the knife made a papery tearing sound.

"That is beyond gross," Lilly commented.

"Yeah," I said through gritted teeth. The knife began to hit bone, and I worked more carefully, exposing the hard fibrous curves.

Soon I began to see the bar code.

Victoria had been a selectee. One of the very elite inside the Eden domes who'd been chosen for Project Elysium. For the trip to EdenHome, which Paul said was nearly prepared. They only needed the Paintbrush of the Gods to begin. But the location of EdenHome was secret. Victoria hadn't known, as she'd defected from Paul's plans years ago.

And there was still the other mystery, the one that had led the first people we'd met outside EdenWest to try to kill us: Harvey, Lucinda, and Ripley had wanted passage on the Ascending Stars. They were a rumor in

Heliad-7, of lights going up into space, of the gods leaving. Lilly and I figured it must have had something to do with leaving the Edens. Maybe the Ascending Stars were some sort of special aircraft that Project Elysium had built. Or satellites or drones to deploy weapons built from the uranium we knew Paul had stolen. Maybe he was building defenses against anyone who would try to stop them. I still didn't know what it added up to. The only thing we were sure of was that Paul needed the Paintbrush to succeed. So we had to find it first.

And maybe we'd need this bar code. To access some place we'd need to get into to stop Paul or, if we failed, maybe even to sneak into EdenHome. It was more likely that if we failed, we'd die; but, though I hadn't thought about it at the time, I realized now that one of the reasons I'd taken Victoria's finger was as a backup plan.

It had to do with one of the first things I'd thought about Lilly. Back when we'd had gills, I'd imagined us finding clean ocean together, living on a beach, a little paradise.

Even though we were Atlanteans with a mission, sometimes I wanted that vision with Lilly, to just be in love with her there. Sometimes I wanted that far more than I even wanted to save the world, even though it seemed impossible that one could exist without the other. And so I'd found myself thinking: if we weren't able to stop Paul, maybe we could use the bar code to sneak into

Project Elysium and be a part of EdenHome. Sometimes it was more than just a thought and almost a wish. We'd be together, and really, how terrible would that be?

Except that it would betray all the people—friends, family, and allies—who had suffered and died for our mission, a list so long now that it took the two of us to remember it. From Anna to Dr. Maria, Leech, and even Seven, to those whose fates we didn't know for sure, like Evan and the CITs, Robard and the other Nomads, our parents, brothers, and sisters . . .

But even though I hated the thought of letting them down, of those lives and sacrifices wasted, hadn't I also suffered and lost? Sure, we'd be turning our back on the rest of the world, but it wasn't like the world had been that kind to us. After all that I'd had to go through, was I really expected to risk my life just for some mission that I'd never even chosen?

Maybe I had chosen it, though. Sure, it started because of my genes, but since then, over and over, when I could have just run, could have just ignored what I was, I hadn't. Or I could have stayed in EdenWest or in Desenna . . . except all those places were traps. Paul would have strapped me to his machines, Francine would have captured me, Victoria would have had me killed. I'd had a choice, but by doing what was right for the mission, I had also been trying to survive.

And so, sometimes I wondered: What would happen if

there came a moment when I had to choose between those two things: survival or the mission? Or worse, between the mission and Lilly? I felt like I knew the answer, like it was obvious, but what kind of hero did that make me?

I finished cleaning the finger, then cut free the single bone that was striped with the black lines of bar code. I wrapped a thin strip of leather around it, and then tied that to a loop of twine. I knotted it around my neck.

"Like it?" I said to Lilly.

"Very savage," she said.

I smiled, but the word stung. *Savage*. I knew what she meant, but . . . it reminded me of bodies strung on walls, piles of corpses in dry riverbeds. Savage was like ruthless, selfish. . . .

I relieved Lilly and focused on flying instead. As we shifted positions and she handed me the sail lines, we kissed, and it was a momentary island of safety, and yet—

The Three will fail.

"What is it?" Lilly asked.

I realized I'd sort of paused in the middle of the moment. "Nothing."

I'd told her about the Terra's visit and about her instructions to find the Sentinel, but I hadn't told Lilly the part about the lie. We had enough to worry about, and I didn't want her to know that I was doubting our mission or for her to doubt it, too. But I couldn't shake the Terra's comments.

It helped to have the sail lines in my hands. The feel of wind and movement brushed the thoughts back. We rose steadily, the ground beneath us becoming more rocky and precarious. An hour later the peaks had risen around us, and we began to wind our way up deepening valleys, following each branch into the moonlit mountains. The air became cold and thin, and the winds less predictable.

The stars begin to glimmer like glass beads. The Milky Way gained depth, feathery folds, and I breathed faster to get oxygen.

"We have to stay hydrated," said Lilly. She dug into the canvas bags of supplies at the front of the craft. Luckily, whoever had been tasked with stocking us for our journey back in Desenna hadn't known that Victoria was planning to kill us all along, because we were flush with water, mango, millet crackers, tapir jerky.

Lilly passed me one of the filmy plastic water bottles a hundred times recycled. The mineral-tasting sips reminded me of the cenote, of the cool and the trees and the sun of Desenna, where, for a moment, I'd had family. It also reminded me of Seven's lips, of her urgent kisses. . . .

But then I pictured her leaking blood and falling from my sight.

"You okay?" said Lilly.

I shook my head. It seemed like every thought I had

eventually led to some dark corner. "Sure."

I tacked back and forth up the barren valleys. Craggy peaks reached to the stars around us. The winds whipped, and after I spiraled up alongside a sheer face, we came out above the entire range, as if we were above the earth itself, close enough to fly to the moon.

"How much farther, do you think?" Lilly asked, wrapping a blanket around my shoulders, another around herself. The temperature was dropping fast here in the high altitudes, and though, like Lilly, I was wearing the jeans and sweatshirt that Heliad-7 had provided us, I was glad for the extra layer.

I checked the maps in my head. "A couple hours. By midnight maybe? Especially if the winds stay calm—"

A shriek of sound like clashing metal tore through the air around us. Lilly grabbed for her ears. The sound whined and then twisted into a static hum. And suddenly there was a tinny voice speaking:

"I DO, I KNOW, I KNOW HOW THE WORLD WILL END."

The voice was a half whisper, a man or a teen, hoarse with frazzled edges.

And it was coming from the vortex engine.

"I KNOW ABOUT THE ANCIENT ONES, THE THREE, AND HOW THEY WILL ASCEND LIKE STARS AND LEAVE US. I KNOW ALL THEIR PLANS. ALL THEIR DEVIOUS PLANS. ALL ABOUT PROJECT ELYSIUM . . ."

He spoke like he was trying not to let someone nearby hear him.

"What *is* that?" Lilly asked, cautiously taking her hands off her ears.

"PLEASE HELP ME," the voice whispered, edged in static. "I CAN TELL YOU HOW TO GET THERE. I CAN FREE YOU FROM THE BLOOD, SO MUCH BLOOD TO COME. I'VE FELT IT ALL . . . BUT WHAT DO I FEEL? WHAT IS REAL?"

"We're picking up a message," I said, "or a recording. The vortex is like a big magnet, reacting with the electromagnetic field of the earth. That's how it creates the antigravity field."

"BU—Y—" the message clipped. "YOU JUST HAVE TO GET ME OUT OF HERE. I'VE DIED TOO MANY TIMES, FELT THE LIFE DRAIN OUT OF MY LOVED ONES . . . WE ARE SO MANY BUT SO ALONE!"

"Magnets are what powered my dad's guitar amplifier," said Lilly. "Sometimes it would pick up a transmission or a stream."

"BUT IF YOU GET ME OUT," the voice went on, "I CAN GET YOU THERE, TOO, I SWEAR—" Rips of static or maybe a crashing sound in the background. "YOU JUST HAVE TO GET ME OUT, GET ME OUT OF VISTA— WAIT . . ." More crashing. "NO, GET BACK! GET OFF—"

There was a final screech and the transmission cut out.

"It must have been close by," I said, gazing warily

around the barren mountains. "Not sure where, though."

"There's something." Lilly pointed off starboard. "That's a light, isn't it? On that plateau?"

I peered at the outlines of peaks and ledges. Something blinked far off. "We should check it out," I said, turning the craft toward it. "Whatever it is, there might be information we could use."

"He said Vista," said Lilly. "That sounds familiar. Have you heard of it?"

"If I have, I might not remember it," I said.

"I don't think it's something I know about from Eden. More like, from pre-cryo."

I tried to think back, but the fog was particularly thick at the moment.

As we neared the light, I could make out a structure, small and square and sticking out of the side of a barren slope. The light flashed through windows on either side of a door. Up a gentle rise from it five large radar dishes stood on a long plateau.

"It's maybe a radar telescope," I said. "Or used to be." There was a long flat strip extending along the plateau, like a runway.

"I'm having that feeling again . . . ," said Lilly. "Like this is a bad idea but also like we're going to check it out anyway."

I shrugged. "I still feel like we're flying blind. It might be a lucky break."

"Yeah," said Lilly, "but it might be the terribly-horribly-bad-and-we-end-up-dead kind of luck."

I slowed and hovered a few hundred meters away. "We could just keep going."

"Hold on." Lilly closed her eyes and pressed her palms together in front of her. She breathed in deeply.

"What are you doing?"

"Sshh," she said, then whispered, "I'm feeling the presence around us, feeling for other life-forms in it."

"You can do that?"

Lilly shrugged, eyes still closed. "I think I can."

After a minute, she opened them. "Weird. There's no one in there. Not as far as I can tell. Could it be a recording?"

"Or maybe the telescopes are boosting a signal from somewhere else." I lowered us toward the structure. "Let's at least take a look." I tried to smile at Lilly. "It's what we do, right?"

Lilly's smile was forced as well. "Don't drink the horchata," she said.

"Agreed." I landed and put the knife in my belt. We gripped each other's hands, and stepped out of the craft.

3

WE FOLLOWED A WINDING DIRT PATH, FAINTLY
outlined by moonlight, up to the door. A metal sign in
the center read:

Welcome to
VISTA
An Exclusive Post-Terrestrial Sentient Holotech Community
Powered by GenSoft and Quarkle

"What is this doing up here?" I wondered.

"Well, no danger of flooding," said Lilly. "I remember
Quarkle. Weren't they one of the big holotech companies?"

"Sounds kinda familiar." I tried the steel door handle, but it was locked. "Do we knock?"

There was a pleasant ding of a bell from inside, and a
click from the door. I tried the handle again and it opened.

As soon as we were through the door, lights flicked on. We were in a small room. Leather couches lined the walls to either side. A cabinet of glassware and dusty liquor bottles against one wall, an ornate deep-red carpet over the middle of the hardwood floor. In another corner was an area of kids' toys, neatly stacked. Ahead of us stood a desk beside a massive steel door that looked like a bank vault.

The walls were adorned with pictures of people, all healthy adults, some with children, smiling out in the sun, playing golf, or dancing in a club. Another showed two people wearing slim jet packs and arcing through the sky, hand in hand. Someone riding on the back of a dolphin, another with his arm around an old guy with wild white hair.

"Is that Einstein?" Lilly asked.

"I think so." These were activities you could do inside this holotech world. There was a slogan on the wall between two photos:

VISTA: The Good Life, but Better!

Another ding sounded, this time followed by the humming of machinery. A final click, and the vault door yawned open.

"Somebody knows we're here," I said.

"This way!" urged the haggard male voice that we'd heard in the vortex. It hissed from unseen speakers. "Hurry!"

I started forward. "Wait," said Lilly. She lugged the desk chair, a heavy wood-and-leather thing, toward the door. "This has *lock us in* written all over it."

"Good point." We wedged the chair in the doorway.

The next room was larger, still square but with a higher ceiling and clean white walls made of rectangular panels that were slightly convex. It was empty except for a single glass case, a cube about a meter tall, floating in the middle of the room, suspended on about twenty red wires that extended out to hooks on the walls and ceiling. The wires vibrated with our footsteps, absorbing the shock so that the cube stayed still. Inside it was a crystal cylinder with pale white light glowing from the center. The only sound in the room was the humming of air conditioners.

"Are you here?" Each time the voice spoke, there was a click like a microphone being activated.

"We're here," I said.

"You heard my signal?"

"Yeah."

"How? How did you hear it?"

"We were passing by," I said.

"Passing by . . ." One of the wall panels suddenly flicked to life as a video screen. It showed a distorted image of Lilly and me standing there. I looked up and spied a single camera eye in the ceiling above the cube.

"You two . . . I've seen you. In APB reports from

Eden. You are the fugitives wanted for murder." His voice lowered. *"The Threee . . ."* He sounded excited, almost hungry. I felt my mistrust growing. "But where is your third?"

"Dead, in Desenna," I said.

"Ah—" His voice was cut off by an eruption of static, then a buzzing. He moaned. "Sorry, I need to relocate. Be right back."

The microphone clicked off, leaving us in the humming stillness.

I saw Lilly looking back at the door. "Let's make it quick."

The mic clicked on again. "Okay." He sounded out of breath. "Where were we?"

"What's your name?" I asked.

"You can call me Moros," he said. "A name that means—"

"It's the Greek god of doom," said Lilly, almost bored, but also eyeing the glass cylinder suspiciously. "I know my myths. That's not your real name."

"Well, no . . ." Moros's voice faltered. He was still breathing hard. "It is my name in Vista. Moros was born here in Vista." His tone thickened. "Born in blood."

Lilly flashed me a glance. "This is an upload colony, right? You're a digital version of yourself, and Vista is a holotech world, like a program that you inhabit?"

"Yes. We all uploaded a few decades ago. Ziiiip! My

dad was a programmer for Quarkle. He helped build the Vista environment. It runs on a fusion battery that should last for as long as the sun lights the earth. The idea was utopia forever, no aging unless you wanted to, no dying, no— Guh!"

There was some kind of snarl and clangs of metal. Feedback whined over the mic, followed by a grating sound and something like wailing in the distance. When Moros returned, he was panting.

"What's going on in there?" I asked.

Moros sighed. "Dying. Chaos."

"It doesn't sound much like a utopia," said Lilly.

Moros laughed between deep breaths. "No. It was, in the beginning." There was a rumble like a distant explosion. "I will show you, but I warn you not to look for too long."

"I'm not sure I want to know," said Lilly under her breath.

All around us, the wall panels came to life, each displaying a camera view of the virtual world inside Vista.

Lilly was right.

Everyone was screaming. Either in terror or in rage. Each screen was like a scene from a different nightmare, combat footage from the end of the earth: a city on fire, smoke everywhere; meteors hurtling to the ground and blowing up homes; a man, screaming, being eaten alive by a pack of zombies or vampires—they were maybe somehow both; another scene of screaming and terror that involved chains and naked bodies; two children crying in a corner, a shadow falling over them. . . .

Lilly shut her eyes and shoved her hands against her ears. I tore my gaze away and focused on the cube, trying to unsee the images and yet I felt them burning into my brain forever.

"I'm over here."

I tried to pick out the whispering voice among the horrors and found a face on one of the screens, up close to the lens. "Yeah, here." He was a few years older than us, his face gaunt and streaked with ash and blood. One eye was swollen shut. The other hid deep in a hollow socket and darted around like a frightened animal. His chest was crisscrossed with straps of ammunition.

"The problem with Vista was that everyone got bored," said Moros. "After about ten years in here, utopia just wasn't that interesting anymore. So, the programmers started adding these survival challenges to spice things up—like an asteroid hit, a zombie uprising, and also twisted stuff, perversions—but they were just games and each one had an end. The last survivor would be declared the winner, and then the system would reset back to normal ol' Vista. So, you'd maybe get your face eaten off by a demon, but then in what seemed like a blink, you'd wake up and find life back to the way it used to be. And then we'd read about what had happened and who had won and watch replays and it was all kind of a rush.

"But then . . . it warped everyone's minds. Made us monsters. The programmers started increasing the challenges, everyone feeding off it, until . . . I don't know what happened. Everybody lost it. I guess . . . who wants to play golf and raise your kids when you could be slitting the throats of your friends and tying up your neighbors? The system got overloaded, and all the terrors started happening at once. And now, the program won't reset. All the programmers are dead. My dad is dead. I've been on my own for . . ."

His gaze went blank. "Years. But I've figured out where the ports are for interfacing with the program— my dad had taught me some stuff before he died—so I can hide and . . . adapt." Moros backed up, and I could see that one of his arms was missing. There was a blank gray circle where his shoulder ended that looked sort of pixelated. "I changed the code to keep from bleeding out," he said. He also had a cyborg left leg.

Now that he'd moved back from the camera, I could see that he was hunched in some kind of closet, surrounded by circuitry.

Something thudded against the door behind him.

Moros sighed wearily. "One sec." He stood and raised a weapon like a chain saw, gunned it to life, and then yanked open the door. A yellow-eyed being with boiled skin lurched forward, hissing, flicking a long lizard tongue. Moros decapitated it with a single stroke, then closed the door. He turned back around, his face still blank, and sighed. "I don't even know what that was. The program's been stuck for so long, it keeps degrading and producing weird artifacts. I got attacked by a bird thing that had my brother's head the other day. I don't know what's real anymore, which is funny to say in here."

"I know the feeling," I said over the screaming from all around. "Can you shut off the other screens?"

"Sure."

Moros fiddled out of the camera's sight, and the horror show around us clicked off.

"What's your real name?" I asked.

"Peter." He gazed into space below the camera.

I couldn't imagine being in a place like Vista, and yet I felt a connection to him, facing constant unknowns, having the world switch on him and show him terrible things.

"And how do you know about Project Elysium?" Lilly asked.

"Vista has gamma link," said Peter, "and the program would download news so we could see what was happening in the real world if we wanted. Like I said, I know how to access the program code, and I've had a lot of hours on my hands these last few decades. I saw little mentions of the project here and there, especially in Nomad transmissions, so I started digging and piecing together what I could find—"

Another snarling creature lurched into frame behind him. Peter turned and cleaved it in two. Green blood splattered on his face, making him cough and spit. He wiped it away miserably. "Forgot to shut the door," he muttered, closing it now.

"How do we get you out of there?" I asked. "Where's your body?"

"It was cremated when I uploaded. The ash is somewhere in Anchorage. It would be so nice to feel real air. In here, it almost seems real, but . . . you can tell."

"So, is there anything we can do?"

Peter sighed. "Yes, actually. There's a manual reset button for the system. If you could do that for me, then I'd at least get to see my family again." Shrieking screams echoed behind him.

"Where is it?"

Peter fiddled at controls out of sight. There was a hissing sound in the room, and a panel opened in the floor between me and the cube. A small electronic console rose up on a metal stand. "I'm feeding you the code now."

I watched lines of numbers flashing by on a small screen on the console. There was a keyboard below this screen and a few other buttons around the side.

"Okay, there."

A command line flashed:

```
Reset: <Enter>
```

"Just press enter?"

"Yes." Peter was breathing hard, like he was nervous. "That's all. It's so easy, but the way it's built, a real person, flesh and blood, has to do it."

I was moving my finger toward the button when Lilly said, "Hold on. If we reset your system, won't you forget everything you've learned about Project Elysium?"

"Oh." Peter paused, thinking. "No, the reset doesn't erase our memories. It just restarts the holotech simulation and reboots all the people to a living state. Unfortunately, everything I've seen is going to stay with me."

I shared a glance with Lilly. I felt like I believed him, or at least wanted to. *Elissa, Aralene, Anna, Carey . . .* we couldn't erase what we'd seen either, but a reset button . . . that sounded nice.

Lilly stayed persistent. "Okay," she said, "but before we help you, you need to prove to us that you know things. Tell us something about Project Elysium."

Peter shook his head, half smiling, and his tone shaded darker again. When he spoke like this, he looked to the side of the camera, like there was someone else there. I thought of it as his Moros voice. "Fair enough. She plays rough, very rough. I like it." Then he shook his head and sounded more like Peter, looking at us again with war-torn eyes. "Well, what do you want to know?"

"Where are Paul and his team right now?" Lilly asked.

"That I don't know. They were in Coke-Sahel, acquiring a target, and then they headed to Desenna, but there's been nothing on them since."

"How about the Ascending Stars?" I asked. "What do you know about that?"

"I've heard the term," said Peter, "but it's vague. Something to do with the project, and it's definitely related to the uranium they stole, and something called Egress, but that's it."

"This is useless," said Lilly. "I thought you said you knew things."

"Lilly . . ." I felt like Peter had mentioned enough key terms to prove that he knew something, or maybe I was just being too sympathetic to his nightmare situation.

"I do!" he pleaded. "How about this . . . . I know that Eden's board of directors are at a facility they call Elysium Planitia. And it's coordinates are . . ." He held up his leg, and we could see that his pants were covered in writing scrawled in black ink. "Here: three point zero degrees north and one hundred fifty-four point seven degrees east. I have also heard them refer to this place as EdenHome."

"That's something real," I said to Lilly.

"Nothing we can verify right now," she pointed out.

Something slammed into the door behind Peter. It bent, cracking like it might give way, and the muffled sounds of snarling returned.

"Now can you reset me?" Peter asked, his voice pleading. "And then I'll tell you more. I swear."

"Tell us now." Lilly kept her edge, sounding like an interrogator. And while I thought that was probably the smartest way to play this, I couldn't quite meet her there. Peter sounded genuinely scared, and I wouldn't wish his world on anyone.

"It's okay," I said, touching her arm and raising my eyebrows. She frowned, but nodded. "We'll reset you," I said, "as long as we have your word you'll still have information for us."

"You have my word." Peter's eyes locked on me. "And thank you—" The door behind him started to splinter. "I can't tell you how much."

"Okay," I said. "Here we go."

I pressed the Enter button. It lit up, and the little screen started scrolling information. The cylinder began to pulse. I heard a humming sound, and looked up to see a panel sliding open above me. A searing white light shot down, blinding me.

"Yes, that's it," said Peter/Moros again. "You're perfect. You'll do just fine."

"What?" I asked. His voice sounded different. Closer.

"Owen . . . ?" Lilly asked distantly.

The screen stopped scrolling and words flashed:

`Initiating Transfer`

My vision began to blur. I blinked but felt like I was losing control of my body. There was a flash of an image in my mind, of a cramped room full of circuitry. A crack made me spin my head and I saw a chunk of the door behind me fall away, but wait, this was wrong. What I was seeing wasn't in the room with Lilly, instead it was . . .

Inside Vista.

4

"WHAT'S HAPPENING?" I ASKED. MY VOICE sounded like it was coming through a speaker.

Good luck in Vista, said Peter, and it was no longer like I was listening to his voice, but instead like he was inside my head. *Your body will be a perfect fit.*

And now I could feel the transfer happening, like I was being fragmented into tiny bits and blowing on a wind. Reality was re-forming around me, from the Vista control room to the cramped closet, while Peter downloaded back into the real world.

Stealing my body.

LILLY! I shouted and yet I could tell it was no longer my real voice. The feel of breathing, of speaking, had become electronic. The world became a closet of controls around me, adorned with flashing lights and the sound of terrible creatures behind me, and I was a one-armed, cyberlegged boy with a chain saw and mad scribblings all over my pants legs.

Sorry, Peter said, his voice distant now, *You were my only chance.*

I spun toward the door and watched it splinter apart. There were three of those red-faced, yellow-eyed creatures, their fangs curved and hung with tattered flesh. I tried to stand but lost my balance on my cyborg leg. I stumbled, claws raked across my chest; the chain saw was heavy and I didn't know how to operate it.

No, this couldn't be happening! After all this, I couldn't die in some virtual world, a lie of an ending for my lie of a life—how could this be it? So incredibly pointless, without meaning, some random computer mutation now sinking its teeth into my thigh . . .

I swung the saw, hitting the creature in the head, its teeth tearing away as my leg exploded in pain, but another demon yanked the saw from my hand. They hissed with glee and lunged and all bit deeper. I tried to kick, but one tore my leg off in a spray of sparks.

And I screamed as the pain grew, Peter's pain becoming my pain and I was dying and dying, dying—

But then the light became white again, and the demons and the pain started to fade.

Error: Transfer Suspended.

No! What's happening?

The snarling, the pain of the closet in Vista faded

and the clean light of the control room began to fill my vision. I saw the room, the red wires, the cube, and the light inside the crystal cylinder flashing red.

"Owen!" Lilly called.

Recipient Contains Mental Pathway Corruption.

Unsuitable for Transfer.

Action Terminated.

"No!"

Peter's voice was outside my head again. And I was me.

I fell back to the floor, a searing pain surging through my skull. I blinked, and found Lilly kneeling over me.

"Are you okay?"

"No! Help me! Help me!"

I looked around her to the wall panel, where I saw Peter thrashing against the demon creatures.

"I'm sorry! Help me!"

"Don't worry about him," said Lilly.

"I won't," I said weakly.

Peter screamed again, and was dragged down out of the view of the screen.

Lilly help me to my feet. "What happened?"

"He tried to download into me," I said. "But . . . the computer rejected me. It said my brain was too damaged, I guess from what Paul did to me during cryo."

"Well," said Lilly, kissing my forehead, "that is one unexpected bonus of having your mind messed with. Come on." She guided me toward the door.

Behind us, I heard the saw buzz to life. I turned back and saw a splatter of green blood hit the screen, and the sound of screaming and swearing and then Peter appeared, his face smeared in blood, his and the demons', and his chest raked with deep wounds.

"COME BACK!" he screamed wildly. "I'M SORRY! You can't leave me in here—" He spun and chopped again.

"Sorry," I said, but couldn't help turning to Lilly. "Maybe we should try—"

"No. He can wait for the next sucker to come along."

We stepped around the chair in the doorway. Lilly yanked it free and I pushed the vault door closed. Peter kept screaming, and as the door sealed shut we heard him cursing us and the demons of Vista, his saw grinding away.

And then we were in the utter quiet of the front office.

We threw our arms around each other. I tried to relax and let the pain seep out of my head. "It would be nice if someone, just once, was honest with us. I felt bad for him, though. That was a terrible way to live."

"They all got what they deserved," said Lilly darkly. "They're just like the people in the Edens, trying to escape from the world rather than live in it. It's everybody for themselves, it seems like, everywhere we go. And it always ends badly." She kissed my cheek and brightened. "So your damage saved you," she said.

"Yeah." I almost smiled. "What do you know. But I wish we'd gotten more information from him."

"We know where EdenHome is," said Lilly, "and the board of directors, if he was telling the truth. I'm not sure what good that will do us, though."

"Me either. We'll need to find a gamma link to check those coordinates."

We stepped outside, into the clear dark and cool breeze, and climbed back into the craft. My head still ached, and I still pictured those creatures, computer code gone wrong, biting into me. Twice now, we'd seen the worlds people tried to build to escape this one—here and in Desenna—seen them both end in terror and scream-ing, seen them devour themselves.

What is of this earth cannot control it, and thus the horrors are unleashed, the Terra had said to me on the roof of the Walmart.

The tide that swallows a people is born of its own darkest desires, Victoria had said just before she died.

And even once the pain in my head had subsided, and we'd put many peaks between us and the Vista station, I wondered if it would ever be any different, or whether we were always doomed to these endings in blood.

5

WE FLEW SOUTHWEST THROUGH THE NIGHT, THE air getting thinner and colder as we pushed higher. We wrapped our blankets tightly around ourselves and over our heads, and I fought the dizziness brought on by the lack of oxygen. The moon crawled across the sky. We arced from peak to peak, mostly silent.

"I can't get all the screaming out of my head," said Lilly.

"Me neither." Vista made me think of Paul. I wondered if his selectees would get bored of EdenHome and become perversions. What if he destroyed the rest of the human race, only to have his precious elite lose their minds?

Far off, dawn began to light the horizon, the sun returning from its journey around the world, ready to burn again. All across the planet, people were starting a new day by taking cover, unaware of the other danger they faced. I wondered: How many dawns did we have left before either we succeeded or Paul did?

Just then, in the ice-blue light, I saw a reflection of crystal. A gleam of skull-like white.

Ahead were the highest peaks in the entire range, a ring of jagged rock, like a crown. At its back, the highest spire of all shot straight up, nearly vertical, a finger pointing to the heavens. Suspended like a swallow's nest on the inner wall of this peak, was a stone structure with curved walls and a giant arcing crystal window, like an eye looking out over the entire world.

As we came closer, I could see more buildings at the base of the spire, nestled within the crownlike ring. Angular structures that mimicked the rock, more crystal windows, and a series of stone catwalks carved into the sheer walls. Some gray-streaked smears remained in the alleys between the buildings.

"Is that snow?" Lilly asked.

"I think so," I said. "This place was probably ice covered for ages."

I dropped below the rim of the crown and flew along its steep sides, keeping the tip of the highest spire in view. I curved around behind it, and here the mountains gave way to a cliff that dropped thousands of meters into a remote valley. The back of the spire was smooth except for a single hole, far up near the top, small and rectangular with an arched top, like a window.

"Which way do we go in?" Lilly asked.

"Not sure yet." I banked back around to the side of the crown and rose until we reached a gap between two of the peaks. We could see the entirety of the small temple complex, including a flat landing area just below. It had walls with giant stone rings for tying off Atlantean ships.

That was where the Eden hover copters were.

"Uh-oh," I said, and immediately dropped back out of sight. Had we been spotted? I listened, but there was only wind. "Now what?"

"How about there?" Lilly pointed to a spot below us, a ledge sticking out of the steep mountainside that was just wide enough to land on, if I was careful.

"It's a long climb back up to the top," I said, surveying the treacherous slope above the ledge.

"Don't need to climb," Lilly reminded, and when I looked at her, she'd started floating ever so slightly off her seat.

I smiled. "You think you can carry me?"

Lilly curled her arm and flexed. "No problem."

I waited for a lull in the wind, then landed carefully on the narrow ledge. I grazed the wall, and had to come around again, but still, it was a move I couldn't have made a few days ago, not with these cross breezes and such a small space, but all the flying had made the craft like an extension of me. I knew it so well, its every reaction to the breeze.

I lowered the sails before they could catch a breeze and pull us off the side.

"What's our plan?" Lilly asked.

I slipped my knife into my belt and gazed up the slope. "Not sure. Head up and get a closer look." Just talking made me breathe hard. My brain felt fuzzy with the altitude, and now, looking up, I saw white spots in my eyes, but also something red . . .

Red and flickering, more like an actual light.

"Owen!" Lilly hissed. She pointed at the mast, just by the vortex. A small red light was dancing there.

Targeting . . .

"Get out!" I shouted, but froze. There was nowhere to go on the tiny ledge.

"Hang on." Lilly turned her back to me. I threw my arms around her shoulders and she dove over the side.

We plummeted through the dark, gaining speed. Wind roared in our faces.

"*Qii-Farr-saaan* . . . ," Lilly whispered, and the blue light glowed all around us. Her skin looked luminous. Then she began to sing a high note, warbling in the wind, and we slowed and leveled out.

As Lilly raced away, I heard a sound like puffing air, and then a streaming whistle. A trail of fire streaked through the sky, but not toward us—

There was a crush of sound and an explosion of fire

and blue energy. The blast wave buffeted us and sent Lilly sideways, our shoulders slamming into the cliff face.

Another whump of air . . .

Another explosion. When I looked back, I saw the last remnants of my ship consumed in smoke and flames.

6

"KEEP YOUR EYE OUT FOR MORE!" LILLY SHOUTED as we hurtled upward.

I craned my neck, looking for the source of the missile strike. It must have been a soldier on the ridge. We'd be hard to hit as a small, moving target.

Except then I realized I was an idiot.

Of course they wouldn't fire directly at us. Paul didn't want us dead—he wanted us in his clutches. Which meant they probably wouldn't have fired at all if we hadn't jumped out of the craft. If I hadn't panicked . . . I should have kept my head! Just taken off . . . now, what did we have left?

"Hang on tighter!" said Lilly.

I gripped Lilly's shoulders as she banked hard and my legs dangled thousands of feet above deadly rock.

"Which way?" she called over her shoulder.

"There was that opening at the top of the spire."

"Got it." Lilly arced upward. I took one look back at

the smoldering wreckage of the craft. Flashlights darted around on the rim above it, their beams crisscrossing in the rising smoke.

The full shock began to sink in: the craft was gone, our supplies, our means to get anywhere, and my power as the Aeronaut was gone with it. . . .

We rose straight up the back of the spire, the heights dizzying my already spinning head. As we closed, I could see that the opening was definitely a little archway, like a castle window.

Lilly slowed as we neared it. Moonlight outlined the inside of the arch, but beyond that it was dark. She edged close to the side and I hopped through, dropping onto a stone floor. Lilly climbed in after me, her light and song fading. Looking back out the window, I saw miles of mountain peaks stretching in all directions, just tinted in dawn light.

We stood in a small room. The floor was bare and damp, the air raw. Our rapid, thin breaths made clouds. The window cast a narrow triangle of faint light onto the stone-block floor, and in the shadows I could see a table covered with large, flat pieces of slate. I ran my finger over one. It was etched with a star chart. Ancient carving tools were arranged neatly beside it. More tablets leaned against the wall. Some were hung on the walls.

"Here," said Lilly. She stood by a dark patch against the far wall. I joined her and spied a narrow stone staircase spiraling downward.

Come home, Kael. Come home, Rana.

"Did you hear that?" I asked Lilly.

She nodded. "My skull is here."

"Leech's, too," I said. I felt that familiar magnetic pull, drawing me toward them.

"And both skulls are calling to you," said Lilly, "even though they're not yours."

I shrugged. "Kinda."

"And we still don't know why."

"No," I said, *but I think the Terra does, only she won't tell me.* Maybe here, at last, we would find out.

I pulled the knife from my belt and stepped onto the staircase.

"Owen, wait."

I turned to see Lilly's eyes wide. "What is it?"

She looked away and shook her head. "Nothing."

I stepped back and held her shoulders. "Tell me."

She glanced to the ceiling, and I saw that her eyes were rimmed with tears. "It's just that . . . Paul is already here. He knows we're here. It's . . . I'm scared of what happens down these stairs."

"Me, too," I said, feeling the sickening wave of hopelessness well up in me again, because what exactly were our chances at this point? I wanted to say what I'd been thinking before: that we should run, but where? The craft was gone. We had no supplies. And there was the

Terra's message, about finding the Sentinel . . . but also her comment that we were a lie. If we were, then all this was pointless.

"But what else can we do?" said Lilly. "This is our destiny, our mission. What we were chosen for."

Again, I thought, *no*, or at least, *does it have to be?* And yet, what choice did we have? So I said, "We know more than Paul does, and we're strong. And you can fly us out if we need it."

Lilly nodded resolutely. "You're right."

"Okay," I said. Only later, when it was too late, would I know how wrong she was.

I started down the stairs, running my fingers against the cool stone walls. Lilly rested a hand on my shoulder and followed close behind. The steps were slippery, the ceiling low, and we had to hunch to fit.

The staircase went on and on in tight spirals. I slipped once, then twice, so did Lilly, but we held each other in the pitch dark, clawing for the seams in the walls. We tried to make our footfalls quiet, but I was so tired, my brain and muscles so rubbery with the altitude and worry.

I started to lose track of time, to see dull flashes in my vision. Had we been climbing down for five minutes? Twenty? It felt like we were tunneling into the center of the earth.

But then we began to hear sounds: distant, undefinable echoes of voices; the humming and grinding of machinery; and finally, a flicker of light.

I could just see the outline of a doorway, the staircase coming to an end, when Lilly gasped and gripped my shoulder.

"What?" I hissed.

She was squinting, her breath held.

"Lilly . . ."

Her eyes snapped open, and she exhaled. "There's something here," she whispered.

"You mean something besides Paul."

"Something ancient. Powerful, and . . . dangerous."

"The Sentinel," I said.

"I think so."

"Can you tell where it is?"

Lilly closed her eyes again, but then shook her head. "No, but, even if I could . . . I don't think we want to be around when it wakes up, no matter what the Terra said."

I nodded and led the way to the edge of the light. We looked out into a high-ceilinged hall. It ended to our left at a massive stone door, ornately carved and shut tight. Two black-clad soldiers stood a few paces away, gazing at it and aiming strange weapons. They looked sort of like guns, except with wide disk ends, almost like small radar dishes. The weapons hummed, as if they were emitting a signal.

"It's in there," Lilly whispered. "It doesn't know we're here yet. Those guns must be masking our presence."

"The skulls are this way," I said, pointing in the opposite direction, the magnetic pull increasing inside me.

"I feel it, too," whispered Lilly. "If we had my skull, I could use its power to take these two, like I did in Desenna."

I remembered Lilly creating storms of wind and light. "Except wherever your skull is, that's where Paul will be, too."

We were still paused in the doorway when a scream echoed from a far distance. Human and in agony. From the same direction as the pull of the skulls.

"Skulls, then Sentinel?" said Lilly.

"Yeah."

I glanced back at the door, thinking we could maybe get the jump on those two . . . but it would definitely be easier if we had Lilly's skull power.

The scream echoed again. We ducked out of the doorway and crept along the wall. The hall ran wide and straight for a while, and then curved out of sight. A battery-powered light stood at the bend, offering weak yellow light.

Around the corner, the hallway became a grand staircase, sweeping downward in a wide arc around a vast, open space, a giant cylindrical chasm that stretched out of sight above and below us.

"Yikes," said Lilly, peering down.

The space was maybe fifty meters across. Below,

stone bridges spanned it here and there at angles, leading to different tunnels. Smaller staircases hugged the inner wall, connecting the bridges and tunnels that weren't aligned with the giant curve of stairs we were on. It continued like this, downward into the gloom.

But not total darkness. Far below, nearly out of sight, there was an ominous glow of red light.

"It's like it goes into the center of the earth," whispered Lilly.

I peered along the inner wall of the chasm and saw more weak battery-powered light spilling faintly from a tunnel two levels below.

We made our way down the wide arc, and then crossed a stone bridge across the chasm. It was narrow with waist-high sides, and when we reached the middle I felt a breath of hot air from below. In the dark and the heat, the bridge felt too narrow, the black, too, beckoning, like some ancient urge to fly was activating, and it was all making me dizzy. Lilly and I held hands and also the stone railings, focusing on each step we took.

We reached the other side and entered an arched tunnel, past the temporary light. The magnetic pull grew. The sound of voices became clearer, and now a tight cry of pain, a weaker, more-defeated version of the one we'd heard before. We moved down the hall as quietly as we could. At the next light, I spied a narrow doorway in the wall of the tunnel and beside it, a vestibule with a bone-spiked hand impression.

The key is inside you.

The door was already open. Electric light flashed from inside, like lightning.

Come home, Kael. Come home, Rana.

We edged in. The light grew, the familiar skull white, along with the sounds of electric circuitry.

My head blurred with that first vision, of the Three on the roof of the Atlantean temple like I'd seen in Eden-West. Lük, Rana, and Kael, kneeling on pillows and about to have their throats slit, their world darkened by ash and destruction. Lük and Rana sharing a tragic glance.

We reached the end of the short tunnel and peered in.

A circular room. A pedestal.

The third Atlantean skull.

A figure stood over it, hands pressed to its gleaming surface, but in the shock of bright light, I couldn't make out who it was.

The skull blazed ghost white, casting shadows around the room, bathing the onlookers, who all wore welding goggles, except for Paul. He stood on the far side, his bionic eyes sparking in electric blue, dressed in his usual shirt, tightly knotted tie, khaki pants, and EdenCorp vest, like this was another day at the office.

Seeing him, it was all I could do not to scream, to run at him with my knife. The man who had lied to me in nearly every way, killed my friends, turned my sister into a weapon . . .

Francine and Emiliano stood beside him, clad in the black of Eden's soldiers. I felt a moment of tightness inside me, a wave of the lost confusion that had nearly drowned me back in Desenna, at having my mother again, only to lose her—

But no. I'd had enough time to remember my real mom, to remove Francine from the spaces she'd tried to occupy. She'd never been my mother. She was just a soldier of the enemy. But she was also a symbol of what I'd lost both in time and in memory . . .

Lilly squeezed my shoulder, giving me the strength to shake off the feeling. I glanced back to thank her, but saw that her touch had actually been to keep herself standing. Her eyes were trembling, the white skull light dancing in them. She wasn't looking at Paul.

My gaze returned to the skull. Its ancient carved face grinned at us, and the person standing over it was aglow, hands on it, the white lighting up his fingers, his veins, radiating beneath his shirt. But this was Leech's skull. Who else could be accessing it? His head was down, hair falling forward, but he was tall, broad . . .

And screaming again.

"Nnnaaa!" His head snapped up, jaw clenched, eyes squinted shut, white light making his own skull glow out through his skin.

I heard Lilly's gasp.

Evan's hands popped free of the skull as if a magnet had repelled them, and he staggered back, panting, the light fading from his skin. Evan, who'd saved us in EdenWest. Who'd said, on the raft before that, that we were *lucky* to be in Camp Eden, who'd suggested working together with Paul. Now, he was, but this didn't look like the partnership he'd imagined.

The skull stayed aglow.

Come home, Kael, it called to me again.

"Did it work?" Paul asked. He checked his watch. "We're in a hurry."

Evan nodded weakly. "Yeah." He doubled over and vomited on the floor.

I tapped Lilly's shoulder and motioned at Francine with my eyes. We'd have the element of surprise if we moved right now. Could we get the skull before anyone could react?

But Lilly didn't look like she could move. She was staring tragically at Evan, her lips trembling. I stepped back, starting to move her out of here. We'd need to regroup—

"Excellent," Paul was saying, and out of the corner of my eye I saw him turn . . .

Right toward us. "And now we have everything we need."

I grabbed Lilly's hand and started to retreat, only to feel the press of a gun barrel in my back.

7

THE SOLDIERS PUSHED US FORWARD INTO THE skull light.

"Lilly?" Evan's voice was weak, made uneven by the tremors racking his body.

"Go to him," said Paul, motioning casually. "He'll be so happy to see you."

Lilly's fingers grazed my arm and I met her eyes. She nodded and then rushed across the room, kneeling beside Evan. I couldn't believe he was here. It meant part of what Paul had told us back in the desert was a lie. He had caught the CITs, but he hadn't cut Evan open. At least there was that.

"Lil," Evan croaked. "Is it really you?"

"It's me, Ev." Lilly sniffed, rubbing his shoulders. "It's me. It's gonna be okay."

"Owen, it's nice to see you again in the flesh." Paul grinned at me, his eyes whirring, and I hated him so much, but I didn't reply. I wanted to give him nothing.

He didn't seem to care. "You look different," he said. "Older. I guess you've had to grow up fast these last weeks."

Ignore him, I thought over and over, and yet I could feel myself shaking. I couldn't take the bait. He wanted to see me lash out, I could tell, to break me down further. Instead I met his gaze and pointed to Evan. "What did you do to him?"

Evan was still slumped on the stone floor, breathing hard. Lilly had her arm around him and was speaking quietly in his ear.

"I altered him to suit my needs," said Paul. "His DNA and brain wave composition, specifically, to make him a stand-in for Leech—well, an improvement: less attitude. I had a full recording of how Leech's mind interacted with your skull, and how the skull interfaced with the brain, from back in EdenWest. I found that with a few tweaks to Evan's DNA, I could make him a genetic duplicate, at least as far as the Atlantean skull is concerned." He grinned at me. "They're not perfect, as you know."

I didn't respond, but I wondered if this meant that he knew all the skulls were calling to me.

Evan started coughing again and doubled over, dry heaving. A thin line of spit dripped to the floor.

"It's left him a little worse for wear," said Paul.

Lilly swore under her breath. Her face was murderous,

but she rubbed Evan's back and kept whispering to him, ignoring Paul.

"The last thing I needed to get into this place was Leech's notes and the sextant," Paul continued, "oh, and a fresh sample of his blood to activate the door. Luckily, he left plenty of that in Desenna."

I fought the anger inside me, fought to stay quiet. "So now what?" I asked.

"Now." Paul smiled. "We have everything we need. I have my three Atlanteans and the location of the Paintbrush of the Gods is now safely in Evan's head. We're close, Owen. Very close to the end of the one true quest, the oldest quest there is. So many explorers have died searching for what we are about to find. And don't think I'm referring only to Atlantis. This goes further, from Ponce de León to Herodotus, back to the dawn of humankind."

His riddles filled me with the same mix of hatred and curiosity I now knew all too well, but I focused on a more important question. "What are you going to do with us?"

Paul laughed, a short, dangerous burst. He looked at me like he was going to speak, but then a voice from a tinny speaker interrupted us: "Sir, we've got activity."

Paul pulled a phone from his belt. "Copy that. We're ready." He looked around the room. "Time to go, everyone. Quickly. The electrodampeners worked to a degree, but now our presence has been detected, and a certain someone is waking up."

Lilly flinched, glancing to the ceiling like she'd heard something the rest of us hadn't. I tried to catch her eye but she focused on helping Evan get to his feet.

The soldiers started to file out. Emiliano moved to Lilly and Evan, taking them each by an arm, but Lilly tore herself free.

"Relax," she hissed, supporting Evan as he leaned heavily on her shoulder. "We're not going anywhere."

Emiliano let her go, but Francine trained a handgun on her. Another soldier placed Leech's skull in a black bag. I saw that Francine had the bag with Lilly's skull from Desenna over her shoulder. As everyone moved toward the door, she looked at me, and I kept my gaze icy, like I didn't know her at all.

"Out," she said to me, just as coldly.

When Paul moved, I noticed a boy behind him in the shadows, wearing a dirty LoRad pullover and sweatpants. He had dark skin and kept his eyes on the floor. Paul glanced back at him and said, "Mateu, *viens.*" It sounded like French. Mateu followed. He looked a couple years older than me, and I guessed that he had been the target of the Eden raid in Coke-Sahel, the one we'd watched in Heliad tactical. Who was he? Why was he here?

We all exited the skull chamber and followed the

tunnel out onto the narrow bridge. I watched the soldier's back in front of me, Francine in front of him, and weighed my chances. Could I knock them both into the chasm before I was hit or shot? Could Lilly grab me and fly us out? I thought to glance back at her, and see if she was thinking the same thing.

Except she was busy talking softly to Evan.

"Don't worry, just keep moving. We'll be all right."

"Lilly," Evan's voice was tattered and thin, "I'm sorry, I didn't want to . . ."

"It's okay," she said.

"We fought as hard as we could, but . . ."

"Sshh, not now. Let's just get out of here."

I heard her kiss his forehead and I told the sliver of jealousy in me to shut up. This wasn't the time. They were friends, and Lilly and I were so much more now, but of course Lilly cared about him deeply. The only problem with that care was that, with Evan's condition, escaping or getting Lilly's skull would be basically impossible.

"Keep moving," Paul said tersely.

We were halfway across the bridge when something thundered from high above, a quick concussion followed by a deep rumble that made the bridge shudder.

"Was that—" Francine hissed urgently.

"The sound of our time being very much up," said Paul. He touched his phone. "Containment team, do you copy?"

The only reply was a hiss of static.

"Containment team . . ."

Another rumble reached our ears, and then, fluttering behind it, a scream.

"It's coming," said Lilly quietly.

"Hurry," Paul commanded and we all started to run.

We'd only taken a few steps when more screams reached us and the sound of gunfire.

A light began to grow up at the top of the wide staircase, cold and white and skull-like. It flickered on the walls, then sprayed out into the chasm. Wind slammed against us, stopping us in our tracks. And a sound grew, a sound like terrible wailing, like knives being sharpened for the kill.

A streak of light burst out of the darkness, swooping from the staircase into the chasm, spiraling like a shark swimming circles above us.

The Sentinel had arrived.

Gunshots exploded from behind me: one of the soldiers, rifle pointed straight up.

"No! I told you don't under any circumstances!" Paul shouted.

The Sentinel screamed again, a sound like razor-sharp icicles, and then dove toward us. It moved like fluid, and it was on us before we could move. As it blurred down I could almost make out its features, a flow of robes, impossibly long hair trailing behind it like a comet tail.

It hit the guard who'd fired in a burst of light. He barely got out a scream before the Sentinel crushed him, literally smashed right through him in a liquid explosion of light, and then out his back and on down through the bridge. The stone exploded and the screaming soldier tumbled out of sight. Others opened fire at the slithering light, but only for a second, as the bridge began to crumble and fall away.

"Get off!" Paul shouted. He grabbed Mateu's arm and ran.

I started after him with everyone else. Two of the guards fell screaming. One was picked off by the Sentinel, another shoved over the side by Francine.

"Owen!"

I turned back and saw Lilly hanging on to Evan as the rock crumbled away around them. And in the moment that I paused the bridge beneath me collapsed and we plunged into darkness.

I heard screams, saw Emiliano falling, too, and looked for Lilly, but rock rained around me. A chunk slammed me in the shoulder. White light blurred. I felt the rush of cold air, then the breath of heat from below. Darkness became complete. I flailed my arms uselessly. What was at the bottom of this chasm? I'd be dead the moment I found out.

"*Qii-Farr-saaan*." A hand grabbed my arm. "Hang on to me!" Lilly shouted. Her glowing form shot by me. I gripped her wrist as she flew sideways and banked upward. "*Nnnn!*" she cried through gritted teeth, holding me with one hand and Evan with the other, straining but dragging us out of the chasm.

I distantly heard the echoes of gunshots, the banshee screams of the Sentinel. I'd seen Emiliano fall, but what had happened to Paul and the rest of them?

Lilly brought us up past the remains of the bridge, back up the wide staircase and into the hall, leaving the fray behind. "We'll go back out the way we came in . . . ," she said, her words labored. She followed the arc of the passageway, and my back scraped against stone. "Sorry!" she called. "Almost—"

The screaming of the Sentinel chased us down like a missile.

It slammed into us, throwing Lilly off course and we hit the wall and then tumbled to the floor. My right arm caught under me and I heard a *snap* like a tree branch breaking and then a wicked, numbing pain burst up and down my arm. Spots exploded in my eyes.

Everything seemed to get quiet. I faintly heard the pop of gunshots like they were miles away. I looked over, the world sideways, and saw one of Paul's soldiers, covered in dust, aiming one of the strange guns with the radar dish at the end. Pulses of high-pitched sound surged from it, but the Sentinel's cry drowned it out.

She swooped down and punched through the soldier's chest, exiting out the other side in a fountain of white light.

The soldier crumpled, gun clattering to the ground.

"Owen, come on . . ." I looked up, found Lilly tugging on my shoulder, and saw Evan staggering to his feet. I looked down at my other arm and saw that my wrist was flipped around, bent at the wrong angle like it had been put on backward. More white spots, more pain like a flood over me . . .

The Sentinel's scream snapped me out of it. I saw the light bearing down on us, but then Lilly began to glow herself, shouting, "Get back!" The Sentinel broke off in a wide arc.

"Only the Three shall pass!" it hissed in a deep, silken voice.

"We are the Three!" Lilly shouted, but the Sentinel bore down on us again anyway, and I stumbled to my feet and we barely got out of the way as she slammed into the wall in an explosion of rock.

"In there!" Lilly pointed ahead toward a vast light. We ran and passed through the broken chunks of what had been the large door we'd seen on the way in.

We moved through dust into a high-ceilinged room. Before us was the immense, convex crystal window I'd seen when we first flew in. It looked out onto a panorama of mountains. The sun had crested the horizon, spraying orange beams across the jagged peaks.

A single chair stood before the window, carved from thick wood. I thought of the Sentinel sitting there, watching the sun rise and fall for ten thousand years, waiting for someone to arrive. For many of those millennia, that view had likely been blurred by sheets of ice.

"Only the Three shall pass!"

I felt the wind of her arrival and spun, Lilly and Evan beside me, our back to the dawn world.

She landed and faced us, burning in white fire, a beautiful ancient maiden skeleton. It was as if we could see her bones and her skin at the same time. Her long white gown seemed at once radiant and tattered, like she was flickering between alive and dead. Her eyes were hollow pits of black, her mouth pursed and menacing.

And now she raised a sword, its silver blade flickering with blue flame.

"I was told to find you!" I shouted at her.

She hissed at me, teeth bared, a sound that froze my blood.

"Stop!" shouted Lilly.

The Sentinel regarded us, her hollow gaze impossible to read. She bobbed up and down, snakelike, sword still held high, ready to strike. "Only the Three shall pass," she said again, her words slithering around us.

"I told you, we *are* the Three," said Lilly. "Now stand down, sister."

The Sentinel's head turned slightly toward Lilly. "You are of the Three."

"Yes," said Lilly. "Thank you."

"And you," the Sentinel breathed, sizing up Evan.

She turned back to me. "But you are not of the Three."

And in a blur she lunged forward and her blue blade flashed.

"OWEN!" Lilly screamed.

My breath stuck, my whole body frozen in screaming pain, fire, ice, all at once. I looked down to see the sword stabbed deep into my chest.

And then a wrenching burning as the Sentinel pulled the blade back out.

My breath tumbled out of me. I collapsed to my knees, grasping my chest. I'd been stabbed, stabbed . . . I looked down. My hands covered the wound, and something warm seeped between my fingers, but it wasn't blood. It was light.

Light, my life, slipping away. I fell back to the floor, my head slamming the rock. Everything spun.

"No! Owen!" I heard Lilly scream, and I saw her face above mine, her hair falling over me. "Stay with me, stay here . . ."

But I was already leaving, draining out, the world becoming a distant thing.

The edges dissolved, Lilly disappearing, the burning in my chest, the hoarse sucking sound of my breaths, all fading away until I . . . was . . .

Gone.

Into the white.

PART II

The Jaguar, Eu, will leap because the Turtle, Ana,
cannot reach.
Qi and An.
Ana is aware that she cannot leap.
Eu is aware that he cannot float.
This is balance. This is Truth.
Qi and An.
One cannot be without the other.
But then one day Eu thinks, if he could tie a rope
around Ana,
He can keep her close.
He can leap as high and as far as he wants,
Whenever he chooses.
And in this moment, the great harmony is lost.
—TRANSLATED FROM A MAYAN CODEX, PRECISE
ORIGIN UNKNOWN

8

THERE IS DARKNESS, BLANK SPACE, BUT I CAN STILL sense it, as if time is moving and I am still a part of it. Maybe I am not dead . . . yet.

Now light.

The white realm, a voice says distantly.

Where? I try to ask.

We are traveling. . . .

The light grows slowly, diffusing around me, but I do not think I have opened my eyes. It is more like I am arriving at this light, arriving from somewhere very far away.

It is not the white of the Sentinel nor the sunrise nor the shadow blues of the Andes temple.

It is crimson, golden, flickering like firelight.

Blurs become lines. Draw geometry, create depth.

There is a room.

A single window looks out on night aglow with amber city light. The other walls are hung with heavy folds of fabric. The wall in front of me has a floor-to-ceiling mirror.

My view of it is blocked by a girl.

She stands facing the mirror, back to me, wearing nothing. Black hair spills in waves all the way to her waist.

I think to turn away, but I can't. I am not in control of these eyes.

Then her arms rise above her head and shimmering black fabric falls over her shoulders, down her back, to her knees.

Rana's head cocks back toward me, and she smiles slyly. "I told you not to look," she says in a soft, ancient language. Back in my—in the Aeronaut's—skull, Lük said we were communicating *beneath language, through the harmony of Qi and An*. That must be how I understand her now.

And so I start to reply, *Sorry*.

But another voice instead answers, "You did."

I feel us grinning.

Rana steps to a dresser and begins to pull her hair back. In the mirror, I see myself kneeling on the wooden floor, wearing black as well.

Not quite me. I recognize the angular face and short brown hair. I am Lük. Is this another skull vision?

No, this is real. Lük doesn't turn, but I do, or I turn my perception, and I find the Terra floating in the gray space beside the windows of Lük's eyes.

Real, I say. *Like a memory?*

You are in this moment. I have brought you here to see.

Brought me here, like, through time?

Time is one of the faces of the Qi-An. I have removed you from your world, pulled you back into the white realm, the foam behind the solid surface of reality. Here, we can travel outside time.

Is my body still in the temple? Am I still . . .

Your body is safe. Right now you are here. I could connect you to Lük because you are similar. Brothers of memory.

But, I say, as the bright white moment, the Sentinel's blade, returns to my mind, *she said I'm not one of the Three.*

The Three will fail, says the Terra.

But am I one of them or not? Am I the Aeronaut?

The Terra doesn't need to respond, though.

I already know. I have maybe known for a while, since Rana spoke to me in Lilly's skull, or even since we were escaping EdenWest.

No, says the Terra. *You are not one of the Three.*

My first feeling is anger. Yet another lie told to me, another way I've been tricked.

It is not like that, says the Terra.

So then what am I?

You are the one that I chose. You are more than the Three. I found you across time and space and have chosen you.

Why would you choose me?

The Terra seems to frown. *Is that really your first question? To doubt yourself? Is it not more important what I have chosen you for?*

Sorry. I feel a wave of embarrassment.

It is true, though, that I had limited choices, says the Terra, *among those who were close enough matches to receive the knowledge of the Three.*

That doesn't make me feel any better.

Owen, most of the universe is shaped by circumstance. This planet would still be ruled by dinosaurs if not for a stray asteroid. That you ask these questions is part of what makes you worthy, that you can see beyond the human veils of ego and selfishness. But they also make you vulnerable to doubt. On your journey you have learned to trust, in yourself, in the moment, and in what you believe in. You must stay strong in these ways for what is to come.

Okay . . . so, you didn't choose me to find Atlantis or protect the Paintbrush of the Gods.

No.

Then what did you choose me for?

That is the right question, says the Terra. *I chose you to save me.*

You? How?

You must watch this moment, this night, and then you will understand.

There is a knock on a door. Rana looks up. Her eyes flash to Lük and she finishes twisting her hair in a long braid.

Lük stands and crosses the room, his black-booted strides causing the planks to creak. He slides a small viewing panel aside, and sees familiar eyes on the other side. He unlocks the door. A boy with shaggy hair steps in. I have only glimpsed him, on the pyramid roof where the Three had their throats slit.

"Ready?" Kael asks. He is taller and thinner, with sharp features and dark eyes. He is dressed in black, too. He pulls aside his long shirt, revealing a thick belt. Loops hold shiny triangular metal pieces with slightly curved points and holes in the centers. I can feel Lük's knowledge that these are throwing blades and that Kael wields them with lethal accuracy.

"Yeah," Lük answers, and he reveals that on his own belt, he carries a device that looks like a slingshot, along with a line of tiny metal darts. These weapons cause a moment of nervousness in him, and I feel him think: *I would rather fly, maybe even far away from here. . . .*

I want to tell him that I know the feeling.

"Hey." Kael is peering at Lük, examining his eyes. "You okay?"

"Fine," says Lük. "It's just . . . this is a big night."

Kael smiles with bravado. "The biggest."

In the distance, a long, low chime sounds, its depth vibrating the walls.

"We should go," says Rana, wrapping a cloak around her shoulders and pulling the hood over her head. "It's about to start." She says this with weight, like this is the beginning of the end; and I can tell that she is serious, like Lilly, maybe too serious at times.

"Right," says Kael. "We wouldn't want to be late for the masters' big show."

He turns and opens the door. Lük follows Rana. I feel his heart rate rising. He pauses in the doorway and looks back at the room, and I feel him wondering if he will ever see this place again. I sense that he and Rana have spent countless hours here, feeling safe, and in love, so much so that Lük has wondered if his sacred mission is even worth it. He has imagined taking Rana's hand and stealing away in his craft to some far island, somewhere perhaps in the northern reaches of Pacifica, where they could just be together. And with every step they take on this night, that possibility grows more and more distant. His heart aches at this, and he doesn't even know what I know . . .

That his dream will never happen.

We step out onto a narrow balcony. Stairs crisscross

the side of a curved building made of stone blocks. A craft like mine floats serenely, tied to a copper ring on the railing, its vortex engine glowing. Far below, I see dark water.

This building is perched on a jagged cliff, and we are in a vast city built on an archipelago of rocky islands. Foamy ocean sloshes through fjords between them. In some places these are spanned by wide, arching bridges, but mainly the city is connected by glowing ships gliding from one spire or pyramid-shaped building to the next.

In the distance, the moon illuminates jagged peaks and curling glaciers on a large land mass.

There is a hum overhead and Lük looks up to see the belly of a huge Atlantean craft sliding overhead, glowing blue, its massive sails billowing in the stiff breeze. It has long, curved markings along the base of its hull on either side of the rudder.

"You know it's a big event when the Polarians make the journey down," says Kael.

"I'm pretty sure that attendance was mandatory," says Rana. "Besides, their city is sinking. The whole north land is going under. The Polarians have much to gain if the Paintbrush of the Gods works."

"I still hate that name," says Lük. "As if Eu and Ana would ever approve of us plying our hand to reshape the world in our image."

In Lük's mind I see them: Eu the jaguar, and Ana the turtle, like the statues I saw in Rana's skull vision, in the courtyard in Tulana.

"There's always Master Solan's teaching," says Kael with a hint of sarcasm as he steps into the small craft, "how our will and the will of nature are, by design, the same."

"Master Solan smells like sloth dung," says Rana. "So, who's driving?"

"That's funny," says Lük, stepping in and taking the pilot's seat.

"I could always fly myself." Rana holds out her palms, two stones glowing blue, and floats up from her seat.

"Well then, may I have the honor of transporting you?" asks Lük.

Rana smiles. "Spoken like a true noble."

"Like a true fool," chides Kael, but he smiles.

I feel Lük's limbs moving as mine used to, untying the tether, aligning the sails, and activating the vortex. He's a better pilot than me, though, trained since childhood; and in spite of the whipping winds, he guides the craft away from the apartment in a smooth arc. He brings them up over the next jutting island, above a tight labyrinth of sandstone buildings lit by globes of light. He picks up speed and banks quickly around the Polarian ship. Its railings are lined with people looking out eagerly, some pointing to different buildings, the spires and pyramids.

"First time in Atlante for many of them, I bet," Kael says. "Probably a big change from mammoth furs and cliff caves."

"What do you know?" Rana snaps. "Polara is a beautiful province, or was. All these people may be rolling their mammoth furs out on our floors soon enough, if they keep losing their land."

Lük rubs her leg supportively. She leans an arm against him and I feel him stir, and there is the doubt again. If only they could run . . .

"You sound like you're going to side with the masters' plan," Kael mutters.

"Well, at the ceremony I'll do my best to heed Master Alara's advice and *look* like I'm siding with the masters," says Rana. "You both need to remember that, too. Our plan will be ruined if anyone suspects. But it's okay to be sympathetic. We don't have to like what's happening to the world. We can love our vortex energy and yet know that its effect on the planet's magnetic fields has had dire consequences. But that doesn't mean the masters are right in what they mean to do. You remember what Alara said."

"Of course I remember what she said." Kael's voice rises. "I've pledged to *die* for what she said. I just want to be sure you're committed, too."

"We all are," Lük says sternly. "Always. If that is what it comes to." And I feel that he can't bear to look at Rana as he says this.

Lük aligns them with the other craft in the sky. There are ships of all sizes, from four-person vessels like this one to giant barges ferrying hundreds. Some are open topped, built for quick transport across the archipelago, while others have decks and cabins and look ready to cross the planet. All the ships are orienting in the same direction, and ahead I see the largest island yet and rising in its center, a giant curving structure.

It looks like a dome.

But as we get closer I see that its exterior is made of stone rings with gaps in between, and the top is open to the night. The rings are connected by staircases that also act as supports. Stripes of brilliant light shine between the levels.

While most of the larger craft settle on the stones of a wide plaza surrounding it, Lük flies to the topmost ring of the dome, where he ties off at a staircase.

"Look at them all," Rana says, peering down at the masses filing in. "Good little lemmings." She sounds like Seven.

"They don't know any better," says Lük. We step out and he and Kael and Rana share a look. "Ready to play the part?"

"Three starry-eyed students of the protectorate," says Kael cynically.

They each produce a shimmering jade disk etched in Atlantean, and affix it to their chests above their hearts, a badge of some kind, then climb out of the craft and ascend the stairs and pass through an arched entryway.

A guard stands just on the other side, in a copper helmet and crimson robe, holding a long staff with a gleaming blade at the end. His gaze is stern until he sees the three, then his face softens into a wrinkly smile. "There you are," he says. "Master Alara was starting to wonder where you'd gotten off to."

"The usual debauchery, Deniel," says Kael. "Wine, weed"—he grabs Rana by the waist—"and wonderful women."

I feel Lük bristle at this. Rana doesn't push Kael away but instead wraps her arm around Kael's shoulder. "Isn't he adorable," and in seconds she has flipped him into a headlock.

"And you are feeling well and ready?" Deniel asks.

"As we'll ever be," says Lük. Deniel pats Lük warmly on the shoulder as he passes, and Lük's nerves rattle again.

The three emerge onto a balcony, the top level of the enormous coliseum, open to the air. Because of the dome shape, this highest ring is also the smallest and the closest to the center, and so it is suspended over the legions of people below and nearly right above a round stage.

Figures in hooded robes are assembling there, slowly making their way up staircases on different sides of the stage and forming a circle.

"There you are at last."

The three approach an older woman who wears the same type of robe as the figures below. Her hood is back to reveal her silver-and-blue hair. Master Alara looks like she'd be in her sixties in my time, but I can sense in Lük's mind that she is well over one hundred.

Much longer life was possible when the world was in harmony with me, the Terra informs me.

Alara leans close to the three. "I need to go down and make my appearance," she says, "and play my part. You have what you need?"

"We do, Mother," says Rana, and I see her eyes have welled up.

"Don't," says Alara, shaking her head, and yet I recognize her face and know that Rana is right to fear. Not long from now, Alara will stand across from them when their throats are slit, though neither she nor the rest of them know this.

She pulls Rana to her, rubbing her shoulder. "The Terra may find worth in our lives yet." Alara closes her eyes for a moment, breathing deep, her nose in Rana's hair, then pulls away and brushes her robe. She lifts her hood over her head, shadowing her tear-streaked face. "I will see you after."

"Good luck," says Kael.

Alara sweeps out, and the three move to their seats. There are two rows in this balcony, and three seats in the front have been left open. The rest are taken by students of similar ages, but none of them speak to the three, only in hushed tones to one another. Lük catches a few wary glances, some leering, and I can feel him bristle at this, but he also thinks to himself, *They don't understand. They've chosen to remain blind to what is really happening.*

The coliseum is almost full, the circle of masters on the stage nearly complete. From Lük's mind I understand that there are twelve masters, one for each realm of Atlantis. I can see the map, the Polarians in Greenland, the Vira Cocha in the Andes, Olmecia on the Yucatán, the Sumer in the Middle East, Jiahu in the Far East, and more in cities around the globe.

We are in Atlante, the capital city, on the edge of Antarctica, its ice-covered mountains nearby. The Atlanteans consider this the center of the world, with the magnetic South Pole as the navel of the planet, and from here all trade and influence flow out over the globe. This location is also important to the masters' plans, to the energy of the Terra and of the planet, though Lük does not know quite the mechanism that the Paintbrush will use to, as the masters say, *maintain the Atlantean way*.

Another low chime sounds. I feel it in Lük's teeth. All the globe lights in the hallways and staircases dim, and for a moment there is a dark like night with only the stars glittering in the black above.

Then light explodes on the masters' circle. They stand, faces shrouded beneath their hoods. The light comes from a ring of crystal spheres on pedestals, one in front of each figure. A voice speaks, deep and gravelly.

"The world is changing."

"Watch out," quips Kael, "Master Solan is using his scary voice."

"Alara says he always wanted to be a stage actor," adds Rana.

I hear Lük chuckle, but his heart is racing. I feel him wishing more than anything else that the world could have stayed how it was, that he could have lived during the height of Atlantean glory, instead of now, during its fall.

"Qi and An spin away from each other," Master Solan continues, "as they are known to do, and all shall suffer until the next cycle of balance . . ."

He stands in the circle with the others but the light grows brighter on him. Everyone listens expectantly.

"Unless," he adds, "we choose to fight."

The crowd murmurs supportively, but also with a note of fear.

"We are born of the nexus of Qi and An," says Master Solan, "our consciousness the note of its song, realized. And so we ask: How then is our will not also the will of the Terra? Why should we stand by, as some suggest, and watch our world fail, watch our cities die because of the planet's whim? Because of molecules and orbits? Must we just *accept* this? I say no."

Shouts of agreement echo here and there.

"Because even if we consider our own role in the rising seas and the darkening skies, should we be ashamed, should we feel guilty that our advancements, our *triumph*, has consequences? Or should we correct as we see fit?"

The crowd begins to show its support in a unison hum. It sounds like a hive, and so much like in Desenna, these hundred thousand people creating a terrifyingly powerful note.

"How can we be wrong to do what it takes to defend ourselves, the Terra's greatest achievement?" Solan calls. "Are we not the work of this earth?"

The crowd responds. "*Mmmmmmmm-QiiiSan!*"

"Are we not the reason? Are we not the purpose?"

The roar of voices grows. Deafening. They stomp their feet, the entire coliseum shaking.

Now Master Solan strides to the center of the circle. "Today we will show that we are not the Terra's playthings! We will not fall because of some antiquated fear of nature! Tonight we will show that we . . . are . . . nature!"

The crowd explodes. The phrase is so similar, for a moment I expect to see Paul down there, leading these people like he leads the Edens, but when Master Solan throws back his hood, arms up in exultation, I see that he is bald with a talon-like nose.

He is showered with adoring cries and screams.

"So dramatic," Kael whispers sarcastically.

"He's a tyrant and a fool," Rana spits.

Lük nods in agreement and squeezes her leg.

Solan waits for the crowd to quiet. Then he hisses, "Let the ceremony begin."

9

"WE WILL NOW CHANGE THE COURSE OF HISTORY!"
Master Solan intones. "Tonight, we will take the power
into our own hands!"

"Some people doubt this will even work," says Kael,
just loud enough that a disapproving student nearby
shushes him.

"If it's not going to work," says Rana, "why do I feel
like I'm going to vomit?"

Solan returns to his spot in the circle, and puts both
hands on the luminous globe in front of him. The other
masters do the same. The globes explode with pulsing
light, a regular rhythm in unison, a strobe effect that
makes the crowd seem to sway in slow motion.

Deep drums begin to thunder. A large door grinds
open on the far side of the coliseum. Silhouettes appear,
moving out toward the masters' circle. As they get
closer, frame by frame in the stop-motion flicker of the
lights, I can see that it is a group of shirtless men, two

in front and two behind, and in between them is an astonishing animal, a gigantic cat wearing an iron muzzle. The muzzle has spaces for the creature's two giant saber teeth. Its shoulders rise above the tallest of the men, its head massive, its legs like thick trees. Its eyes flick back and forth above the muzzle, and its great ribs expand heavily with each giant breath.

Sinassa, the Terra says sadly. *The great queen of Eurasia.*

Each of the men holds a colossal chain attached to one of the cat's enormous legs. They lumber with a clanking sound toward the stage, where there is a flurry of activity.

More people have appeared in the masters' circle. Smaller hooded figures. Lük knows they are apprentices. They make circles with a dark powder on the white floor, overlapping rings of various sizes. One figure creates a solid disk a meter wide in the very center, then bends over. There is a lick of sparks and the powder alights in purple flame.

Sinassa sees this and begins to struggle, head lurching, and it is clear that she could toss these men aside, tear their limbs off, but there are too many soldiers in the wings, too many spears.

Be calm, Sinassa, the Terra says sadly.

Sinassa lowers her head again, docile as they lead her up the steps. The purple plume has died down to lavender embers. They bring her to the center so that her head is directly above these. One of the men produces an obsidian blade. Like Desenna . . .

Sinassa raises her head and offers a last, defiant roar that for a moment silences the drums and the murmurs and even the breathing of all in the coliseum.

The blade slices through her throat. Blood pours into the embers.

The Terra weeps.

Rana squeezes Lük's leg. "Such a beautiful animal," she says thickly.

Steam rises from the embers. Sinassa slumps and the blood slows to a trickle. She collapses to her side and her giant ribs expand in one last gasp before she falls still. As the men drag her away, the steam increases, becoming a vortex of spiraling black smoke that grows, reaching up and out of the top of the coliseum.

"We call you to us!" Solan shouts over the roar of the smoke.

It is time, says the Terra.

Though I can still sense her image beside me, a bright light begins to glow throughout the coliseum, illuminating everyone. I assume that it is coming from above, that the Terra is being summoned from somewhere far away, but then I see that the light is coming *from* every single member of the audience. Rana, Kael, and Lük, too. They all glow from within, just like Lilly did when she flew.

And then the light begins to move out of them, right out of their chests, the light becoming streams leaving every single body and flowing toward the spiraling smoke column. There is a little tug of pain inside Lük as the tail of the light snaps free, and he slumps back, all of them slump back, and the streams coalesce, creating a vortex of light that reaches as high as I can see.

And there is more energy arriving, streaming into the coliseum from the sky. Lük twists in his seat and we can see that the light is coming from all directions of the night, as if being drawn from the entire planet.

The wind whips everyone's faces. Some turn away. A girl near us weeps, clutching her chest. Lük feels so sad and empty. Even just breathing feels like a burden.

Now there is a deep rumble and the center of the stage begins to grind open, revealing a great blue swirl of light. It looks like a vortex engine, only hundreds of times bigger. It increases speed and whines in a deep vibrating tone. The energy rattles Lük's bones.

The light above, the energy of the Terra, begins to be drawn down into the blue vortex. As it does, the sky suddenly ignites with lightning. Clouds boil and thunder crashes, as if the heavens are furious at this betrayal. Hail falls, dashing against us. People shield their heads. The wind becomes so strong Lük can barely open his eyes.

The column of light is sucked in faster, and as it blurs

there is a sound like screaming, like the cry of a star in pain, something white-hot and luminous. Rana doubles over. Lük throws his hands over his ears. It is the worst sound he has ever heard. . . .

The last of the Terra's light reaches the vortex. The scream dies as if its throat were slit. The hail ceases, the thunder rolls away, and the vortex slows, its whine cycling down, its blue glow darkening to silver. Everyone breathes again, cautiously lifting their heads and pulling off their hoods.

The vortex stops spinning. The silver liquid becomes still. The masters' globes reassert their light.

The crowd is stunned. Stunned by the power but also by fear.

"What have we done?" whispers Rana. I feel that Lük agrees. Even though they knew that this was wrong, that this should not have been done, the truth of what has happened, of what they've lost, overwhelms them still. The Terra is gone. Its light gone from them all.

And Lük feels empty inside in a way that he does not even want to recognize. Something has been taken from him, something that I have never even known. The music of the Terra, of Earth, and the harmony of life itself has been wrenched from him and everyone in this coliseum. Perhaps, judging by the light show, from the entire planet. There is something hollow inside each and every living thing now, a cold absence and a lack of connection, like a whisper of doubt making everyone fear that they are actually alone in the universe.

A new crunch of stone sounds, a new grinding of gears, and the silver pool of mercury begins to roil.

"Behold!" shouts Solan. "The Heart of the Terra!" The masters' globes grow brighter.

An object breaks the surface of the silver pool, something smooth and square. It rises, and we can see that it is a large cube, perched atop a stone pedestal. The mercury drips off and the sides of the cube are revealed to be pure crystal with copper edges, transparent except for a slight rainbow shimmer of refracted light.

And when everyone can see inside, there is a collective gasp of thousands.

Inside the cube, sitting cross-legged, is a girl.

A girl I have known since I drowned in Lake Eden, who swam to me through the dark, her long hair flowing behind her. Who appeared to me in the tunnels beneath the lake, her heart glowing blue, and across the world since. She is dressed now as she would be when she came to me: the crimson dress, copper belt, hair back, wearing the necklace with a carving of what I now know was Sinassa.

The Terra, imprisoned in her crystal cage.

She sits serenely, her face relaxed and unflinching. Her hands rest palm up on her knees. Only her eyes move. She looks slowly around the entire coliseum, and as her gaze falls on the spectators, they weep, throw their arms over their faces, cry out in anguish.

Her lavender eyes sweep up even to our heights.

Rana gasps, squeezing Lük's leg. Lük clutches her arm and feels in the Terra's gaze that sense of loss, of aloneness, and worse, the sense that he knew of another way, a better way to feel, not moments before, but he cannot find it now, and he fights the urge to cry.

"We have betrayed her," says Lük.

"Not for long," Kael mutters grimly.

I see that Master Solan is noticing this reaction in the crowd, that other masters are murmuring to one another with concern. Maybe they did not expect this. Maybe they didn't realize the true scope of what they were doing. Solan leans toward his neighbor and speaks something urgently. One by one, but with less conviction, the masters' hands return to the control globes.

"Citizens!" Solan calls, his voice booming over the sorrowful whispers. "Fear not! For now begins our salvation!"

A light appears above and we see a large Atlantean craft, its hull oval, lowering into the coliseum. Thick ropes with copper hooks at their ends drop from its sides. The men who guided Sinassa reappear and link these around the cube. They step away, and the crystal cage begins to rise.

Lük is afraid to look, but as the Terra is lifted from

the coliseum, her eyes have closed. Her face is calm.

But when she is exactly level with us, her eyes flash open.

Only you can free me.

Lük does not hear this.

But I do.

The crystal cage rises out of the coliseum, and the great ship arcs off.

"Return to your homes!" Solan calls. "Be safe, and tomorrow we will wake to a new dawn!"

Rana tugs Lük's arm. Her gaze is fierce, Lilly-like. "Let's go."

Lük nods. The three stand and move quickly around their stunned counterparts. As they exit the balcony, Deniel steps in to stride beside them.

"This is it, then," he says.

"This is," says Kael.

In Lük's thoughts I see that this is the only time when the mysterious Paintbrush of the Gods, placed deep in the mountains, will be lightly guarded. The three needed to make an appearance here, so as not to arouse suspicion, and now, with the ceremony ending, they have a small window of time before the masters can return to their work. This is the best moment, perhaps the only moment, they will have. I can hear Lük repeating a thought to himself as they board the craft and he guides it away from the coliseum. *Tonight we will end this.*

10

"DON'T GET TOO CLOSE," SAYS KAEL.

"I know." Lük angles the craft lower, hanging back, skimming the building tops but keeping the crystal cage in his sight.

They fly over the outer islands, over giant stone wharves, and between towering lighthouses and then across the surging black sea. The moon lights the wave tops and in the distance paints the jagged Antarctic mountains.

Lük strains against crosswinds. He looks over to see Rana checking a timepiece. Multiple dials spin above its gear works. "How long do we have?"

"If Alara was right, the ceremony will just be ending. The masters' ship will have priority. They're probably boarding now."

Lük presses harder on the pedals and the craft lunges ahead. Waves crash against black cliffs below, the water dotted with chunks of ice, and now we are over a grassy plateau. The mountains rise steadily, glaciers in their seams.

We follow the ship carrying the Terra through a deep valley in S curves. After a few turns, the surrounding mountains are mostly covered with snow.

"There it is," says Deniel.

The valley meets a headwall, and the transport ship flies straight into a massive cave hung with icicle teeth. Lük flies far left of this entrance, up along the side of the valley wall, and then over the headwall.

Behind it, fields of ice stretch to the horizon. Waves and folds of glacier look as if an ocean was flash frozen. It sparkles in the cold moonlight.

Lük brings the craft around the craggy peak above the cavern entrance, to the back side of the mountain. He descends toward steep icy flanks, to a small tunnel entrance with a narrow landing spot beside it. He expertly hits the target, luffs the sails, and ties them down.

Deniel grips his staff. Kael checks his throwing blades. Rana pulls twin curved sabers, held in worn leather scabbards, from the seat compartment of the craft. She belts them to her waist.

"Nice," says Lük, referring to the blades. "You brought the minions."

Rana runs a finger down one leather side. "My father's swords. I will make him proud."

Lük reaches into the same compartment and produces

a heavy leather case with a thick strap. It is rectangular and he is very careful as he slings it over his shoulder.

"Don't trip," says Kael. It's the first time he's smiled, a cockeyed grin. It reminds me of Leech.

Silence falls over the three. They pause in the whipping, icy wind, their eyes darting from one to the other. No one dares speak.

"To battle," says Deniel, and rushes into the tunnel.

"What he said," Kael adds, and the three follow, plunging into darkness.

Lük feels Rana's hand find his. Their feet scuffle on cold rock. Minutes pass, the tunnel straight and sloping downward. The angle increases, and their boots begin to slip.

"Here," Kael whispers. He moves Rana's hand, who then guides Lük's to a cord along the wall, strung between rough stone rings.

They continue deeper for what seems like ten more minutes. Finally, there is light, a deep red glow.

The tunnel levels out and meets another, running at right angles. This one is taller. Overhead, carved arches hold the mountain at bay. The red glow comes from both directions. Water drips from the ceiling. Breaths of steam slip along the walls.

"Which way?" Rana asks.

Kael produces a thin gold sheet from his pocket, and twists it in his hands. A map is etched into its gleaming surface. "It should be . . ." He turns. "This way to the vents."

"How much time do we have?" Lük asks.

Rana checks. "Not enough."

They jog down the passageway. Hallways open in either direction, and occasionally I catch glimpses of machinery in Lük's peripheral vision. Giant metal gears and arms. The clouds of steam grow thicker, sometimes billowing in sudden, deafening hisses.

The tunnel joins another, widens, and then Kael halts them at a four-way intersection. The tunnel straight ahead leads to a large chamber, where we can see a glimpse of the transport craft, soldiers scurrying around it.

"This way," says Kael, heading left. They run through darkness for another minute before arriving at a metal catwalk that spans a chasm, a fissure that extends into darkness to each side, and above and below. Five wide copper pipes run vertically through the center of the space. A catwalk branches to each. Lük knows that these are cooling vents from the Paintbrush.

Kael leads the way to the center pipe. Its surface is beaded with condensation. We can hear the hum of air inside. The catwalk ends at a hatch in the side of the pipe. Deniel turns a handle and yanks it open, and a rush of hot air spills out.

"It looks like a tight fit," says Kael, peering in.

Rana leans in and takes a look. "It will have to do."

She opens her shoulder bag and unfolds a small black cloth, revealing eight teardrop-shaped jewels. Lük recognizes them as Falcon Hearts, and I feel his heart racing. They are planning to levitate down this pipe, deep down into the cavern where the Paintbrush is located. Lük doesn't mind heights if he's flying a ship, but this kind of levitation has never been his best skill.

Rana passes out the crystals, two per person, then holds her own to her lips. She closes her eyes, whispering, "Be with me, spirit," and then blows on them. They ignite in brilliant blue. She cups them in her palms and then spreads her arms and rises slightly off the ground.

"I will go first," says Deniel nervously. "Seniority." He performs the same ritual with the crystals and begins to float.

"Remember, control your speed," says Kael. He checks the map one more time. "We should emerge at the far end of the cavern. There will be a plateau on the east wall. It should be obvious."

"Right." Deniel is breathing hard. He pulls himself through the hatch, then lowers out of sight.

Kael and Rana follow, then Lük, who closes the hatch behind them. They descend, lit by the blue of the crystals, hands guiding along the blackened interior of the pipe. It's not quite wide enough for Lük to fully extend his arms, and I sense him tensing, thinking about the kilometers above and below. He wishes for the wide-open spaces of the sky.

The descent is long, deep into the earth, like traveling down vessels toward its heart. I imagine the tons of rock and the sense of darkness and weight is almost too much to handle, and I'm not even the one actually stuck in this spot, having to breathe the hot, mineral-tasting air.

Ten minutes down and the heat is becoming unbearable. Lük is drenched in sweat, wiping drops out of his eyes. The motion causes him to lose focus, and his speed increases. His feet bump Rana's shoulders.

"Sorry!" he whispers. And then he voices a fear that has been growing. "I'm having a harder time with control."

"So am I," says Rana. "Something has changed. I feel like I have less control with every minute."

"Get ready to slow down," Kael calls. There is light now, below. Red light.

Lük focuses on the crystal, on the sense of space around him, and starts to slow his speed, but I can feel that it's a struggle. He has lost some sense for it that he once had.

"Deniel, slow down!" Kael calls urgently below.

"I'm trying, I—" Deniel's hands and staff rake against the sides of the pipe. "I can't quite grasp it, I . . ."

"Something's wrong," says Kael. "Ow!" He bounces from one side of the pipe to the other.

"Kael!" Rana calls. "This is because they've taken

the Terra," she says between rapid breaths. "We've lost our feel for it."

Rana slows hard, and Lük slams into her shoulders. "I can't hold it!"

Rana begins to sing, a high note like Lilly has sung. She glows brighter, but then the note catches in her mouth. I hear her gasp. "I—I can't find it! I've lost the music!"

They slide free of the pipe, into a massive cavern space beyond measure. Lük tries to stop himself, but his speed only increases. His worry turns to panic, but Rana grabs his arm and pulls him sideways, angling downward toward a narrow ledge that curves along the side of the cavern. Below it, at the bottom of sheer cliffs, stretches a wide river of glowing magma.

"Kael!" Rana shouts. She pushes Lük toward the ledge. He is able to lower himself the rest of the way and lands hard. Rana darts back, her whole body glowing, and she grabs Kael. The moment they have slowed, they both shout.

"Deniel!"

"I can't slow down!" Deniel's robe flaps in the wind. He loses his staff, his arms and legs starting to pinwheel. Falling faster . . .

"Deniel!" Rana screams. "Kael, let me go!"

Kael is gripping Rana by the shoulders. "You can't! We've lost the music!"

They watch helplessly as Deniel's speed increases. He's too far down now. He stops screaming and pulls his arms in, wrapping them around his body. He is free-falling, and Lük thinks he has been like an older brother to them, all their lives, and it is not fair that he is about to die and there is nothing they can do.

Two seconds before Deniel reaches the bubbling magma, he bursts into flames. His body disintegrates on impact, leaving only a hiss on the glowing surface.

Rana and Kael hover there for a moment in shock, then slowly float over to the ledge. Rana is fighting tears. Lük wraps her in a hug, and she buries her face in his shoulder.

"We're losing our connection to the forces," says Kael after a moment. "What will this world be, what kind of future can there be without the Terra?"

"I should have known," Rana mutters. "It felt wrong. I should have warned him, or we should have gone another way . . ."

"Don't," says Lük.

Rana pulls away, her eyes fierce. "Why not? His death means nothing!"

"It does if we succeed," says Kael. "Deniel chose to be a part of this mission. Now we need to finish it. For him. For everyone."

"But . . . ," Lük says, and what he is about to say ignites a deep fear inside him. He glances up. "Those vents were going to be our escape. How are we going to get out if we can't find the music?"

Kael stares at the ground, Rana at Lük, and more tears well up. She doesn't need to answer. Lük already knows. While they may try . . . they are probably not going to escape.

"It was always a risk." Kael sighs.

I feel Lük remembering his wish back in the apartment, to run, to turn away and flee instead of facing this. And now, it's too late. I find him thinking of his family. His parents, his younger brother. They've already lost one son, Lük's older brother Maris, a soldier, and Lük has not seen them very often since he came to the academy. The visits home have been brief. Too brief, now, it seems.

"We need to keep moving," says Rana.

The question of where to go is obvious. The three turn and gaze across the cavern. It stretches out of sight into blackness, a vast space large enough to hold a city. Huge chunks of rock, the size of icebergs, regularly topple away from the walls and splash into the magma river with explosions of sparks. The ledge that the three stand on grows wider as it stretches away from them, becoming a plateau, and in the distance a huge section thrusts out like the bow of a mighty ship.

Perched on this triangular point is a vast tower of copper and brass metalwork.

The Paintbrush of the Gods.

The masters' secret creation. Their scientists and alchemists have been working on it for hundreds of years.

It resembles a sort of gigantic telescope, with a triangular base, filled with gears and glass balls, and then a huge cylinder that is angled downward, aimed at the magma river. Behind it are rounded structures arranged in rows reaching back to the cavern wall. Lük thinks they are the turbines, twenty electromagnetic vortex turbines each strong enough to power all the lights of Atlante. And in spite of their mission, Lük can't help but to feel awe and wonder at the sight of this great device.

"Come on." Kael starts to jog toward the Paintbrush. Lük and Rana hold each other for another second, then lock eyes. Lük nods slowly, hating this, but they run.

The magma cracks and bubbles below them, and waves of heat wash over the three. Rumbles signal new falls of rock crumbling away.

Lük knows, from Master Alara's teachings, that this is a spot where plates of the earth's crust meet. The Atlanteans do not call it plate tectonics, but they think of the earth as Ana's shell. The Paintbrush is placed on this fault line that stretches from beneath Antarctica up the spine of the South American continent, along North America, and around the Pacific Ocean, though none of these landforms are quite the same shape in Lük's mind as they are in mine. The fault line is a deep, strong subduction zone with a spiny backbone of volcanoes, always active and moving. The Paintbrush will send a beam of vortex energy deep into this fault, causing a chain reaction of volcanic eruptions around the globe, releasing ash into the skies that will cool the planet. There will be some tectonic upheaval, but the Atlanteans have built monitoring stations at various points along the Paintbrush's path: in the Andes, along the Pacifica islands. They believe they can temper the system, release the energy if it gets too intense. Most of the masters are confident.

But some, like Alara and other scientists and alchemists within the realms, do not believe that the Paintbrush is safe. They believe that the power unleashed cannot be controlled and will cause certain disaster. This is why the masters have trapped the Terra, because they believe that adding her energy to the process will ensure their safety. She is, they believe, the force of life and the Atlanteans are the highest life-form, and so, by design, she exists to serve them.

Alara and others think this is folly.

And so this plan was formed. Alara could not trust any of the masters, or any in the military, and thus she had to turn to her students; and she has asked this difficult thing of them because they are capable, and because they are just slightly too young to be taken seriously by the masters or their bureaucrats or their generals. And yet they can be lethal, and they are fiery and idealistic and can act on their hearts' passions without compromise.

Lük knows they must act, or all may be lost. Yet with every step closer to the Paintbrush, he wishes more and more that they could turn and run instead.

The three reach the curved walls of the vortex turbines. They hum with potential energy, blue light glowing out through copper gratings. A path between them, paved with giant stones, leads to the Paintbrush.

"Alara said there is venting at the base of the Paintbrush," says Lük and he pats the heavy bag he carries. "If we place the device there, we can bring down the whole plateau."

They are about to move, when Kael holds up his hand.

They hear the sound of approaching boots, and now a bright light glows from the tunnel at the far end of the turbines. The soldiers appear, carrying the Heart of the Terra atop poles that they support on their shoulders. They march right past, and Lük can see the Terra, still sitting, eyes closed as if she is meditating.

The soldiers reach the base of the Paintbrush, and then two begin to turn a powerful crank. Gears whine and the crystal cage is lifted until it is even with the center of the long telescope-like cylinder. Another soldier operates a pulley that opens a side panel in the cylinder, and then the cage slides into place. It looks as if the Terra will be used almost like a lens, the energy beamed through her and she will refract it like a prism, though Lük knows it is more complicated than that.

The soldiers finish and head back out, except for two, who remain near the Paintbrush.

Kael nods to Lük and Rana, and then he takes off along the outside of the turbines.

Rana counts silently down from ten, and then motions to Lük with her eyes. They stand and walk out onto the pathway, making no effort to hide themselves.

The guards turn in surprise and then stride toward them, wielding spears. "Stop! Right there."

A shadow darts out behind them: Kael, both arms cocked back. He snaps first the right, then the left, and throwing blades flash. One guard staggers, crying out, the blade buried in his shoulder. The other is hit in the back of the head and topples over. Rana and Lük break into a run, Lük pulling out his Y-shaped copper slingshot. He loads one of the metal darts, careful not to touch its toxin-coated tip, and shoots it on the run. It catches the staggering guard in the sternum. He looks down at it, already woozy from the shoulder wound, and then collapses.

The three run, and Lük takes the lead. The Paintbrush looms above them now, a marvel of copper and bronze and glass, elegant curves and cylinders, even more impressive close up, with all of its intricacies. Lük can't help but consider that maybe this should be done, maybe they should use this fantastic power. . . .

"There," says Kael. He's pointing to a round grate at the base of the structure.

Lük shakes away the doubt and kneels. Together, he and Kael remove the grate. There is a row of glowing glass tubes that transport the energy from the turbines. Lük opens the heavy bag he's carried and pulls out a polished block of metallic stone: magnetite. His fingers find a seam in the top and he pulls off a heavy lid, revealing a chamber full of bright yellow powder. He rummages through his bag for a small dagger and a leather satchel that is damp to the touch. He loosens the drawstring and removes a spool of twine, soaked in oil. This will be the fuse for the bomb. He unspools the twine, placing one end in the powder, then he closes the lid, and places the box atop the glass tubes.

He scrambles back from the vent, heart racing, unrolling the twine for a few meters then cutting it. He rummages in the bag one more time and produces a flint.

Kael joins him. "Ready?"

"Yeah," says Lük. "This is will give us thirty seconds to get up that tunnel."

"Sure wish we could fly," says Kael, and the look he shares with Lük says he knows it's not enough time.

Lük sees that Rana is still over by the Paintbrush. She's staring at the wall of wheels and levers and glass tubes. "Rana," says Lük. "Come on."

"Wait . . ." She peers closer, her brow furrowed.

"Let's go!" Kael hisses, checking over his shoulder.

But Lük sees Rana's eyes widening. "What is it?" he asks.

"There are handprints . . . ," she says absently, gazing into the machinery.

"What?" Lük asks.

"Our names," she adds. Rana's eyes flash to Lük and Kael. She is deathly pale. "Look at this."

Lük steps cautiously over, his body humming with worry, the fuse shaking in his hand. Kael joins him. Rana points and Lük examines the wall of gadgetry. There in the center is a flat panel with three handprints. They are recessed in metal, and in the handprints, tiny white spikes stick up at regular intervals. I want to tell Lük that I know these all too well. Above each handprint is a name etched in copper: KAEL, RANA, LÜK.

"Why are those there?" Kael asks numbly.

"Because they're for you!"

The voice booms through the cavern. Lük whirls to see Master Solan sweeping out of the tunnel, flanked by soldiers. The one beside him holds Alara, her hands bound behind her back. The other masters follow right behind in a procession, hoods up.

"That's right!" Master Solan calls, seeing their stunned faces. "The Paintbrush needs three people to operate it. And who better than you?"

11

"LIGHT THE FUSE!" RANA SHOUTS, HER FACE WHITE.
Lük is in shock, and I feel the spike of fear and panic but
certainty. . . . *Yes, light the fuse, we will die but it has to
be now*—

Only just then he feels a terrible pain and staggers
back, a short arrow sunk in his shoulder. The fuse slips
from his numb fingers.

And then the guards have reached them. Strong arms
fold around Lük's shoulders.

"Yes, well, here we are." Master Solan strides toward
them, hands clasped behind his back. He looks down at
Lük's explosive. "Magnet charge. That would definitely
have caused some damage. Luckily, you all have reeked
of treachery for months, and you"—he turns to Alara—
"for years."

"Ask the Terra whose cause is more treacherous," she
says defiantly.

Solan ignores this. "So, what do you think of my

extra design feature? I thought it would be appropriate for you three to be the ones to save us, since you were so determined to ensure our destruction."

"We'll never help you," Rana says bravely. "You'll have to kill us."

Master Solan smiles. "I don't have to kill anyone. You're going to operate the Paintbrush for me."

"No," says Lük.

"Really? You sound so certain. . . ." Master Solan keeps smiling. "Bring them in."

"Solan!" Alara calls. "This isn't necessary."

Solan turns, his eyes narrowing. "Of course it's not *necessary*, but what good are gods if they are not artful? If they do not teach lessons. And we will be artful gods."

More soldiers emerge from the tunnel, and they are carrying huge rectangular objects. Steam rises off their glassy surfaces. As they get close, I hear a little moan from Rana.

Lük knows what these are, too.

Caskets.

Coffins made of ice, from the catacombs that the Atlanteans built into the glacier, which holds the dead all the way back to the ancient kings.

There are three huge blocks, water dripping from their sides. The soldiers place them on the ground and slide their heavy, translucent lids off.

Lük tenses all over, and I feel him trying to hide his

horror. Lying in the middle casket is Maris, still in his cadet uniform, who died in the Pacifica trade uprising two years ago. Lük can barely breathe, flashing back to the funeral, standing in the icy catacombs, singing the song of the departed with his sobbing parents, his stoic little brother, Elden. . . .

And he knows that the man in the front casket is Rana's father, Marcon, who died suddenly of a wasp allergy, whose twin swords Rana carries. The third casket holds Kael's girlfriend of three years, Diala, murdered by the Assuye sky pirates in a raid on her airship as she returned from her studies in Tulana.

None of the three can speak at first.

"What is this?" Alara asks fearfully.

"Our alchemical studies have revealed an added benefit of this concentrated state of the Terra that we have constructed," says Master Solan. He moves to the Paintbrush and climbs a spiraling staircase to the crystal cage, where the Terra still sits silent, eyes closed. He pulls a lever and gears begin to whir. There is a sound like scraping rock and the cage begins to glow. The light gains intensity. Solan throws another lever and a thin metal spear shoots into the cube and stabs the Terra in the shoulder. Her eyes flash open, but her expression remains unchanged.

Something brilliant and white flows out of her and down a recess in the spear. Solan produces a small stone cup from his robe and maneuvers it into the machinery. When he climbs down the ladder, Lük can see that the contents of the bowl are a glowing white liquid.

"Blood from the Heart," says Solan, "the essence of life itself." He steps over to Marcon's casket and pours a single drop of the glowing liquid between Marcon's frozen purple lips. He moves on, doing the same to Maris and Diala.

"What are you doing?" Rana asks weakly.

"I am showing you the power that we have harnessed, which can be yours."

Lük, Rana, and Kael stare at their lost relatives, and in Lük I can feel the pain flooding out of a locked room, all the sorrow he felt, the regret that his brother was in the wrong place at the wrong time, the guilt that Lük hadn't been there to fight alongside him . . .

And then, white light begins to glow all over Maris, spreading from his chest out to his fingers and toes, glowing up in a corona over his heart.

In a fit, his chest moves.

His eyes open.

All I can think of is Elissa, rising from the cryo tube, a horror returned.

But Maris's eyes look human, normal. He coughs wickedly, and then, incredibly, sits up stiffly and looks around, his skin still blue. One of the soldiers faints. Another rushes to the side of the nearest turbine and vomits.

"Where am I?" Maris croaks with dry vocal cords.

It happens to Marcon. It happens to Diala, and then all of them are awake, alive, back from the dead and looking around, and trying to understand this place they are in, these coffins . . .

And the three are watching their loved ones return.

"Dad . . . ," Rana breathes, crying.

"Di," says Kael, shaking all over.

"Maris," Lük says, the shock rendering him nearly mute.

"This is the power of the Heart of the Terra," says Solan proudly. "The Paintbrush can bring back the whole planet, and then we can achieve our greatest yearning, overcome life's greatest foe. We can conquer death."

"You don't know the consequences of the power," says Alara quietly, trembling at the sight of the resurrections.

Solan ignores her. He looks at the three. "This is my gift to you. In return, you will run the Paintbrush for me. Please, don't make me beg."

Lük and Rana and Kael share overwhelmed, teary glances. This is too much, and to have these loved ones returned. . . .

"Rana? Is that you?" Just the sound of her father's voice is tearing her apart. "What is all this? I was in Pacifica, that wasp nest by the beach. . . ."

"Kael, there were pirates. . . ."

"We swore to protect the Terra," says Kael, staring at Lük and Rana and not at Diala, as if looking at her would undo him completely.

"I know," says Lük.

"Lük, brother, what are you d—" Maris's words are drowned out in a choking fit. He grabs his neck and starts to double over.

It happens to Marcon and Diala, too. They contort, their combined struggles for breath deafening.

"What's happening?" Rana screams, her sanity shredding.

"I only gave them enough to find their way back to this life again," says Master Solan. "If you want them to remain here, then please activate the Paintbrush."

"Oh, gods, I can't, I can't," Rana sobs.

I feel Lük exploding inside, crushed—he can't lose his brother again, can't bear that emptiness. And I feel him thinking, trying to tell himself that they don't know that the Paintbrush *won't* work. They don't know and maybe it will be all right. Maybe it will make things better, but even if it doesn't, at least they will have their loved ones back. . . .

It is Kael who steps to the handprints first. His eyes are glued to Diala now. "I'm sorry." He stares at his love, shaking with each choking gasp she makes.

Lük and Rana join him.

As Lük places his palm against the tips of the white

spikes, he gazes up at the Terra and thinks, *I'm so sorry.*

The Terra gazes down at him. *Beware the gods and their horrors*, she says, but again, I am the only one who hears it.

Lük presses. His hand ignites in burning. I know this pain. Rana hisses as she does the same, and Kael, and the pain grows and the blood flows.

For a moment there is only silence.

And then the entire cavern begins to rumble. The turbines spin up, glowing electric blue. The gears of the Paintbrush begin to whir, to churn, and the crystal cage lights up in blinding white.

The entire cylinder of the Paintbrush, a giant weapon now aimed at the magma blood flow of the planet, hums and vibrates. Sparks begin to fly from its joints.

And the energy is traveling through Lük, Rana, and Kael, overwhelming them with warmth and light and stars and eternity, and it feels like the most horrible pain and the sweetest delight and maybe like dying or living forever in a day or something, so much something. Lük is crying and screaming and silent and time seems to lose meaning.

"Behold!" Master Solan shouts over the wind that whips through the cavern.

Lük opens his eyes and through the white heat that he has become, he sees an enormous beam of energy erupt from the Paintbrush, firing into the magma, causing plumes of fire and lighting the molten rock to a blinding white. The energy of life, of the earth, of the stars and the universe . . .

Lük barely hears the first scream, but he can hear the second. He and Rana and Kael are wrapped in folds of white energy but Lük is able to turn his head, and beyond the light he sees Master Solan, his face wide with ecstasy or terror. He is screaming. . . .

And then bursts into flames, his robe on fire and white light shooting from his eyes and mouth. In a moment his body has become a charred silhouette, crumbling to ash.

It happens next to a nearby soldier. Then another. The masters start to flee for the tunnel, but few of them will make it. Their bodies begin to burn and burst before they can reach safety.

Lük thinks to run, somehow hears Rana thinking to run and Kael, too, as if their minds are connected by the energy, but then a voice speaks to them, the voice that only I have known:

Stay with me, children, in the safety of my light.

The Terra has spoken and when he hears this voice, Lük feels that he has never truly known the world, or what it means to be alive, until this moment.

What is happening? Rana asks.

No vessel can contain that which cannot be held, says the Terra. *Qi and An. The quest to become gods has unleashed horrors. Using my energy in this way will ravage the earth. There was nothing you could have done.*

More screaming. Chunks of the cavern walls begin to break away. Masters are crushed beneath toppling boulders. One by one, the turbines explode in glorious plumes of lightning.

Lük feels the shrapnel and rock, the flares of magma, all passing near him and maybe through him, but he is safe in the embrace of the Terra's light, a horror he has helped to unleash.

Everything shakes and blinds.

But then for a moment there is silence.

Go. Now, my children, says the Terra. *And remember me.*

Lük tries again and this time his hand comes free. He staggers back, leaving the light, stumbling over chunks of rock. He reaches out and finds Rana's arm, blinking as his eyes adjust. He turns to see the devastation. Wreckage and rock everywhere. Most of the plateau in either direction is gone. The magma crashes in terrifying waves against the cavern walls. Each impact peels away columns of rock.

"Rana!"

Lük and the others look over to spy Alara, singed and bloodied, waving from the exit tunnel.

Hurry, children!

Lük hears a strange whine and looks up to see all the light sucking back into the Paintbrush, and its very matter seems to be rattling, becoming molten, and Lük feels certain that it is going to explode.

"Go!" Kael calls, thinking the same thing.

Lük runs, taking Rana's hand. They vault across the wreckage, around the charred impressions that were once soldiers and masters and . . .

His feet splash in water between two twisted pieces of copper. The ice coffins—

"They were already dead," says Rana, her voice shredded. "Say it."

"They . . . ," Lük manages, but that is all. It's Rana's turn to pull him along. She's right, he knows, but the image of Maris returned will haunt him. Had there been another way? Could he somehow still have his brother back? The guilt will stay with him forever.

They reach the tunnel and duck inside, and Lük takes a last glimpse at the mighty Paintbrush of the Gods as it hums and vibrates and seems to be drawn in molten light.

And then there is a deep, sizzling sound, and they are thrown to the ground and shield their heads as a blast of energy sears past them.

Then it is dark.

Lük gets to his feet. He helps Rana up. They peer back into the cavern. The magma lights it in ominous reds. The plateau is dark but not totally. Lük sees that the Paintbrush of the Gods is still glowing like a hot burner, steam rising from it. Only a faint white light remains from the crystal cage.

"We have to go back for her," he says.

But a new tremor shakes the ground, and everywhere there is the sound of crumbling rock. The ceiling begins to fall in great slabs.

"We can't," says Alara. "We have to get out."

"The Terra—" says Lük.

"Is lost," says Alara.

Run, the Terra says to them. *What is lost shall be found.*

And so they do. They escape the tunnel and arrive in the entrance cavern. It is all coming down. Fallen ceiling has already grounded the transport ship. The masters' craft, here now, too, has smaller ships tied to its sides. The Three and Master Alara pile into one of these small craft, and Lük flies them out, dodging the debris, and then back to Atlante, where the first seismic shocks and tremors are arriving, the sea roiling, the ice and rock cracking. The Paintbrush of the Gods is gone, but its work has been unleashed, and the world is convulsing, changing . . . *all by our hand.*

The Three will fail, I hear the Terra's voice. This is not a message for Lük, it is for me.

And now I am leaving, pulling back away from Lük's mind, but as I am, I see in a blur what is to come:

They will evacuate, journey north, the masters gone,

society and the world collapsing. They will race the ash clouds to Greenland, to the last stronghold city of Polara. Alara's disciples will prepare the skulls, prepare the temples to hide them in, while the three prepare themselves to be sacrificed, to preserve their memories and knowledge forever, to help save future life from this same tragedy.

The millions dead, the dead raised only to die again. . . .

Over and over the cycle repeats.

They will kneel on pillows under an ash-filled sky as the world plunges back into ice. They will wear white and try to be strong and look at one another with tragic, knowing eyes because this must be done. Alara and the surviving clergy will offer words to the Terra, but she will not hear because she is trapped in a cage and buried, and the earth will not know her song, the coming civilizations will not know her music, because it is lost, and for ten thousand years, they will make the same mistakes, on larger and larger scales, rising and falling, because they cannot see another way, they have never known the music. . . .

And Lük will take his last breath and then squeeze his throat tight as the blade meets it.

There will be a searing white pain.

A sense of leaving.

The last thought he will think is of Rana's beautiful face, her beautiful hair and high cheeks and wide hollow eyes . . .

Black eyes . . .

Dead eyes . . .

But all does not end after that.

12

FIRST A DULL BURNING. THE COLLAPSING ATLAN-
tean world still a blur . . . then my eyes opened to a
warm orange light, the soothing relief of a setting sun, in
stripes across arches of stone.

I blinked and recognized the shape of a high ceiling,
a large room, and beside me, a huge window of crystal
panes like an eye, looking out on a sky of imperial blues,
a sliver moon already cresting overhead.

I had to sort out my sense of time. It felt like years
had passed, or minutes or millennia, but no matter
which measurement, each was infinite and infinitesimal
at once.

Owen. You must hurry. They are coming for me.

I tried to move, but couldn't.

The sun faded from the ceiling arches.

The world went black again.

○ ○ ○

Later, I felt pain distantly, like sticks rubbing together. Broken bones.

Eyes open.

The sun had set.

Stars infinite in the sky, a brushstroke of cold Milky Way. The ceiling arches in shadows.

I felt the tingle of my arms and legs, the beating of my heart, pressure of stone against my back, the systems coming back online, technicians throwing switches.

"Did you see . . ."

I pulled my head from the cold stone and found her sitting in her throne.

The Sentinel. Sword by her side. In the giant chair, she looked small. I'd assumed she was old, but without her shroud of fury she looked more my age. She glimmered in ghost light, but I could see more now: her black hair flowing around her threadbare white dress. Her bare feet. Her mouth pursed and small in her thin, smooth face.

Her eyes still vacant holes of black.

"See?" I croaked. The images from the journey seemed both like memories and like dreams, things I knew but couldn't trust. Collaging, fragments in an already fragmented head.

"Did you see . . ."

I sat up and was distracted by a scream of pain. I

looked down at my ruined right wrist. The skin around the contorted joint was swollen and purple. Just looking at it made it hurt more.

"Did—"

"I heard you," I snapped. My jaw ached. My head pounded. "Did I see. See what?"

The Sentinel just stared at me. I had a weird sensation, like she was familiar.

"You are not of the Three."

"Yeah, I know. And you stabbed me in the chest." Except I looked down and realized that whatever her blade had done, my chest seemed to be fine and moving in a normal living, breathing way.

"The Terra asked me to help," she said. Her voice was low and flat, but still slightly girlish. "To send the one who was not of the Three."

"Yeah, well, you sure did that."

"Did you see . . ."

"I don't remember what I saw! Let me think." I turned away from the Sentinel's dead gaze, and looked out on the silhouetted mountains and the stars, trying to piece it all together.

The Terra wanted me to see why the Three would fail. Back in Atlantis, it was because the masters used the power of the Terra to resurrect loved ones. They'd discovered that the concentrated power of the Terra could restore life. But what did that have to do with now?

"Did you see . . . L—" The Sentinel sounded like she was searching for a word.

The masters had built a trap into the Paintbrush and the Three had failed. Master Solan had been as twisted as Paul. Not only did he want to succeed in his goals, he also wanted to break the spirits of those who opposed him. He didn't have to design the Paintbrush to specifically use the Three. He'd done that because he'd wanted to be *artful*.

I wondered what it was about power that made someone like that: it wasn't enough just to achieve your goal, you also had to relish in the suffering of the people who opposed you. To flaunt your power.

Yet the power of the Terra had been too great, and the force unleashed by the Paintbrush threw the earth into chaos.

But what had I seen? Why would the Three also be destined to fail this time? Unlike the masters, Paul would have no idea about that power of the Terra. He'd have no way of knowing it— Wait. Unless . . .

I turned back to the Sentinel.

"What are you asking me?"

"Did you see . . . Lü—"

And suddenly I saw her. Right there in front of me. "Did I see . . . Lük?"

Though her face was mostly light, and her eyes absent,

I saw some ripple of relief wash over her.

"Lük."

"You're Rana," I said.

"Rana," she repeated, as if she was remembering it.

"But you died: you had your throat cut and you went into the skull."

She nodded. "We died, only to discover that we could not. Though our knowledge was transferred to the skulls, along with a piece of our souls, though the blood drained from our bodies onto the stones, we . . . lingered. We linger still."

I felt the pieces coming together. "This is because the Terra's energy flowed through you, isn't it? In the Paintbrush?"

"Paintbrush . . . I had forgotten its name. Lük," she said, like she was glad to have the word back. "The exposure to the Heart of the Terra made us immortal in a way. But we're incomplete. Never to die but never to be fully alive."

"How did you end up here?" I asked.

Rana sighed. It was a frail sound, like wind through a crack in a door. "Once we saw what we had become, we chose to be watchers. The skulls could be left dormant until we activated a signal, along the magnetic beams of the planet, which would cause them to reach out for the lost Atlantean code.

"At first we thought we could remain among the

living, but eventually, as the knowledge of the ancients was lost to the new world, we became feared, monsters. And we could not fully explain who we were or why we existed because this would expose the secret of the Three.

"And so after thousands of years, I grew tired of hiding, of trying and failing to connect. I found this place, with its shreds of our culture. It felt like home. And so I have lingered on. I do not know what became of the others, Lük and . . ." Her mouth moved like it was trying to reshape a word.

"Kael."

"Yes. I lost them, in the centuries when we were hunted and feared."

"I know that at least one of you did a similar thing. I'm not sure who, but Paul found one of you in Greenland—sorry, Polara."

"Where we were sacrificed. Where our earthly bodies lie frozen," said Rana.

"That's right," I said. "Paul found your bodies, and that's where he got the genetic samples to search for the Atlanteans in the first place. And . . ."

Then it hit me. "That's how he knows."

"Knows what?" said Rana.

"If Paul saw Kael in Sentinel form, and also saw the bodies," I said, my pulse pounding, "he probably figured out what you are. And if he knows that the Heart of the

Terra has that kind of power . . ."

I remembered his words from the skull chamber, which felt like days ago: *the one true quest, the oldest quest there is.*

He'd already practiced cheating death once, but only by bringing the Cryos in EdenSouth back as mindless drones. Now he would have the power to conquer death fully. All his experiments, the bodies in the Eden lab, the program that raised the Cryos, maybe this was what he was really working toward all along.

The power of immortality.

I struggled to my feet, everything sore, my wrist absolutely burning. "How long have I been out?"

"A day and a half," said Rana.

A spike of panic surged through me. "What happened to Lilly and the others?"

"Your enemy, Paul, had too many soldiers. They escaped. I think the Medium girl, my sister, could have gotten away, but she would not leave her wounded friend."

"No," I said, hating and admiring Lilly's loyalty, "she wouldn't. Why didn't they take me?"

Rana's head cocked. "Because you were not here."

"Not here? At all?"

"When I stabbed you, you disappeared until just moments ago."

"Okay."

"Also likely because you are not of the Three."

"No," I said. "I'm not." Lilly, Mateu, and Evan were the Three. Evan standing in for Leech. The Three who would fail. Did Paul know that part? How could he? After all, the actual Three didn't. Only me.

I wanted to think through it more, all of it, not least about how I had actually time traveled, but Paul had a head start and I needed to hurry.

First, I needed to know where they were going. The Mariner's knowledge I'd had led only as far as this place.

"Are there any bodies here?" I asked Rana. "Of soldiers?"

"I threw them into the chasm," said Rana. "They dishonored this space. Also, they were beginning to smell."

"Ah," I said. They might have had a gamma link pad I could have used.

"I did, however, keep this." Rana indicated a black bag beside her in the shadow of the chair. Just my looking at it incited a white glow. "It is mine," said Rana, "I think. I can't enter it, but that is how it feels."

Come home, Rana, the skull called to me, glowing, as if it only needed my attention turned toward it.

"Yeah," I said. "Lilly's—and your—skull. Did you kill the woman who was carrying this?"

"It was dark," said Rana with a shrug, "but I do think I remember a woman's scream. And when I saw the glow in her bag, I rescued it from the chasm."

A little burst of adrenaline coursed through me, thinking of Francine being gone. The part of me that had wanted vengeance felt cheated. I should have been the one to kill her, not that I could actually imagine killing someone. Still, I was the one she'd wronged most. Maybe I'd have a chance with Paul. Paul who now had Lilly. It always came back to him. And I could all too easily imagine evening the score.

But something about the glowing bag bothered me. "And the soldiers didn't come back for this? Try to get it from you?"

"No. Perhaps they were too afraid." Rana sounded proud.

"Yeah, but . . . they need that skull. Lilly needs to know how to communicate with the Terra. Isn't that what your skull teaches? How to be the Medium and talk to the Terra?"

"Yes. The Medium is the one who can talk to the Terra by singing her soul. Then she is the one who can actually free the Terra by answering the Terra's question."

"What question?"

Rana seemed to shrug. "No one knows. But the shamans divined that the Terra could be freed by answering a simple question that she would pose to the one who could speak with her. That was the true role of the Three. Not just to protect the Terra but to free her."

But the Three would fail, and so the Terra had chosen me instead. My worry grew, making the skull glow brighter as well. "Maybe Lilly had already communed with the skull. Maybe she already knows. But when I was in the skull, Rana—sorry, you—didn't tell me about the question."

"The skulls are designed to reveal more information the closer the Three get to the Heart of the Terra," said Rana. "It was a defense mechanism: in case of capture, it would keep the Three valuable and alive and keep the secrets. It was also to protect the Three from corruption of the spirit."

"What's that mean?"

"It was believed that the Heart of the Terra is so powerful, even the most courageous would have second thoughts about freeing her."

I turned all this over, struggling to put it together. It seemed like Paul would have known, or at least suspected, this feature of the skulls. And yet he'd left it behind without a thought. . . .

But maybe that made sense, too. If Paul was after the immortality power of the Terra, he'd have no need to free her from her cage. He didn't need the skull, just Lilly, to help run the Paintbrush, to activate the handprints.

After that, though, she'd be expendable.

"Okay, I've got to go," I said, wanting to move, needing to move. . . .

But then I remembered my craft was gone.

I slumped back to the floor and looked out the window at the endless mountains. No supplies, not even boots to hike out in. And hike out to where in the sun and heat, and lethal cold at night? I wasn't getting out of here soon, or likely ever.

"What is it?" Rana asked.

"We came here in an Atlantean craft," I said.

"The one hidden with the Aeronaut skull?"

"Yeah."

"That was Lük's favorite ship. We once flew it cross hemisphere, to see the mammoth migrations in Siber. I miss him."

"Yeah, well, it was a great ship. It got me and Lilly all the way here, but it's gone now."

"Where is it that you need to go?"

"To Atlante," I said. "Those men that were here, their leader, Paul, has the three Atlanteans. He's going to find the Paintbrush and use it. And there's nothing I can do."

Rana sighed again, like a night wind through the Yellowstone caverns. "Poor boy," she said.

"Yeah, poor me."

"You are not of the Three."

"Right, I know. Are you going to stab me again?"

"You are of the One. Chosen by the Terra to save us all."

"I guess, but I'm not exactly having much luck at that."

Rana stepped down off her throne. "I will help you." She slid her sword into its scabbard, and I saw that she still had the twin blades, one on each hip. "This way. Bring the skull."

"Wait, where?" I picked up the skull bag with my good hand, slung it over my shoulder, and followed her. I kept my broken wrist by my stomach, trying to keep it from moving, but every step caused deep waves of pain.

She walked out the wrecked door. "It is this way."

Rana led me back down the wide staircase around the central chasm. We spiraled farther down than the skull chamber, crossed a stone bridge, and ducked into a tunnel, the carved walls lit only by her ethereal white. The passageway led straight for a while, then opened up into a wide space. Her light began to describe angles in front of us, and now I saw familiar wood and copper seams.

It was a craft. Quite a bit larger than the one I'd flown. It was maybe twenty meters long, of a diamond shape. Rana floated to where ladder rungs had been carved into the hull. We climbed up to a deck. Two copper masts lay flat, ready to be raised and attached to bronze fittings.

Sails were rolled and stowed against the folded booms. Near the front, a semicircle of crystal glass as tall as me stood on its side, shielding an almost nautical-looking steering wheel from likely winds. There were pedals in the floor.

I gazed around, getting to know the ropes, imagining how the craft would move in the wind. But something obvious was missing. "No vortex engine."

"Here." Rana was standing over a trapdoor. I opened it by pulling up a metal ring. We dropped into a small, dark compartment; and in Rana's light I could see a large black sphere, as wide as the spread of my arms, made of gleaming obsidian.

"This is one of the larger-scale vortex engines." It was ten times the size of the one in my old craft. Rana indicated a lever on the wall. I had to push hard, and it lowered with a heavy click and then gears began to grind. A section of the craft's hull slid open. A gleaming silver antenna extended down from the sphere, down beneath the craft, and I saw that it was headed for a circular notch in the floor. When the antenna hit this, there was a rumbling of rock and two sections of the floor spread apart. As they did, blue light seared my eyes. Beneath the floor was a swirling pool of vortex energy nearly as wide as this craft, but its glow was dim. It still had power, but not nearly what it had probably held ten thousand years before.

But it was more than enough for our purposes. The antenna lit up nearly molten and the light surged up into the black sphere. There was a familiar whine that eased my worried mind, and the giant vortex turbine began to hum deeper and stronger than anything I'd ever felt before.

The blue light from below faded, the last charge of this great Atlantean battery being sucked dry, and when the swirl had returned to its mercury silver, the antenna lost its glow. I threw up the lever and the system closed.

As we moved back to the deck, I could already feel that we were hovering off the ground.

I took the wheel with my left hand. I was right-handed, and wondered if I could pull this off. The wheel hummed with potential energy, like Sinassa, ready to pounce. Rana floated beside me and placed a hand on the wheel. "I can help. Let's go."

I glanced at her, standing there, twin swords at her waist. "You're coming with me?"

"Your enemy, Paul, has an army. I will be yours. The army of the Terra. Also, I know how to get there."

"Thank you," I said.

"And when it is over, I will beg the Terra to free me from this lingering."

There were rock walls on all sides except forward, where blackness beckoned.

I pressed the pedals and we leaped forward. "Whoa."

I could feel Rana looking at me. "Lük was probably way better at these things," I said.

"Yes. But you're doing well enough."

I flew into the darkness, guessing the passageway led straight ahead. After a few moments, a hint of silver beckoned. I increased our speed, and we hurtled out into the starlight. Looking back, I saw that we'd emerged from a cliff face, far below the high spire where Lilly and I had entered days—it felt like years—ago.

I brought us up, level with the peaks, and moved to try to lift the masts and unfurl the sails. After struggling with one hand, my broken wrist throbbing with every movement, Rana glided over and helped. Their rigging wound down into the deck, so that the ship's wheel could control them. Once we had it set up, I asked, "Which way?"

"Higher."

"I meant which direction."

"I know," said Rana. "First, higher. This is a distance craft, meant for the curve of the atmosphere, the upper wind currents, where the air is thinner and faster. Then, south."

13

THE MOUNTAIN PEAKS FELL AWAY BELOW US AS WE rose into the night, higher still until, far to the east, there was a meniscus of daylight. The temperature dropped, and the air grew nearly impossible to breathe.

Rana pointed to a lever by the wheel. I pulled it, and with a whine of pulleys and gears, the crystal windshield slid over our heads, more emerging from the deck, until it created a glass globe around us. I found locks to fasten it down, and then warm air began to filter in through small vents in the deck, keeping us warm and able to breathe in the thin, high air.

"Now . . ." She yanked on the bottom of the wheel, and with a snap it flipped up to a horizontal position. She slid a compartment open in the center of the wheel, and a glass ball rose up. There was a sphere inside the glass, striped with glowing orange lines.

"Those are the magnetic field lines of the planet,"

said Rana. "They run from pole to pole and are particularly strong in certain places. We must angle until we can line up with this one." She pointed to the glowing line that was nearest to a meridian etched in the glass. "It will lead us to Atlante."

"But Atlante was destroyed," I said.

"Yes," Rana agreed. "We will have to see what shape it is in. I have heard that it was covered in ice for most of the last ten thousand years."

"You've never been back?"

"No."

I oriented to the force line, and once I was aligned with it, I climbed higher and pushed the pedals to the floor.

We hurtled above the clouds and nearer to the stars, so high that there was always dawn, first to the west, and then to the east.

The ship was fast, maybe five or six times the speed of Lük's craft. Flying it reminded me of those first moments when we'd taken off from Lake Eden, the feeling of having this power, this control and purpose . . . and of having Lilly by my side. The purpose was still there, but the ache of missing Lilly was worse than ever, especially not knowing where she was or what had happened to her while I had been in the white realm.

Owen, hurry. The Terra's voice again. *They are very*

close. I pressed down harder on the pedals, the wind out-side the glass becoming a roar, and hoped we weren't too late.

Rana hovered next to me, her eyeless gaze aimed straight ahead, her mouth always curved down like she was sad.

"When was the last time you saw Lük?" I asked her.

"In ancient Egypt. We had made our way to Sumeria after the fall. We lingered there for many centuries, but it was never the same. We couldn't touch, and we were no longer whole, a part of us lost to the skulls. And people began to fear us, not just because we were spirits but also I think because we were reminders of some memory they had lost, that they knew was back there in the past somewhere, some better sense of the world. They maybe even felt a sense of guilt over losing the Terra.

"They called us *gidim*, or shades," said Rana. "We drifted through Egypt, during the earliest dynasties, and I briefly became a sort of psychic guide to a daughter of Pharaoh Khufu. But they turned on me. They always turned on us. After that, I retreated to darkness. And I lost Lük, somewhere in that time."

"I met him," I said, "in his skull."

Rana turned toward me. "And did you see the great city of Polara before it was lost to the ice?"

"I did. It was amazing."

"Such a place could only exist in the Terra's music.

The majesty, the magic . . . This world has been dead a long, long time." She sighed. "You don't still have it?"

"Lük's skull? No, it smashed on the journey. I'm sorry."

"It's just as well," said Rana. "Better not to be reminded of things that can never be again."

I wondered if freeing the Terra could bring that magic back into the world. I didn't think Rana was necessarily right that the world was dead, but it was definitely out of balance. People in my time thought it had been that way for a couple hundred years or so, since the rise of industry and technology, but the truth was that humanity had been out of balance for much longer.

Night passed and we followed the long spine of the Andes south until they became a tail of jagged islands. Then we crossed over an ocean. The sun began to rise, its light catching the whitecaps of the stormy sea, and painting, in the distance, the brilliant whites of the last place on this earth where ice still ruled.

The great Antarctic continent gathered dawn light, nearly blinding us. The ice had long since pulled back from its shores, revealing a rocky black coastline, but behind its collars of mountains there was still more ice than any Great Rise could melt.

"Follow the coast," said Rana, pointing. "See those mountains just inland? Behind them used to be the great valley that led to the Jaws of Sinassa."

"Is that the cave with the icicles and the tunnels down to the Heart of the Terra?" I asked.

"Yes, but the world has changed since then. I do not know what we will find now."

I brought us down along the black coast as the sun cleared the horizon. The oceans were blue here, bluer than I'd ever seen. There was none of the pollution like around the other continents, the oil slicks, gyres of garbage, and brown clouds of plastic sludge. There was the occasional boat carcass, at one point a cruise ship lying belly-up, and some piles of wood that had drifted here from the washed-away cities, but there were also stretches of unspoiled beach; and at one point, we even spotted the gray backs of whales. No one up north still believed in whales, and it made me wonder if Rana was wrong. Maybe there still was a future as magical as the past, maybe it was still here, hiding just out of our sight—

Owen. They've found me . . .

My head exploded with a white noise as the Terra's voice twisted into a scream. It sounded like a cry of pain but electric like sawing and also like Lilly's singing. All of that at once. She was hurting. . . .

"Repeat!" A voice interrupted my thoughts. "Proceed on your current course and bring your craft down."

"We have guests," said Rana.

I blinked tears out of my eyes and looked out to see that we were no longer alone in the sky. There were aircraft on either side of us, sleek metallic arrows with short wings and high tails. Their bellies were hung with missiles. They had no cockpits but spikes of antennae instead. Drone fighters. And they had markings on their sides, showing red-and-white stars and three letters: ACF.

"Lower your craft immediately or we will be forced to shoot you from the sky." The drones weren't the source of the voice, though.

Ahead, I saw two giant helicopters rising over a ridge near the coast. They faced us like predators waiting to pounce.

I wondered if I could outrun them. Probably. But they were right where we needed to get to. And that screaming . . . the Terra needed us.

A sharp series of cracks sounded, followed by the popping of fabric. I caught sight of the sails flapping with new bullet holes, as a gun mount on the port-side drone swiveled to take more shots.

"Would you like me to destroy them?" Rana asked, sounding like she'd enjoy it.

"This is General Mendes," a new voice spoke. "I'm leading this operation. Your name is Owen, Owen Parker. We know who you are and we're after the same thing. Land your craft and we can proceed together. Otherwise, we're on a mission to apprehend an enemy of the state and I cannot let you interfere."

I stared at the rhythmic flicking of the helicopter

blades. My feet flexed over the pedals. There wasn't time for this. Lilly . . .

"Bring her down, son," Mendes called. "We're not the enemy here, and neither are you."

The urge to run was so strong . . . but I let the pedals up and adjusted the sails to luff in the wind. I wondered if this general could be trusted. Every adult we'd put our faith in on this journey had let us down, but I couldn't save Lilly or the Terra if I was dead. I didn't know what other choice we had.

I dropped low over coastal cliffs and headed toward the ridge where the helicopters waited.

"Look," said Rana. She pointed to a high bluff of rock. "The great beacon of Atlante."

A half-crumbled tower stood at the edge of black cliffs. It had square sides that narrowed like an obelisk. Most of one side was eaten away. It rose to a crumbled pile, with one finger of wall still sticking skyward.

"It held the eternal light of Atlante, to guide all sailors home from the skies." Rana sighed. "This was once the first island of the archipelago."

I flew over the tower ruins and beneath the helicopters. On the other side of the ridge, I found a triangular delta, where a river of milky glacial water crossed black sand and met the dark blue ocean. Here and there, fallen buildings and stone walls stuck up from the gray river silt. The far wall of the valley was crisscrossed by crumbled staircases. The ruins of Atlante.

Three large ships were beached on the delta's edge. The ACF used hovercraft destroyers, as few normal boats could navigate the trash-filled oceans with any speed. Better to skim over it. Each hovercraft had a heli-pad on the back. A third copter hovered over the far side of the delta. Troops were streaming off the boats, as if they'd just arrived, their boots splashing in the water and digging into the black sand.

I landed beside the river. A cold breeze washed over us. It was still winter, down here at the navel of the world, and this was maybe the only place left where the word *winter* had any real meaning. This was the coldest air I'd ever felt.

By the time I'd pulled the lever to lower the sails, and the other that opened the crystal windshield, soldiers had surrounded us, rifles raised. I could see them eyeing Rana uncertainly.

"What is she?" General Mendes stepped through the line. He was older, his mostly bald head peppered here and there with silver hair. His face was weathered, his nose tinted with NoRad. His barrel chest stretched his silver-and-white fatigues. The soldiers all wore a similar fabric, the sun blinding as it reflected off them.

I glanced at Rana, now transparent in the faint sun-light. "She's a shade," I said. That likely wouldn't make much sense to them.

"Atlantean?" asked Mendes, as if the concept didn't faze him.

"Yes."

"So she's, what, a ghost or a memory or something?"

"Basically." I heard murmuring among the soldiers and felt like I should add: "She's a friend. I know it sounds strange . . ."

"Strange? All of this is strange." Mendes spoke over a stiff breeze tinged with salt. "More like impossible. But, it doesn't really matter what's possible or not. I've seen enough to know that you trust your eyes, not what you want to believe. But you're sure she can be trusted?"

"As long as you are kind to him," Rana answered.

Mendes squinted at her for a second. "Fair enough." He motioned for us to come down. "We need to get moving, so . . ." He turned and stalked off without finishing.

I climbed slowly down the side of the craft. Rana joined me, the black bag with Lilly's skull over her shoulder. The soldiers flanked us, but not too close.

The helicopters were landing farther up the beach, where the delta stretched back into a valley with steep black mountain walls. I could see ice shrouded in the cliff folds, deep in the shadows where the valley twisted out of sight.

Soldiers were in motion everywhere. A unit had gathered at the entrance to the valley. Others were massing around the helicopters. I was guided to General Mendes as he stood with other officers and looked over a computer pad.

"Okay," he said to them. "Send the scout team in." There were shouts, and the soldiers by the valley entrance formed two tight lines and began jogging along the edge of the gray river. "We want to preserve some element of surprise," Mendes continued. "High altitude surveillance shows the Eden team is up that valley, but the walls and the ice get real tight, according to the recon."

"Here's more data, sir, from the silent drones' pass." A soldier tapped his pad.

Mendes swiped at images, then held the pad out for all of us to see. "Looks like this is where we're headed."

This was a view deep into the valley, where the rocky sides ended at a solid wall of blue ice with a narrow fissure down the center.

"Looks like the heat signatures are about a kilometer into that ice fissure. That's where our mark is." Mendes sighed. "Copters aren't going to fit in there. Drones burn too hot for that ice. Reaching them on foot is going to be tough, too."

I found myself measuring the fissure in my mind, and imagining Lilly in there in Paul's clutches, forced to place her hand on the Paintbrush's spikes.

"I can fly us in." The words were out of my mouth before I'd even realized I was thinking it.

Mendes looked at me evenly, no surprise. He glanced

over my shoulder. "You want to take our team in on your ancient flying machine, there?"

The circle of tall military officers gazed down at me, unconvinced. I felt a rush of nerves, but looked back at the ice canyon. "I can fly that."

The officers looked expectantly to Mendes.

He smiled. "From what I've heard, son, I'll take my chances with you. You're one of these . . . Three, I understand?"

I almost said no, and then I worried that Rana might, but she stayed silent and I realized that I didn't need to reveal my true nature. "Yes," I said. "I'm the Aeronaut."

Mendes nodded. "Surveillance drones caught your escape act in the Rockies. Damn fine flying. We can probably fit ten men on your craft there. Corporal . . ."

A soldier stepped forward. "Yes, sir."

"Get platoons formed for everyone else. Have the helicopters set up a distant perimeter, so as not to draw attention. Send our best ten commandos over to me at that ship and—"

"General . . ." Another thought was escaping my mouth before I could stop it, and I thought about how I never used to act this way around adults, never used to speak up, but then again, a lot had changed in a few weeks. "Your goal is to take out the Eden team?"

"Affirmative."

"And what about Paul?"

Mendes smiled. "He's dead or alive for us, though alive would be preferable. We'd love to get him in front of a tribunal. Why, what's your goal?"

"Same, but . . . there's a girl," I said, expecting someone to laugh, "part of the group in there. She's a hostage, another one of the Three, she—"

"Lilly Ishani," said Mendes, reading off his pad. "Resident of EdenWest and noted murder suspect."

"She didn't—"

"We're not worried about those charges," said Mendes. "The real murderer is Mr. Jacobsen. He committed an act of war against the ACF by attacking our Cheyenne Depot, not to mention stealing critical supplies. And I have no doubt the list of his crimes is more lengthy than I know. Anyway, don't worry, the hostages' lives will be of paramount importance to us. Now, let's go, men. Make it happen."

Mendes stepped through the group and put an arm on my shoulder, turning me back toward the craft. "You were in Desenna, I understand?"

"Yes."

"Northern Federation humanitarian team is there now. Some kind of horror show, as I understand it . . . Cryos brought back to life as killing machines, missile strikes that killed scores. Like that place wasn't bloody enough . . ."

The memories surfaced as he spoke. I realized how

hard I'd been trying not to think about all of it. "Yeah."

"I'm sorry you had to see that," said Mendes.

Elissa and I used to wish on rocks thrown into the cracks. Cracks in the seams of Hub that we were sure led straight to the center of the earth.

Carey jumping off the cenote ledges.

Seven never counting to three . . .

I tried to focus. "Me, too," I said.

I led the way up the ladder of the Atlantean craft. The commandos followed, packing onto the deck until there was barely space to move. Rana hovered beside me by the wheel.

"All our evidence points to Eden being after some kind of weapon," Mendes continued, "the Paintbrush of Gods, we've heard it called."

"It's a machine," I said, "that can change the climate. But it's dangerous." I wondered if I should mention the Heart of the Terra, its power, but it seemed best not to complicate things. And I wondered: Could anyone be trusted with knowledge of the Terra's true power? If I was really going to free the Terra, it was probably best that no one know.

"No doubt," said Mendes. "We've been monitoring Paul and the Edens for years, had spies in and out, but cracking their Project Elysium plans has been tough. Especially since we can't locate their board of directors. We had a mole in that operation back in the early Rise.

They had corporate offices in Dubai while the domes were being built, but our attention was turned during the War for Fair Resources, and by the time things settled down, we'd lost track of their whereabouts."

"I know where they are," I said. "At least I think. We found coordinates."

"You did? Where'd you get those?"

"Long story."

"Corporal," Mendes called, "we've got coordinates here. Need you to send the birds to check them out."

"I'm not sure how much battery range they've got left, sir," the corporal replied.

"Damn batteries," Mendes muttered. "You know how easy life was back when there was gasoline any time you needed it? You could fly a spy plane around the globe as many times as you wanted." He looked at me. "Can you relay those coordinates?" he asked.

Somehow I remembered them. "Three degrees north and one fifty-four point seven degrees east."

"Yeah, we're not going to be able to suss those out until we get a recharge," reported the corporal. "And we don't have any satellites passing over that vicinity anytime soon."

"Figures," said Mendes. "Well, stay on it." He looked around the deck. "Everyone here?" Then he patted me hard between my shoulder blades. "Take us in, Owen."

14

I MOVED TO THE CONTROLS, MY NERVES RINGING, and yet for the first time, I felt like I was entering a confrontation with Paul where I actually stood a chance, with a real army behind me. As long as we weren't too late . . .

We rose over the delta and I flew into the valley, following the snaking course of the chalky river back into the black mountains. We passed over the scout team in moments. The distant winter sun couldn't reach in here, and the shadows remained cold and dark. The walls were damp and striped with ice. These surfaces hadn't felt the heat of the sun for months.

The valley narrowed to a canyon, its sides becoming sheer and black and tall. The blue sky receded above us.

"There it is," said Mendes.

Ahead, the canyon was blocked by the twin walls of blue ice, striped in thin lines of brown, ice built up over millennia, the deepest layers older than Atlanteans, maybe than the first humans.

My hand flexed on the wheel of the ship, twitching back and forth to get the sails just right. There was a wide enough space to enter about halfway up the wall. I lined up with it, and flew into the ice.

The light became dim and pure blue; the air chilled and our breaths made momentary clouds. Somewhere below there was a faint sound of rushing water.

We left the weak daylight behind, winding through the walls of curving glassy ice, and I considered that it would be nearly impossible to turn the craft around.

"Can these things fly backward?" I asked Rana.

She stared ahead intently. "I don't remember ever trying."

"Things should get a little wider," the corporal said, scanning his readouts, "about a kilometer in. There may be a vent to the surface there."

"Stay alert, team," said Mendes. One of the soldiers had handed him a helmet and a pulse rifle. I felt for the knife in my belt, but wondered what good it would do.

Owen . . .

The voice of the Terra accompanied another scream in my head . . . but this time it seemed distant.

Rana flinched.

"What is it?" The ice leaned closer on both sides and compelled me to whisper.

"I don't know," Rana said quietly. "Something like screaming."

The Terra spoke, from far off it seemed now. *He is taking me, Owen. All will perish. He—* Her voice cut off.

The sides narrowed further. There was no daylight above. Only cold blue. The craft nicked an edge, causing splinters of ice to fall away.

"Careful," said Mendes, his brow knotted with concern. "You're doing great, though."

"Thanks." I resisted the urge to get a more steady grip, to try anything with my useless right hand. Luckily, after a few more twists, the fissure began to widen a bit.

There was light up ahead.

"Weapons hot," said Mendes, giving his team a thumbs-up. The soldiers lowered targeting visors and adjusted their rifles with a series of clicks and hums.

We rounded another corner of glassy blue. The light was brighter, reflecting on the walls like stars.

And there began to be shapes in the ice. Dark geometry, rectangles of shadow with darker forms inside them, blurred by the ice.

"The tombs," Rana whispered.

"Lord," said Mendes, whispering, too, "are those bodies?"

"The catacombs of the kings," Rana added, her head sweeping from one side of the fissure to the other.

The bodies were everywhere, but if they had once been organized in orderly rows, the Paintbrush had thrown them into chaos: the ice coffins at cockeyed angles and refrozen within these walls. There were hundreds, or, as I peered deeper into the ice, maybe thousands.

And I remembered the bodies in Atlante, when Master Solan had rolled them out, had brought them back . . . I remembered when Paul had raised the Cryos . . . and now I found myself flashing from shadow to shadow, corpse to corpse, some merely impressions, some close enough that I could see the bronze of their burial head-dresses, the silk of their gowns and the gleam of their copper breastplates, sometimes even the mat of their white hair . . . and I couldn't help but imagine them starting to move, to rise against us.

But even then, I didn't know that what Paul had in mind was so much worse.

Another scream sounded, heard by no one else but me and, from her wincing, Rana.

And the Terra's desperate words: *If he takes me, all will perish. Life will go dark.*

Her voice dissolved into a scream that brought tears to my wincing eyes. She was in so much pain. Like she was being torn apart.

Muffled cracks sounded from ahead, muted by the ice, and all the soldiers tensed.

"Sounds like gunfire, sir," said the corporal.

"Yes, indeed it does. Stay sharp, people."

"I am going to go ahead," said Rana.

"Wait now," said Mendes, "we don't want to—"

"I won't be seen," said Rana. She lifted from beside me and floated ahead of us, the skull bag hanging below her. Her light glimmered for a moment in the window walls, but then she was out of sight in the curves of ice.

I kept a wary eye on the toppled stacks of shadows in the ice walls.

"Careful!" Mendes called.

My hand slipped, cold with sweat, and the craft nicked the wall again, jarring everyone aboard. "Sorry." I had to focus! But those screams in my head, those gunshots, and now the stillness around us . . . If Paul and his team were in here, why was it so *silent*?

"Registering approximately thirty heat signatures," the corporal whispered, "one hundred meters ahead."

"Activate your targeting sites," ordered Mendes. "Remember, Eden forces, not hostages."

I brought us over an outcropping of ice. Even the sound of the river had faded beneath us. There was only the low hum from the vortex, a shallow breath of the cold wind slithering through the fissure, and the rapid breathing of the soldiers and me.

The light grew brighter. There were bright beams just beyond the next turn in the ice. The bodies between us and whatever lay around that corner were backlit, tan colors of skin, the glimmer of jewels and weaponry. . . .

"Status?" Mendes asked the corporal.

"Fifty meters and closing," said the corporal, "but the readings are uneven. There must be interference. . . ."

Mendes held up a fist. "Ready . . ."

I brought us around the final turn.

We banked into a wide space, the ice walls bowing out to create a cylindrical cavern. A narrow chute opened to the sky and a beam of winter sun bore directly into the space, blinding to our eyes. It illuminated a far wall of ice, the end of this fissure, and reflected off brilliant lines of metal and crystal, complicated angles and gearworks.

There, before us, frozen in the wall: the Paintbrush of the Gods.

It stood in silent majesty, the sun beaming on it, encased in ice except for the nearest girders and gears, which protruded toward us. The ice curved around it, filled its spaces—

Except for a large hole near the top, along the diagonal path of its great telescope-like cylinder. There, the ice had been neatly cut away in a square, forming a hollow cube and immediately I knew what was missing.

I also knew then that we were lost.

But it still took me a moment to accept it, to take it all in.

And that moment cost everyone their lives.

"Where are the hostiles?" Mendes asked.

"They should be right here," said the corporal, confused.

"Sir," a soldier called, still speaking barely above a whisper. His gun was pointed directly below us, into the deep shadows.

I brought the craft to a hover. And when I peered over the side, at first I saw nothing but the green ghosts of light from the sun and the Paintbrush. But then, a pale white glow. Rana was far down there, on the floor, where the ice curved in a still flow between jagged black boulders. There were deep blue cracks, and other black forms . . .

Human shapes.

Bodies.

But not frozen, not Atlantean, these were black-clad bodies in helmets, with gold visors that reflected the sunlight.

"Those are Eden forces," said Mendes.

"They're dead, sir," said the corporal, "or almost dead. Heat signatures are fading or out."

My head whipped around wildly. "Where are the—"

"I've got a positive ID on a hostage, sir," one of the soldiers called, voice rising on rapid breaths as he aimed a sensor at the cave floor. "Male, facial recognition confirms Mateu Owante of Coke-Sahel, age seventeen . . . deceased."

"Positive ID on a hostage," another soldier called.

"Evan Reynolds, resident of EdenWest, age sixteen, deceased . . ."

No.

"Positive ID . . ."

No.

Rana's light was growing now. She was so far down and there was something glowing in her hands, something pale white—

Come home, Rana.

The skull. She had the skull out, and as its light grew I could see the shape of a body lying twisted on the ice beside her, beneath the skull light

A body—

Dark hair spilling away. Clothes smeared with dirt.

No. The blood . . .

"Lilly Ishani of EdenWest, age sixteen . . ."

No.

Lilly, not moving . . .

None of my muscles wanted to work, my brain didn't want to work. I felt a scream building up in every fiber, in every thought, a single terrible note as I stared down at the bath of white light where Lilly lay on the icy cavern floor. . . .

And then a voice called from above. "Sorry, Owen!"

I twisted my head up, like it was made of lead, along with Mendes and every soldier and weapon and we saw, high above us, a silhouette standing on the surface rim, a lone figure in the sun, a monster.

Paul.

"We only took what we needed!" he shouted. "Gotta run!"

He motioned with his hand, like he was waving a wand, then turned and disappeared from sight. Paul, the treacherous, murderous . . . I felt a blinding rage. All I wanted to do was kill him, a hundred times over.

But a shrill beep echoed through the ice cavern—

Followed by a thump of air, and a low, deep concussion of sound that made my ears scream in pain.

"Sonic charge!" Mendes shouted.

The world seemed to shudder, and then the ice began to break apart all around us.

My head whipped around, back to Lilly, far below—

"Get us out!" Mendes shouted, gripping my shoulder. "This whole place is coming down."

I felt my body shutting down, seizing up, all of this, Lilly, no, no, no . . .

"Go, kid!" said Mendes.

The first chunk of ice slammed against the craft.

"HANG ON!" I screamed, my teeth grinding. Down or up? I had no idea what to do. Lilly— but NO, I slammed the pedals and spun the wheel, in lurching motions because I only had one weak hand to fly with but still I launched us forward and banked the craft into a steep climb. Everyone with me would die otherwise, and Paul would escape.

Blistering cracks sounded from every direction. Huge chunks of ice began to fall away on all sides. The vortex whined and we shot straight upward toward the window of daylight, ice dust refracting the sunbeams into clouds of diamonds.

Splinters and chunks smashed off the craft, buffeting us side to side. One soldier was impaled with an icicle, another slammed in the head, both falling away, down into the ice—

The ice.

LILLY! I was leaving her behind, down there, I couldn't . . . but Rana was there, and we had to go we had to . . .

We neared the top. The crushing sound of collapse growing louder. Ice all around us.

We weren't going to make it.

Slivers in my eyes, chunks slamming from all sides, a sound like the end of the world everywhere—

But we were close, just reaching the rim of the hole, sunlight catching the bow of the craft. The sky and distant mountains became visible, the sea of ice.

And for a moment, what was maybe only a second, I saw: A thread, like spider silk, gleaming in sunlight, leading straight up into the sky.

An impossible line of thick silver wire, its end affixed to a giant metal pylon sunk into a bare slab of black rock.

Paul, at the top of a set of metal steps that led to some sort of pod, an oval structure that seemed to be attached to the wire, with two other soldiers following, all looking miniature before the pod and the wire stretching up out of sight.

Paul, turning and shooting those two soldiers point-blank.

Disappearing into the pod and slamming the door.

And then with a great magnetic hum the pod shot upward on the thread at a speed unimaginable, reflecting sunlight and looking like a firework . . .

Like an ascending star . . .

This I saw, all in a moment—

But not the lip of the ice rim exploding free.

"Incoming port side!" Mendes shouted.

We were almost there, cresting out of the cavern, sunlight on our faces now—

When the shard of blue crystal as large as our craft slammed into us.

With two hands, I might have been fast enough to avoid it.

Maybe not.

There was screaming.

The craft breaking apart.

And we were falling.
The daylight fading.
Cold.
Lilly.
All lost to the ice and darkness.

15

THE MORNING AFTER I ARRIVED AT CAMP EDEN, I drowned for the first time.

The next night, I drowned in the night air, before learning of my gills, before diving deep and finding my sense of balance and purpose in the underwater world.

Three weeks later, I drowned in the ice.

At first, I hung on to the wheel with my good hand as the ice crashed into the craft, the crystal windshield protecting me. I was still trying to work the pedals, to drive us out, to avoid the chunks raining down.

Until the windshield smashed. The ship keeled backward over itself, and in a blur of light and cold and the shouts of the soldiers and numbing pain I was separated from it and everything became darkness.

For a while.

Owen.

My eyes opened and there was cold, and light in

shadowy blues, and faint forms. I couldn't move. Everything stuck in place. Pain in my leg, my wrist, a throbbing
in my head, but it all felt far away. My vision was blurred
and cold and I could feel the press of ice against my eye-
balls. I couldn't blink.

I was maybe upside down.

Pinned in the ice.

Fingers stuck in place, every inch of my body pressed
and held still, muscles trying to twitch in panic but
nowhere to go.

No movement.

Distantly, I heard screaming. Desperate, animallike
howling. Another person trapped.

Then thudding. Like a head against a wall. More
wailing.

I flexed my legs. Nothing. Arms. No. Mouth—

Stuck half open, ice jammed into it, melting in a freezing trickle down the back of my throat. The cold aching
against my gums. Tongue pinned in place.

No—

I could feel my heart beating wildly, desperately trying to move blood, to make heat.

Oh no.

This was different from the lake bottom. In Eden, I'd
felt detached, as if my death were happening to someone
else. My whole body had been changing and gills I didn't
even know I'd had were in the process of saving my life.

And I hadn't known how to fight, back then. When I'd drowned, I'd only been two days removed from a secret twenty-five years in cryo, still having weird imaginings of technicians, feeling like some sort of passive thing that couldn't act on its own, a frozen body, which I'd actually been, without knowing it.

Since then, I'd tasted survival and blood, felt power and felt it taken from me, felt true and felt betrayed. I knew how to fight now, had fought so hard, only to be here frozen again, back in ice, trying to move. . . .

Can't move . . .

Can't move, can't move . . .

The distant muffled screaming became sobbing.

Became silence. Became death.

No, no, no.

Parts of me were going dark. Technicians turning out the lights on this hellish experiment that was my body. Technicians were easier, I knew now. Let me imagine someone else was in charge, that someone pulled the levers, turned the dials, that I wasn't just me, dying here, alone, frozen and manipulated by Paul, activated for a purpose by Atlantean alchemy . . .

Lied to by them all. Even the Atlanteans had lied to me, without meaning to.

Used. Moved like a puppet, even through time, even by the Terra, beaten and broken, failed, and . . .

loved . . .

Lilly.

Oh no.

I'm not your math teacher. You don't need to give me your whole name.

No, Lilly, no.

I remembered that sunshine, and her red bathing suit and the pearl polish on her toes. How she spun her life-guard whistle and how in that moment, on that dock, I had really believed that getting her to like me was the most important thing. Foolish, stupid me, thinking about a girl, when I was an experiment and a lie, weeks away from dying in the ice, as if she could possibly have been the most important thing compared to all that.

It was like I already knew you. Like we were already past all that.

Stupid Owen who thought that girl might be his ally, against what he had no idea. Who thought he might have found a friend. Who thought he might have found love.

Or maybe I'd been right, on that dock. Right about Lilly. We'd come so far, never could have made it without each other . . .

Only for it to end like this.

Oh, how we had no idea.

But maybe Lilly did. Her sad smile sometimes, the way she got distant, angry, frustrated that all we could do wasn't enough, the way she pulled away in Desenna, when it seemed that we weren't meant to do this together.

There had always been a distance with her, as if inside she had always known, or feared, that this was how we would end up.

Cold. The ice. Can't move. My jaw going numb. Eyes no longer able to focus. Freezing . . .

She was somewhere below me, now. Somewhere so deep in the ice . . . both of us trapped in a tomb at the end of the earth. The white realm, where we would die.

There would be no getting to her in time.

Four minutes, that's how long I'd had to survive drowning in Lake Eden, except with my gills I'd made it ten. How long was it in ice? How long did I have? No gills this time. No—

No Lilly.

There's not much more we can do, I imagined the technicians saying sadly. All the way back to the beginning, like I'd been drowned from the start.

"Owen."

There was a light.

And I felt something, not a warmth, but an energy passing through me, a sense of electricity. It bled out in front of my eyes, coming from within me.

"It's me," the voice said.

Lilly . . .

"It's Rana."

I could hear her, her voice so close it was like it was coming from inside my ears. I tried to talk back, but my mouth, filled with ice . . .

"I am with you. I can keep you here, on the border," she said.

I felt a surge of energy. Rana was inhabiting the same space as me. She was literally inside me, or around me, like our two bodies had merged. I could feel the energy through me, radiating in every muscle and fiber.

"I will stay with you."

Lilly . . . I wanted to ask. Rana had been down there with her. I'd never heard that soldier say if Lilly was deceased or not. There was still a possibility.

But unlike the Terra, Rana couldn't hear my thoughts.

I felt my body calming, there in the ice, as Rana inhabited me, her lingering power of the Terra keeping me from fading.

Time passed, formless.

I heard another muffled moan somewhere in the ice.

Someone succumbing.

I tried to remember the death rite of Heliad-7. *Be at peace. . . . You have played your part . . . now we . . . we . . .* My brain was too slow.

Too cold.

Then, in the distance, a rumble, like thunder . . .

One . . . two . . . three . . . Mom would count, Elissa and I with our blankets pulled tight up to our eyes.

Or machinery.

"They are coming," said Rana. "Digging down. You

only need to hold on a little longer."

I tried to be calm, the feeling of blood in my head, the cold at my edges, the blue everywhere, and the electric sense of Rana between my molecules.

Thank you, I thought to her, but she didn't hear me.

And all I could think of was Lilly, but I couldn't bear to picture her at the bottom of that chasm, an object tossed into a well. Better to think of the last time I had seen her, in the Andes, fighting breathlessly to save us, heroically.

Better to think of her arcing through the clouds, carrying me to safety.

Of those nights between Desenna and now, flying down the ruined coast, when we had been free of our last horrors and before we'd known what was next.

Secret nights when it had just been us, and the wind and the rain and sky, and a blanket beneath trees in the shade, pulling it over our heads to keep out the sun and mosquito hum.

Double brownies for the rain virgin!

They seemed so short now.

Those days.

But there was still hope. There had to be.

The rumbling became a metallic whine. The sound of crunching ice. Whining of turbines.

"Hang on, Owen," said Rana.

As we waited there, I felt like I could feel the ten

thousand years that she'd lingered, the world she'd watched change; and in her energy I felt like I knew that during that entire time, every moment of those three million days, she had been incomplete, brokenhearted because she had lost a love that had fit her right, like feeling safe with someone watching you dress, the last simple moment she and Lük had shared, that night in Atlante.

I knew now that she had never recovered, and if I got out of this ice and Lilly didn't . . .

Neither would I.

The light grew brighter. Blurs of movement. The flutter of helicopter blades.

"I will find you, later," said Rana. "There is something I must do. Do not despair, Owen. I am sorry about Lilly. But you must survive. And we will fight on. Promise me you will fight on until the masters fall."

I couldn't reply. I had no idea what to say. To fight on. Or to fade. That seemed easier.

I felt Rana's light leaving, felt the raw cold sinking back in, my blood thickening and slowing, my brain going fuzzy on the carbon dioxide of my weak breaths . . .

Fading . . .

"I love you, Lilly," I tried to say through the ice.

Seventh time.

I should have said it four thousand more.

If you really love me, then run with me, she'd said. *Get out of here alive. Because if you want to just stay here and die, then what you just said to me is a lie and I will hate you for all eternity.*

Okay, I thought, *I will live. If I can.*

Scraping. A giant shove and the ice moved around me.

"Here!"

Brilliant light. Silhouettes. Soldiers.

Hands pulled me from the ice.

And I knew that I would live. And I did not know if that felt like a relief or a curse.

They wrapped me in blankets and put me on a stretcher and loaded me into a helicopter as the winds howled and the weak winter sun set. I tried to speak, but couldn't make the muscles work.

"Try to rest," a medic said.

There were other bodies around me. Nearby I saw Mendes. Unconscious but alive. As they'd pulled me out, I'd been grimly aware that there was a different helicopter for the bodies whose faces were completely covered. Most of the soldiers were over there.

The copter lifted off. Before the sound of the whupping blades overwhelmed everything, I heard the pilots say, "Lieutenant says call it. It's getting too cold. And besides, it's been too long. Anyone who's still down there is long gone."

Long gone.

We rose into the sky as the sun sank.

Darkness fell on the grave of the ancients.

Darkness fell over me.

I remembered the chocolate blue of the cenote, in the fading light of day . . . *See ya,* I had said to Lilly.

See ya, she had replied.

And I had climbed up to the surface and when I'd looked back she'd been gone, as if she'd never been. As if I'd had a glimpse then, though I barely realized it, of this.

Of now.

Of the utter emptiness of the world without her. Of breathing while knowing she was no longer.

I felt, too, a vague tingling, the beginnings of the guilt that would probably burn me for the rest of my life, a creeping hollow sense of failure not only for not saving her—

She pulled you from that chasm in the Andes. You couldn't do the same?

but also for every moment I didn't spend loving her better.

Really? You went out with Seven and her friends instead of pleading and screaming and dragging Lilly, if necessary, with you? Or just staying by her bed?

The warmth of the copter and the blankets began to thaw my limbs, and with their return came a flood of pain. When the medic asked me if I needed medicine, I

said yes, and he stuck a needle into the skin between my
fingers, and as I slipped away I only thought:

Lilly.

Please.

No.

16

Before the beginning, there was an end
Three chosen to die

Three coffins on a gray beach.

To live in the service of the Qi-An
The balance of all things.
Three guardians of the memory of the first people
They who thought themselves masters of all the
Terra

Simple boxes built from the wreckage piles.
The boards warped but still flecked with paint.
Three coffins at the edge of a cobalt sea.

Who went too far, and were lost
To the heaving earth
To the flood.

It has taken me two days to build them. Rusty nails pulled out with my teeth, hammered in with a rock now streaked with the blister blood.

I don't know why I bothered.

I could have sunk them in the waves, like Leech,

In the smoke, like Elissa,

In the silence, like Anna,

In time, like my parents,

In the ice, like . . .

Three who will wait

Until long after memory fades

And should the time come again—

But it won't.

This time, it is finally over.

This time, they are never coming back.

What's lost is lost.

Once, in a temple, beneath a lie, I said I wanted to be true. I wanted to see truth.

I have been true.

But still I sit here, as gentle waves lick the coffin edges.

I have not set them afloat.

Because to do that, I'd have to see.

See the truth.

Of what is inside.

And I cannot face that alone.

Around noon, General Mendes finds me.

"Heard you ate something today," he says as he sits down in the sand beside me with a groan. I feel him smiling at me. "Progress."

"I guess." I pick up a handful of sand and sprinkle it over the smooth black surface of the pressure cast on my right wrist, watching it stream off. There's still a faint pain there, but at least the bones are set and the healing has begun, though I'm told it will take weeks.

"It's not surprising," he says. "No one can resist Caesar's millet pancakes."

"Pancakes are good."

The sun is rising over the rolling ocean. Each day, here at the end of the earth, it draws a lazy arc across the lower third of the horizon, before retiring in the early afternoon.

I stretch out my legs and let the diagonal, golden rays light my face. You can only just feel its heat. Here, you don't even need NoRad. You can live bright without cutting out anyone's heart.

"So, I think we've pretty much covered it," Mendes says. "Any other details that have come back to you?"

"Not really."

Over the last day and a half, I have told Mendes my story, everything I can remember and more, from the moment I drowned in EdenWest.

It is all told, now.

I gaze down at the coffins.

The story is over.

"Any new recon?" I ask him.

"We finally got the drones charged up enough to send them to those coordinates you gave us."

I turn to him. "The board of directors?"

Mendes shrugs. "There's nothing there, just open ocean. Unless there used to be an island, or they had a boat stationed at some point, I'd say you got some faulty information."

Moros had lied, then. "Elysium Planitia," I say.

"What's that?"

"That's what my source said their base was called. That was probably a lie, too."

"Well, I'll run it and see if anything turns up," says Mendes.

A few larger swells break against the black beach. Clear waves with white foam tips. A black object bobs to the surface a few meters beyond the breakwater. I've seen one before. A seal. Another long-forgotten casualty of the Great Rise that still exists down here.

But of course it does.

After all, this is the place.

The beach I'd imagined running away to, with Lilly. The place where the water was trash free, the fish still the work of a god who gave a damn, of a Terra that wasn't imprisoned. I'd imagined it to be tropical, something turquoise and coral like I'd seen in books. Instead, it's black and blue, but still . . . here it is. . . .

Lilly . . .

"We finished the excavation," says Mendes around his cigar.

"Yeah?"

"That Paintbrush of the Gods," says Mendes. "Pretty impressive. It seems to work on some kind of fusion technology. We barely understand it. Mercury and induction and it uses the magnetic field of the earth and its relative gravity. Same kind of thing that powered your ship."

I listen. I wish it interested me.

"Anyway, the machine is useless without whatever Paul took from it. This, Heart of the Terra." When I don't reply, Mendes checks his watch. "Listen, we need to pull out of here at eleven hundred hours. So . . ."

"You can leave me here."

"No, I can't," says Mendes. "Sorry. You're coming with us."

"I know."

He rubs my back and it feels fatherly, and I miss my dad so much I nearly sob. It has barely occurred to me how far from me he is, how long ago it really was that I saw him. That, if he is alive out there in this world now, he is very old.

Most likely, he is dead, too.

"Tide's going out," says Mendes.

"Yes."

"Let me help you do this," he says. "Come on, son, it's the least I can do."

Before the beginning there was an end,

Three chosen to die

Three coffins on a gray beach.

The meaning of the legend is very different now.

Why should we save this world, Lilly said once, *when things like this can happen?*

I never want to get up. I don't want to live this next moment. The one I know is coming. Tightness creeps over me.

I realize I am holding my breath.

I let it out.

Pull up my legs, brush sand from my calves.

And stand.

The coffins are perfectly lined up. A wave rushes between them, hissing on the sand.

I take a step. Another.

And the bodies come into view.

The excavation team found Evan first. He died of a bullet to the brain. The medic, a gentle man for a soldier, named Grayland, said that based on the path of the bullet, he would have felt nothing, and experienced at best a second or two of disjointed memories before he was gone.

There are no funeral homes on the empty coast of Antarctica, nor in a fleet of military warships. But they have experience with the dead, and Evan's face has been washed of the blood splatters, and a clean bandage covers where the bullet entered his forehead.

I focus so hard on his closed eyes, on his broad body between the boards.

The medic said there was evidence of neurological tampering. Of cognitive substitution. Of Paul's messing with another head, tinkering to make Evan a better version of his problem child Leech. Had he ever seen any of us as actual people, or just toys in his lab?

I stop at the foot of Evan's coffin. Mendes, his silver uniform pants rolled up, steps half into the surf by Evan's head.

I have been thinking about what to say to him. Not that I need to say anything. He is just a body now. I know that from when Leech died. The light, the person, they are gone. But I want to say something anyway, so at least Mendes, or that seal or the wind, hears it. Or just so I do.

"I never liked you," I say to Evan's still face, "and you never liked me, but you probably would have lived. You would have lived, if it hadn't been for us. Or maybe that's not true. Maybe you would have ended up an experiment, anyway. I don't know. We did what we thought was right. I want you to know I'm not sorry for what I did, but I am sorry for what I didn't do. I could have been stronger, confronted you sooner. We could have come up with a better plan. Maybe worked together. And then, maybe . . . you'd still be alive. I don't know. I'm sorry."

I stop there. It's nothing grand, but if Evan were still here, he wouldn't want any more from me. I nod to Mendes and we lug the box out into the surf. The first cold wave hits us in the thighs. The coffin begins to float. We push, and Evan is given to the sea. His coffin bobs over the swells, beginning to take on water. The coffins are only meant to get the bodies far enough off shore so that the tide can carry them away. Hopefully, they won't wash back up. Or maybe they will. It was all I could think to do. Mendes offered me a military service out at sea, with the pyres, so that the bodies become ash and briefly light the dark.

I declined. The blisters, some sense of effort, seemed like the least I could do.

The next box is Mateu. Grayland said he was still lingering when the ice crushed him. I wonder what it must have been like for him, a boy living in a slum in Lagos, completely unaware of all this drama, to be grabbed from his life, flown halfway around the world, for a handful of days to be one of the Three, to witness wonders and horrors and then to be shot at point-blank range. I never even spoke to him. Never had the chance.

"You were the rightful owner of the Aeronaut's

knowledge," I say to him. "You never knew that. You lived a life having no idea what you were connected to. I don't know, maybe that was better than knowing, since knowing just leads to death, but you no doubt deserved better than this. For that, I'm sorry."

We set Mateu to sea. Evan's casket has moved far off shore, and looks half-submerged.

I step back to shore.

Turn.

It is time.

Oh, I do not want it to be time.

Mendes puts his hand on my back as I face the third coffin. I built this one more carefully than the others, with attention to the joints, using the straightest pieces of wood that the trash piles at the far ends of this beach had to offer. The straightest nails. So it would float the longest.

Grayland said that, like Mateu, the worst-case scenario was that Lilly had been in an unconscious fog, her memories wild and unhinged, a sort of sugar-rush dream, if the bullet didn't kill her instantly. And that would only have been until the ice fell on her.

He couldn't be sure, though, without a body.

She'd been too deep in the chasm. They couldn't dig down that far. But even if she had somehow survived the collapse, she would have succumbed to the cold within short order. Bottom line, Grayland had said, she wouldn't have suffered.

I had listened to this, and yet that whole first night I did not sleep, could not sleep with the thought of her down there, lost to the ice, never to see her face again, never to know for sure if she was gone.

And, worse . . .

To hope. Because I knew Rana had been down there with her. And Rana had power. She had kept me alive, and so there was still a chance . . .

And maybe that was why Rana had appeared along the river yesterday morning. Because she knew that to move on, I needed to lose that hope.

I spied her at dawn, from the hovercraft deck, standing at the edge of the milky glacial river . . .

Lilly's blue body floating beside her.

Beautiful Lilly Ishani.

Oh . . .

It is time to look.

Hello, Lilly.

She lies in the box I built for her. Her clothes have dried. Her hair is neatly gathered behind her shoulders. Like Evan, she wears a clean white bandage like a head-band, covering the hole in her bluish skin. I put it on myself. Her face is still smeared with dirt.

My Lilly.

Rana slid her down through the chasms and fissures, to the glacial river, guided her out from beneath the ice.

So that I could be sure.

I look at her now and I do not know how to understand that she is just a body, that she is just the material that housed a life, without that life in it. The skin the same temperature of the air, structures made to hold something now departed. Like the houses on the coasts, the empty walls can fall away, bones and lungs can be turned back into molecules, can be turned back into energy. Flesh can rot. Bacteria can gnaw on brain stem. It doesn't matter, now. The light and the heat of the life inside are gone.

She is *gone*, and suddenly I feel like I hate that this body can still be here, hate that it can lie there reminding me of every moment we spent together—

Me-O-Mys!

while also being a cruel joke version of her, a cheap knockoff of the real thing, a cold and dead and empty trick that only reminds me that we are terminal, that we are born to die and that if we really knew that every day, why the hell would we . . . anything?

So many times on our journey I had thought of just turning the craft around and running, running for the nowheres of the world where no one would have bothered us, and yet those notions were as cruel a joke as this body lying before me. It was all useless.

We were doomed to this from the moment we met. I started building this coffin on this beach the first time

I looked into her sky-blue irises on that Eden dock and thought I'd found someone who would be careful with my anxious feelings, my pathetic cowardice, my lame, stupid heart.

Lilly, Lilly, Lilly.

I was the weapon of your destruction, but was there any other way?

I will never know.

If she could hear me right now, she would probably tell me to shut up.

Because all these thoughts change nothing. Still she lies here before me, lost. I can't even fully measure how alone I feel. It is as if there is an enormous shadow falling over me from behind, and if I turn, the loneliness will be there in a big nothing so great it will devour me.

That might be easier.

I think of Seven stepping off the pyramid in Desenna and feel like I get it. Right now, that would definitely be easier.

"It's okay," says Mendes, as if he can hear my thoughts crushing inward on themselves.

"Yeah." But it's not okay and I don't think it will ever be.

All of this and more is why I have nothing to say to Lilly. Not now. Not like this. I have thought back on our weeks together and decided that I said most of it while she was alive.

Enough of it.

Doesn't matter if I didn't.

I look down at my left wrist. The leather band there is still damp. I gave it to her by the sea, just after Desenna. The bracelet I made for my father.

I'll be your memory, Owen Parker.

This morning I unsnapped it from her cold, wet wrist. My memories will be mine, and they will haunt me.

But I do have one thing to say.

"I love you, Lilly Ishani."

Eighth time.

I put my hands on the wood edge, hold my breath, and push.

The first wave we meet is bigger than I anticipated, and it slaps against the wood and water sloshes over Lilly, and I want to scream in pure rage that not even this can I control. I can't even get this last thing right.

Crushing my chest to hold back the tears, I keep pushing, my feet pedaling against the sand, but my casted hand slips off the wood, the bones, recently set by Grayland, burning inside, and I am thrown off balance and slip and stumble and lose my grip. Water soaks me. I stagger back to my feet and reach for the coffin, but my fingers miss, and I swallow a mouthful of salty ocean, coughing violently.

She is out of my reach, bobbing over the swells, out onto the sunlit ocean.

"Lilly!" I scream, and a sob breaks free. Tears finally fall.

I lurch forward, another wave catching me in the chest.

"Lilly!"

"No, Owen, don't." Mendes grabs me by the arm and drags me back out of the waves and suddenly I know that I did not say enough, did not do enough. There should have been more. . . .

I . . .

"I'll give you a minute," says Mendes, "but if you go and drown, I'll be very disappointed."

I sit there, listening as he trudges away, and catch my breath, the surge of crying receding, numbness setting in.

I watch the box ride the waves. Better built, Lilly's will stay afloat longer. Beyond that, Mateu and Evan are faint lines on the swelling sea.

Some time passes, the winter sun sliding sideways.

Finally, I can speak.

"I remember," I say to the body of Lilly Ishani, "when you said you were letting me go. You said it just in case, just in case we weren't meant to be together until the end. But we were, Lilly, we were. And I am never letting you go, no matter how much longer I live. I am keeping you with me, until the end."

Waves crash. A gull calls nearby.

My thoughts go dead like static.

When I finally stand, shivering and wet, I find Rana glimmering at the top of the beach. She watches with her dead gaze.

I do not speak to her.

I only nod.

She knows what this means, and she disappears.

It is time to head out with the soldiers.

I join them, and when Mendes asks me how I am holding up, I tell him I am fine. And when he asks me if I know where I want to go next, I tell him that I do.

The request surprises him. It is out of their way.

But he sees the look in my eyes.

The look of someone with plans.

And he agrees.

All along, we have had to guess what Paul has been thinking.

But he is not the only one with unguessable plans now.

He is not the only one with death on his mind.

PART III

"I USED TO SAY THAT I KNEW HOW THE WORLD WILL END, BUT NOW I THINK IT'S REALLY ENDING. HELLO, WORLD, IF ANY OF YOU CAN HEAR ME, MOROS LIVES ON—PROPHET OR FOOL, YOU DECIDE—LIVE FROM THE NIGHTMARE INSIDE VISTA. BUT WHO'S IN THE NIGHTMARE NOW? OUTSIDE, IN YOUR REAL WORLD, SOMETHING HAS CHANGED. YOU FEEL IT, DON'T YOU? IT'S IN EVERY TRANSMISSION I HEAR, IN EVERY MESSAGE AND SIGNAL-CAST I INTERCEPT, IN EVERY BELLICOSE POLITICIAN'S RANT AND EVERY BEDTIME SONG. SOMETHING HAS SHIFTED, OVERNIGHT IT SEEMS. WE'VE BEEN DYING FOR A LONG TIME, BUT THIS FEELS LIKE DECAY. ALL GROWS MELANCHOLY AND VIOLENT. IT'S AS IF WE HAVE LOST SOME INNER LIGHT, SOME PART OF OUR SOUL. I SEE IT EVERYWHERE, AND FOR ONCE, I WONDER IF I AM BET-TER OFF IN HERE. DARKNESS IS FALLING, CHILDREN, AND DAWN FEELS FARTHER AWAY THAN EVER BEFORE."

17

THE HOVERCRAFTS BUZZ NORTH IN THE DARK, over the turbulent sea, away from the monochrome coast. They fly smooth, skimming above the water, their hum constant, through the walls, into your bones.

I sit in my tiny room. Sit on my lower bunk.

The coffins have probably sunk by now.

I eat dinner silently in the galley, at the end of a table of soldiers who are laughing and joking, blowing off steam. They grow quiet when one talks low, then erupt in raucous peals of laughter. Most of them are thinking about the leave they get after this mission. The girls they will see.

I just eat. Try not to listen.

After, there is a mission debriefing, but I am not allowed into that. I hang out up on the bridge deck, face in the cold and spray, wrapped in a wool blanket, engulfed by the deafening roar of the hover engines from this ship and the two that flank it.

I watch the forward lights highlight the wave caps. As we move north, there is more trash in the water. At one point, we pass most of a wood building with a window still intact, reflecting brilliantly in our lights.

I stand there and my fingers play with my necklace, rolling Victoria's finger bone between the pads of my index finger and thumb.

Unlike everything else lost, the dead stay with me. Or maybe that's wrong: the dead don't live on in my mission. The dead are just dead.

The stars are out, the moon gone. The wind is cold, and feels more lonely than usual. Even beyond my emotions, there is something desperate and afraid about the dark tonight. It feels like it could go on forever, like dawn is far away, too far beyond the horizon and we will not find it again. I try to ignore the feeling by tracing constellations and counting shooting stars.

Alien or trash?

I have seen seven by the time Mendes comes and finds me. I'm only counting to know how many she's missing.

"How you holding up?" he asks.

I press down on what is a new feeling in my gut, a part of me as dark and angry as this night, that wants to answer, but I won't let it. "Fine," I say instead.

"Sorry you couldn't come to the debrief."

"I understand."

Mendes lights a cigarette. I like the sweet smell of it. "Want one?" he asks.

"Nah," I say, but it feels like habit, old me. Why not have one?

But I don't.

"I came to tell you the latest," says Mendes.

"Thanks."

"Ship's doctor ran over all the bodies we pulled from the ice, and confirmed that the bullets that killed Eden's men, and the hostages, came from the same three guns: those of the two soldiers who we saw Paul shoot and what we assume was his gun."

"He only took what he needed," I say, remembering Paul's words.

"Yeah. He murdered his team and took off with that Heart of the Terra thing. We're categorizing it as an energy source, at least for briefing our commanders. . . . Is that close enough?"

"Close enough."

"And you said his goal had been to acquire the entire Paintbrush of the Gods."

"That's what he *said* his goal was, but he always lies," I say. "And what about his escape?"

"That," says Mendes, "was a space elevator. Light insertion variety. They were used experimentally maybe fifty years ago—I think the Japanese had one that linked to their space station—but not since the Rise. Paul probably got the technology from the People's Corporation, or maybe someone on the Eden board had ties to a defense contractor.

"Either way: it means that EdenCorp has a space station, or a craft—hell, I don't know. We figure they probably built it back during the war, or maybe bit by bit covertly in one of those domes of theirs. Since the Rise, N-Fed satellites only cover a portion of the sky at any one time. If they had the right intel, they could avoid detection."

"The Ascending Stars," I say.

"Yes, that gamma link legend of the Ascending Stars seems to refer to this space elevator, or maybe Eden has a few of them. We reviewed seismic data from as many observatories as we could find. Linking that elevator to the ground causes a significant magnetic discharge. Turns out, there have been countless anomalous readings from southern Oceana over the last couple decades, but they were spread out just enough that they hadn't been noticed. Well, also, no one was really looking."

"A space station," I repeat.

"Looks like it. We got intelligence from the Russian kingdom, and it turns out they've spotted a large craft in orbit, bigger than any of the old space stations. They thought it was ours. At any rate, that's likely where Paul is."

I gaze up at the stars.

If he takes me, all will perish, the Terra said to me. *Life will go dark.*

Right before Paul took her off the planet. The Terra meant take her from earth. If the spark of life is taken, the earth will die out. Did she mean at first or slowly? Doesn't matter. Without the Terra, life will end. Paul, the selfish bastard, has taken it for himself.

This could really be the last night of humanity, of life on this planet. Paul has stolen its heart, has taken it trapped in an ancient cage, taken it to the stars. How many days, or hours, can a heartless body survive?

"The other thing is that lead you gave us," says Mendes. "Elysium Planitia. It turns out your coordinates were a match after all. We were just looking in the wrong place. Elysium Planitia is the name of a place, but it's not here."

"Where is it?"

Mendes blew smoke into the wind. "Mars."

"Mars," I repeat. "The planet."

"Yeah," says Mendes. "Telescope imagery confirms a base there, a dome, not the size of an Eden here on earth, but . . . Can you believe that? Eden's board of directors aren't even on earth."

"Actually," I say, "I can." Because what kills me is I've already seen EdenHome. I remember, what seems like so long ago, in the lab at Camp Eden, six screens that showed the Eden domes. And the one that said EdenHome . . . had a view of a rusty orange landscape with an amber sky. We thought it was a desert. We were right, but just not about where. Project Elysium. The location is right in the name. I tell myself we could never have conceived of it.

But then I remember even more. When the board of directors appeared on the screen in the skull chamber, back when Paul tried to hook me up to Lük's skull, they'd seemed to almost be floating, with stars behind them. They'd been at EdenHome, in lower gravity, far from here.

"The ship is called *Egress*," I say.

"Telescopes are also picking up evidence of heavy mining on Mars," says Mendes, "for water and uranium, we think."

I hope the mining dust isn't interfering with visibility on the driving range, Paul had said in his report to the board, the one we'd watched while flying to the Rockies.

You're so funny, Lilly had said to the screen.

She might be alive if I'd put these clues together, somehow. . . .

Don't think about that.

I wonder if Paul had ever really planned to save earth, or if all along he'd intended to leave it behind, a dying planet left to die, to take the spark of life, the Heart of the Terra with him, the key to:

The one true quest. The oldest quest there is. Paul's words in the Andes.

It's so obvious now what he meant.

The quest for eternal life. The most selfish wish, to never die, Paul had put it above all else. He and his board of directors and his precious selectees, they'll be sipping off the Terra's blood like vampires, living forever in EdenHome.

And now that Paul has the Terra, the exodus could be anytime.

"So," Mendes finishes. "That's all we know at the moment."

"What are you going to do?" I ask him.

Mendes shrugs. "There's not much we can do. My mission authorization doesn't exactly extend to Mars. Plus, the ACF hasn't had a space program since the last century. The Northern Federation security council is meeting this week, and they will be voting on a resolution whether to authorize a military operation against the Edens. But, while Paul's forces did attack Cheyenne Depot and steal the uranium, it was a lot easier to make a case against them when we thought that was for weapons."

"What's it for?" I ask.

"Fuel," says Mendes. "Their spaceship is giving off a massive radiation signal. We figure it runs on fusion drive rockets, using uranium as the fuel source. It will definitely shorten their trip to Mars. Thing is, they no longer pose an existential threat to the planet. They're just a bunch of rich people leaving. It's going to be hard to justify shooting that ship down."

I could give him a reason, explain that taking the Terra is indeed an existential threat of the highest order, but I don't. A security council of bureaucrats would never believe such a thing anyway. And I don't want them to.

Because then they might get in my way.

"I understand," I say, and I try to sound upset.

"Look, Owen, I'm sorry. Just know that I want the bastard brought to justice as much as you do, and the minute he comes back down to earth, the minute any of them do, for a coffee or a new crate of synth eggs, we'll be there."

"Okay."

Mendes shivers. "I'm heading in. This has been a long day. Longer for you."

"I'm going to stay out a bit," I say.

"Suit yourself. And you're still sure about where you want us to drop you off tomorrow? I'm damn close to overruling you on this one."

"My nephew is there," I say, as I have before. "He's an adult now, but, you know . . ." I point to myself. "Cryo."

"Right." Mendes shrugs. "Okay, try to get some sleep. I know that's been tough for you. If you ask the cook for a very modest amount of whiskey, he's been authorized to treat it as a strictly classified request."

"Thanks."

After Mendes is gone, I lean on the railing and watch the sky. Four more shooting stars. When I see through the bridge window that it is midnight, I move. I stay outside and walk the port deck, around large oval exhaust stacks, to a narrow deck at the stern of the ship. Here, I can see the southern stars behind us, stars I grew up without, romantic constellations like the Southern Cross and Scorpio and Libra.

I shiver against the damp dark. My healing wrist aches. With my other hand, I twirl the bone at my neck.

After a minute, one of the stars begins to dance, to bob and flutter among the others. It arcs with the winds, drawing close. And lands beside me.

"How are you?" Rana asks.

"Lingering on," I say.

She makes a little whooshing sound, and though her mouth stays small and curled, I think this is a laugh.

"Ready?" I ask.

"All is ready."

I turn and enter the nearest door, Rana trailing behind me, her skull bag with her. Most of the soldiers are asleep, the halls dark. I head to the center of the ship and then down the main stairs to the lowest of the three decks. We follow this hall to a solid metal door. I knock.

Footsteps. The door opens and Grayland, the medic, peers out. He is busy with patients during the day and saves most of his work in the morgue until night. This is the morgue.

"Owen," he says. Everyone learned my name quickly. I am their orphan case. "What are you d—"

Rana slides up into his space like a cold chill, inhabiting him, not quite in the gentle way that she did to me in the ice, but also not in the instantly-killing-him way that she attacked the Eden soldiers in the Andes. His skin starts to glow and she clenches and the energy released has the effect she told me it would: His eyes go wide and he is paralyzed, the electric currents of his body interrupted.

I move quickly into the morgue. I know from the galley talk and from what Mendes has told me that one of the last two men Paul killed was the Peace Forces unit commander, distinguished from the others by a set of three green stripes on his shoulder. I slide down the aisle of sheeted bodies, checking under each, my breath making clouds. When I find him, I move to his right side and throw up the sheet.

"How are you doing?" I whisper to Rana.

Her voice comes back muffled by flesh. "I could do this all night, except this man has an odor."

This makes me smile. Almost.

I take the man's right hand and I drape it over my cast. The fingers are stained with a blue dye. I pull the white-handled knife from my belt.

Once, I would have hesitated. But time is short. For us all.

I slice down into the plump middle digit of the man's pinkie. The cold, dead skin pops and splits apart, the nearly bloodless tissue tough like dry meat. I cut down, hit bone, grate laterally, and cut back up. I have to hack at the skin flap. Once it's free I scratch down with my fingernail to be sure. . . .

There. A burst of adrenaline courses through me. This was the first key. . . .

I clamp his finger between the metal table and my cast and I press down with all my weight and I saw against the cold rigid tendons, down into the plasticlike cartilage until there are cracking sounds and the pinkie is severed.

I slip it into my pocket and place the hand back up on the table, stuffing it slightly under the back of the man's thigh. I put away my knife, replace the sheet, and hurry back to the doorway, making sure to stand in exactly the same position as I was when Rana stilled Grayland.

I will be off this boat in the morning. With luck, Grayland has no further work to do on that body between now and then.

"Okay," I say.

Rana slips from him, around me, and down the hall out of sight.

Grayland wobbles on his feet, wincing and rubbing at his head. "Ahh," he says. He looks up and it takes him a moment to focus on me. "Oh, Owen, sorry . . . just got dizzy there for a spell. What can I help you with?"

"I just couldn't sleep," I say. "Wondered if you'd found anything new."

"Ah, no. I've just been filling out paperwork and getting fingerprints."

Fingerprints—but I remember the dark ink on the tips and curse myself for feeling nervous.

There is no need to feel.

"You shouldn't be hanging out here around the dead anyway. Go on, get some sleep."

"Yeah, okay," I say.

"You're shipping out in the morning, I hear," says Grayland.

"Mmm."

He sticks out his hand. "Well, it's been a pleasure knowing you."

He's reaching for my right hand, but realizes it's in the cast. "Oh." He switches to his left, but my left hand is in a pocket with a finger, and so I reach with the cast anyway.

"Oops, sorry, habit."

We both pull our hands back. Grayland laughs. "Well anyway, you have a good one. Stay safe."

"You, too," I say. I start down the hall, my breath held, and he closes the door. With each step, I expect to hear the door open but it doesn't, and soon I am on the next deck up and in my little stateroom.

Rana hovers beside me as I sit on the narrow bed. I examine the commander's finger and start to whittle away the rest of the skin to reveal the bar code. She watches, saying nothing.

When it is done, I slip the finger under my mattress and lie back. I close my eyes, but sleep feels a million miles away.

I think of the wide palm leaves above our heads and the way Lilly would curl against me. The echo of her body makes me tense. I try not to think of it, but the memory hovers like a mosquito.

The weight of her arm on my chest . . .

Her hair against my neck . . .

I try to imagine I am there, and for a second or two it works but then I remember that, no, I am not there, and when I can't take it anymore I open my eyes.

Rana sits on the floor, staring into space.

"Do you ever sleep?"

"A shade needs no sleep," says Rana. "There is never a break from this world. There is always a cold wind, always the feeling of the emptiness."

I gaze up at the metal crossbars of the ceiling.

"What if you inhabit me, like you did in the ice?"

"That would seem like a strange thing to do."

She is probably right.

But I think of sleeping beside Lilly. I think of hearing

her breathing. The times she would snore. "Try it, anyway."

There is a slight whistle of a sigh, and then I feel the buzzing sensation of Rana entering my space, filling my seams, occupying the same electron orbits. There is an electricity to it that is not warm but more like brimming. I see the light around the borders of my vision and I feel something like less empty.

I close my eyes.

"This is maybe better," she says. "Less hollow."

The humming of her presence makes it harder to think, harder to know up from down.

Harder to miss.

"Yes," I say, and sometime soon after, I sleep.

18

THE SHIP'S HORN WAKES ME. GRAY LIGHT THROUGH the window.

Rana has left, as is our plan.

I have barely moved when I hear faint shouting and the crack of a rifle. Then another. And now the spray and heavy thumping of a machine gun.

I sit up, still dressed. Mendes got me gray pants and an olive T-shirt, standard issue for the troops, along with a black LoRad jacket. I reach beneath the bed and slip my only other possession into my pocket.

The engines roar and the boat turns sharply. I hear shouts from up on deck and the clomping of boots. There is a shrill knock on my door. My heart lurches, worried that my handiwork last night has been discovered.

But it's the corporal. His face is troubled. "General sent me to get you. You ready?"

"Yeah." I follow him up to the bridge deck. Dawn is stifling, the sky a dirty brown, the water slicked with rainbow swirls and stinking of oil. Smoke fills my vision, smelling like burned rubber, and I wonder where it's coming from until I notice the flicker ahead of us.

The water is on fire. A wall curving away from us in both directions.

More gunshots sound. The corporal instinctively puts a hand on my shoulder.

"This place . . . ," he mutters to himself with a note of disdain.

There is a sound of thumping bass from somewhere beyond the wall of flame and smoke.

This is the Flotilla city of the Indian Ocean. Compared to the others in the Flotilla network, built on the garbage gyres in each major ocean, this one is modest. But it is considered the most dangerous, a lair of pirates, secret lords, and exiled kings, perpetually surrounded by fire.

Another crack of bullets sounds. An engine roars, and a speedboat bursts through the flames, carving apart the smoke and zooming toward us. Gunshots crackle after it. The driver of the boat, a short, sun-scorched man, shouts and throws something back over his head: a grenade that hits the water and explodes in a plume of flames.

"Target acquired!" a soldier shouts.

"Hold your fire!" Mendes calls from the bridge. "Let him go. It's not worth the bullets."

The boat speeds past us, and the driver wags a middle

finger in our direction. I watch him pass, then notice another boat on fire in the distance.

"Owen." Mendes joins me on the deck. "Things are going sideways," he mutters.

"You were right about this place being dangerous," I say, and I feel that deep foreboding inside again, freeing the adrenaline. This is crazy. It's not going to work—

No. No doubting.

"It's not just here." Mendes looks down at his computer pad. "Since we went to bed last night . . . a reactor meltdown in Siberia, a coup in Sweden, a mass live bright suicide on Mauna Kea. There's even a report of a new pandemic spreading out of the Indian refugee camps in the Himalayas." He looks at me. "It's like the world lost its mind overnight."

Or its heart.

Mendes nods toward the sea of fire in front of us. "We did make contact with the Flotilla, and things are somewhat stable there, for a den of mercenaries and pirates. They're playing nice, though. I think they know I have torpedoes trained on them." Mendes turns to the bridge. "Take us in!" To me: "Better step inside."

The boat nudges forward into the flames. They lick at the bow and the smoke engulfs us. Chunks of debris add to the fire in spots. Two soldiers appear on the forward deck in flame-resistant suits and begin hosing down the ship in white spray.

After a minute of smoky silence we emerge on the other side, the boat sliding over a line of strung-together junk, mostly foam chunks of docks and buoys, that seems to keep the oil slick mostly at bay. There are small boats here and there, with men spraying a similar white substance at the fire when it tries to advance. The light is still ashy and brown, but the sun filters through.

Ahead of the ship is what at first looks like an island, but as we draw closer reveals itself as a floating mass, the entire structure undulating on the water with groans of old wood and rusty metal.

It is a spill of cockeyed triangles, everything built of flotsam. It rattles with a thousand loose joints. Water plunks and splashes beneath its decks. Masts and antennae jut out as docking points, with all manner of boats tied off on them, sloshing against one another. A crammed labyrinth rises behind the makeshift docks, slanted structures built from driftwood and sheets of metal and car doors. In one spot a plastic sandbox has been used as a wall. The carcasses of inner tubes have been stretched to create canopies. The structure builds on itself like a little kid's first Lego castle—

Elissa—

Some structures dangle out over the edges; some seem to have been built out of the inside of others. There are ropes and pulleys and things tied in place with lengths of power line and shoestrings. It smells like tar and burned rubber and dried fish. Hundreds of people crawl like ants both through the smoky alleyways and over the outside of the superstructure. Others sit on ledges and walls, feet dangling as they smoke or drink from brown bottles or fish for who knows what in the sickly tea-colored water.

It doesn't seem like a friendly place.

But then I see a figure standing on one of the docks, waving his arms over his head at us, large metal poles held high that flash in the muted light. And I see a familiar sight tied off behind him.

The *Solara*. Its twin hulls and mast and sleek metal decks cause a strange pain of nostalgia in me. I remember that long day on the boat . . . before I'd seen any of the horrors of Desenna, and everything since. It had been the first time we'd been safe since escaping from Eden, and it seems like some better place in my mind. So much I didn't know then that I know now. How nice would it be to wake up in that little cabin and realize that everything since had been a dream?

Except then I might have to live it all again, and maybe that sounds worse.

The man waving isn't someone I've actually seen before. He lowers the metal poles and I see that they are crutches. His left leg ends at a bandaged stump. He wears a long leather coat in spite of the heat, its shoulders and forearms fitted with mirrorlike plates of metal, along with a cowboy hat and what look like flying goggles, his face shaded in a tightly cut black beard. It all says Nomad.

As we pull up, two soldiers drop to the cockeyed metal dock and tie off ropes. They stand, guns at the ready. The *Solara*'s deck is lined with men and women armed with rifles and crossbows, and you can feel the lack of trust thick between Nomad and ACF. The blood in their past is all too recent.

"Is that your nephew?" Mendes asks, looking at the man on crutches.

"I think so." The story is that he was younger than me, but my time in cryo means he's much older now. Of course, he's not actually my nephew at all.

"That's got to be strange," says Mendes.

"Yeah, but it's okay." My heart rate rises. I'm still no good at lying. "I'm just glad I was able to find him." Then I add something that is closer to the truth: "He might be the only family I have left."

"General!" a soldier calls from the bridge. "We're getting urgent orders from command. We need to scramble for a code one crisis up north."

"Sounds like we need to get a move on," says Mendes. "Suddenly the world is falling apart. Here, let me walk you down."

We make our way to the gangway and climb down the steep staircase. Soldiers kneel, rifles poised, at each side of the base.

I step onto the wobbling dock and find the man leaning on his crutches before me. A woman climbs down from the *Solara* and joins him. She wears jeans and boots and a similar coat.

"Pyra and Barnes did not die in vain," the man says. This is the code we agreed upon when I contacted him yesterday over the gamma link.

"Nor did Tiernan," I say.

The man nods. "It's good to finally meet you, Owen."

Before now, Erik Robard had only been a voice over a phone, one I heard while the Nomad strike team was trying to pull me out of EdenWest. I was able to get word to him through Nomad chat spaces.

He'd been part of a group of refugees waiting to get to Desenna. On the night it was attacked, he was being picked up by a team from Heliad-7 in the *Solara*. Which is why Serena, the medic I met on board who'd known Dr. Maria, is with him now.

"Hi, Owen," she says, looking me over for injuries, her eyes lingering on my wrist. "How are you holding up?" She glances at Mendes, and the anger and mistrust is palpable.

"I'm fine," I say. I nod to Mendes. "If it wasn't for them, I'd be dead." I have an urge to say more, to start gushing about all the events since Desenna. Of all people, Serena feels like someone I can truly trust, even though we only knew each other for a few hours . . . but now is not the time to get into it.

I turn to Mendes. "Thank you so much, for everything."

He claps me on the shoulder. "Be in touch if you need anything and I'll see what I can do." His eyes meet mine. "Good luck, soldier." He looks at Serena and Robard, his face stern. "Keep him safe."

They don't reply. Robard nods stiffly.

Mendes starts up the ladder but pauses. "Owen."

"Yeah?"

"I know you've had a tough time," he says. "You've probably lost your faith. Of course you have, after all you've been through. In times like these, faith comes and goes. It's your soul you need to keep track of."

The statement rings cold inside me. I don't like the feeling, and I can't find a reply, so I just nod and turn back to Robard.

"Thanks for coming," I say.

"Well, your message couldn't be ignored."

A spray of gunshots sounds from somewhere in the Flotilla. Serena flinches, and I see the Nomads up on the *Solara* tensing.

"And," Robard adds, "I think it's not a moment too soon." He turns and motions to the *Solara*, and four of the Nomads sling their rifles over their shoulders and slide down the thick ropes that hold the ship to the dock. Robard looks back to me. "Ready?"

"Yeah."

A horn sounds and engines roar. The ACF soldiers jump to the gangway and hurry up it as the ship starts to back out, rising from the water and retreating into the smoke. I see Mendes on the bridge. He salutes me, and I am glad for him but also feel a sense of regret, of guilt.

He would not salute me if he knew my true plan.

The Nomads, on the other hand, are eager to help.

We move as a unit up the dock. The Nomads keep their primitive rifles aimed, two in front and two behind.

Serena walks beside me. "Lilly and Leech . . . ," she says after a moment.

"They're gone," I answer, holding back a wave of sadness as I say it.

Serena seems to sense that I don't want to talk about it. "Owen, I'm so sorry."

I shrug. "Thanks. The Three was only a myth anyway."

Serena doesn't respond to this, and I don't want her to, so I change the subject. "You survived the Desenna attack."

"We happened to be on our way to bring in more Nomad refugees. Just luck, really. As was being with Robard when he got the message from you."

"How were you injured?" I ask Robard. The bandages on his leg look fresh, and he is not quite steady on his crutches.

"I was in a convoy that was attacked by an ACF

assault force. We were just minding our own business, actually, en route for supplies after your attempted rescue from EdenWest. The ACF came out of nowhere one night and boxed us in a canyon. It was a slaughter. I only survived because they wanted to interrogate me. They thought we'd attacked some military installation."

"I saw that," I say, remembering the firefight we'd seen while flying from EdenWest to the Rockies. "We flew right by. I'm sorry we didn't help."

"They had gunships," says Robard. "There was nothing you could have done. Bastards took out families."

It's hard to reconcile this with my time with the ACF soldiers. "They know it wasn't you, now," I say, in case it helps. "Paul was behind that raid and the ACF knows it."

"It would have been nice if they'd listened when *I* told them that."

The light dims around us as we make our way into a tight alley. Doors and shrouded corridors split off at angles. Shadowy figures lean out here and there, looking first at our guns, then our clothes and possessions. Children and rats scurry across our path, sometimes hopping from one tin roof to another above us. At one point, two boys toss slimy projectiles at us that turn out to be gray-colored jellyfish. They splat, one on the pathway and one on Robard's coat. He flicks it away casually.

"We've kept what you learned about the Ascending

Stars secret," says Robard. "But given the strange events these last twenty-four hours around the globe, people will start to suspect something soon."

"Do you have any word on when the selectees will begin to leave the Edens?" I ask.

"Our sources think it will be any day," Serena says.

Which means this has to work.

We reach an intersection of dark, narrow alleys and ladders, some leading up and some down. Sour-smelling water drips down the brown-streaked walls. Smells compete to overwhelm us: cooking meat, rotting trash, and human waste.

Robard checks a small scrap of fabric on which he's drawn a little map. He points to a rusty metal ladder leading up to another level. "This way."

There is a peal of chesty laughter from somewhere behind us. The thump of bass music starts up again, rattling the walls all around us. It's louder now, like we are getting closer to the Flotilla's heart. An old woman peers out a cracked window, her face gaunt, one eye swollen shut.

"Try to touch as little as you can in here," says Serena, and I notice that she's wearing leather gloves.

We climb to the next level, where the smell of the burning water reaches us on the ocean breeze. Clothes flutter above. We pass through patches of hot, hazy sun. The thudding bass rattles our teeth, growing ever louder.

Robard counts doors and stops in front of one that is hung with the bones of fish and who knows what else, strung on frayed rope. The skull of some kind of rodent stares out from the center of the door.

The music makes the door pulse.

Robard turns to me and leans on one crutch so he can put a hand on my shoulder. "You're sure you want to do this?"

"Yeah."

"It's a good plan," he says encouragingly. "I mean, it's crazy. And you know you don't have to . . ."

If only that were true. "I know. But what other option is there?"

"Okay, well, this is the best place for the job. And she knows we're coming." Robard presses a button on the door.

The bass extinguishes inside. There is a click and a red light ignites and scans us.

Silence.

"She knows we're coming," Robard repeats. He sounds nervous.

The door opens and a thin Asian man greets us with the glowing point of an electrically charged hand saber. His face is crisscrossed with scars and yet he is wearing plain green pants and a shirt like he works in a medical clinic.

"We—" Robard begins.

"Payment," the man says quietly, the knife unmoving.

Serena holds out a small dirty canvas bag. The man quickly pulls it open and thumbs through the N-Fed credits inside, his lips clicking as he counts to himself. He stuffs his nose in and takes a big sniff of the money. He considers the scent, eyes closed, like he's tasting a fine wine. Then wags the knife at us. "Inside."

We find ourselves in a cramped room bordered by cluttered shelves of jars and heaps of equipment. Green lights of charging batteries blink everywhere. There is a wide metal exam table in the center. It is covered in a thin white sheet that only mutes the stains beneath. A bank of computers stands at the far end. A medi-arm hovers over the table. These portable surgical machines are in many of the remote colonies and outposts, a sort of all-in-one basic surgeon. All it needs is one doctor to operate it. The air is still and stuffy, heavy with heat and laced with the scent of bleach.

"Welcome." She stands beside the table, tall and thin, with tan skin and a shaved head. She wears bright blue rubber gloves and a black apron over a tank top and black pants. As she turns to us, I see that the side of her face is tattooed with a snake that starts behind her ear, curls around her chin, and then wraps around her neck like a collar. Her accent sounds like English is not her first language.

"You are Dr. Viram?" Robard asks.

"Indeed." She turns back to a table of instruments: scalpels and other pointed and curved devices. "My credentials are on the wall if you need to see them."

I find a series of diplomas hung there on the corrugated metal.

"You studied at Oxford on Helsinki Island," says Serena, impressed.

"I graduated in three years, including residency. Your next question is why an accomplished doctor is working in a place such as this."

"No," said Serena. "I get it. These people aren't any less important than those in the Northern Federation or the Edens."

Viram doesn't respond but she smiles lightly.

"How can you pay the bills?" Robard asks, noting the surgical machine, and glancing at his own leg. One of these might have let him keep his foot.

"Well," says Viram, "you are not the only customers who will pay a premium for an anonymous treatment. And, believe me, I am giving you an extreme discount."

When she finishes arranging her instruments, she looks at me. "You are the patient."

I feel the old nerves: Owen, who didn't like having attention called to himself. But I press down on those fears because they do not matter anymore. The old me is of no use now. "Yes."

She nods. "Three procedures, as I understand it."

Her tone is so even, like a teacher's. I have to keep myself from asking if that's okay. "Please hand the examples to my associate."

I remove the Eden commander's finger from my pocket, the necklace with Victoria's finger bone from my neck, and hand both to the assistant. From the crowded shelves he yanks a device that looks like a microscope, plugs it into the central generator on the floor, and then sets it up on the exam table, as there is no room anywhere else.

Outside, the longest volley of gunshots yet.

Viram glances at the ceiling. "Things are beginning to deteriorate." She gazes right at me. "Those of us who believed in the Three, in the teachings of Heliad-7, are starting to know in our hearts that the Three have failed. We wonder if there is still reason to hope."

I have to look away. Her statement feels like a challenge, as if it is all up to me now. As if she suspects my true plan. I tell myself, as I have before, that she can't know, nobody really knows, what it is like for me right now. The only people who truly knew are gone.

The assistant looks at each bone under blue light. The magnified image appears on the computer screen.

Viram studies the bar codes.

"They look identical," says Robard.

"Yes . . ." Viram leans in and her finger traces the vertical engraved lines on the screen. "Here is the difference. This spacing. If we make a change there . . . we should be fine. Save that data," she says to the assistant. "Now, Owen, it is time to get on my table. Take off your clothes."

I disrobe, clenching my teeth against nerves; and once the microscope is moved, I lie down on the sheet. The light of the medi-arm blinds me and I feel the fear of the underground Eden lab creep back into me, the fear that I am someone's lab rat all over again. I think of Anna's ribs being spread open. It is sweltering in the room. My back sticks to the sheet.

"We will start with the finger." I feel a dull pain as Viram picks up my casted right hand. The fingers were purple and are now a sickly patchwork of yellow and brown. "Not the most elegant work on your wrist here," she says. "Military. We'll fix that up, too, free of charge."

The assistant attaches sensors to my chest. Serena takes my left hand. "We'll be right here."

I nod and say, "Okay," but it comes out a croak. I'm so scared, too scared. But I won't show it.

The assistant straps my shoulders and thighs to the table.

Viram leans over me, now wearing a surgical mask. She has lovely brown eyes. The medi-arm begins to whine to life, its lights brightening. The string of bulbs lighting the rest of the room flickers to brown.

She holds out a syringe and moves it toward my hand.

"I can't put you under, but I can numb your hand. Shall I move the screen so that you can see?"

I think no, but then I say yes. I want to see the saw tearing apart the cast fibers, revealing the lumpy purple mess of my wrist.

Want to see the moment when the skin of my right pinkie resists, before the scalpel cuts through and the blood flows.

When the skin is peeled back and pinned in place.

The medi-arm lowers, a green sensor scanning.

It hums louder, gathering energy, preparing to work.

19

THE BEST PLACE TO VIEW THE VAST DOME OF EdenEast, Rana tells me, is from the top of the great pyramid of Giza. She promised to take me there when I last saw her, because that is where we will meet up again.

By solar sail, it is a two-day trip from the Flotilla around the Horn of Africa and north through the Red Sea. I spend most of it in a fog, lying in the *Solara*'s infirmary, taking pain medication. There is a vague burning in my finger, a dull throb from my now-cast-free wrist, the pain on my thigh. And my eyes . . .

I keep them mostly closed.

Serena keeps an eye on me, but I learn from our brief conversations that she does not approve of my plan the way that Robard does. I think she wishes there were another way.

But the reports that we hear on the Northern News Network suggest that time is running out:

*The pandemic that was carried initially by the
elephant cockroaches has now officially spread
to humans, and the entire Asian continent is
being locked down under quarantine. . . .*

*Fighting has reached a fever pitch today in
Lagos . . . fears of collapsing into civil war. . . .*

*Repeated transit bombings have led Copenhagen
to declare martial law. . . .*

*The number of cases of radiation poisoning in
Siberia is expected to top twenty thousand. . . .*

*Massive die-offs of pronghorn . . . reportedly
just lying down and succumbing to the sun . . .*

*Fires in the French deserts that have jumped the
containment lines . . .*

"The whole planet," says Serena sadly as she removes
the bandages from my right hand and wrist. "It's dying."

We have slowed and are nearing the shore, a deso-
late, moonlike expanse of the Egyptian coast. The Suez
Canal to the north is controlled by fierce pirates, so we
are docking here to meet Robard's contact and will travel
overland the rest of the way.

"These are looking pretty good," Serena says, running her fingers, the nail polish still black, over the stitches. I hold up my hand and look at my finger. It is a bit swollen and blotchy. The stitches are small and clear and expertly done, located on the inside of the finger, on the opposite side from where I now carry a bar code.

Dr. Viram used the two samples to create a fake one. There is some small chance that her fabricated code will actually match someone's in the Eden system. If that is the case, it's better to have a mix-up with an existing selectee than to be identified as either an enemy of Eden or a deceased soldier, as would have been the case if we'd copied Victoria's or the commander's code.

And even if there is a mix-up, it should still work, because I have the second necessary form of identification, which I will need for getting into an Eden dome to begin with.

You don't need a selectee code for that.

All you need is a retinal scan.

But it can't be Owen Parker's retina. He's already in their system.

Serena removes more bandages, and I try, for the first time to open both eyes at once. As I do, Serena watches a computer pad carefully.

It takes a minute for the blur to begin to reset itself. The colors are not quite aligned.

"I'm calibrating the depth sensors now," she says.

Focus begins to clear.

"And now the movement oscillator . . ."

I try glancing to my right and left, and there is a weird splitting of the information, but then it syncs up. The information from my real eye . . .

And my bionic one.

An artificial eye with a retina matched to a forged identity in the Eden databases, assuming Robard's contacts are able to hack the system. Getting access to the selectee information is nearly impossible, but the regular old citizen information? That is much easier.

Suddenly, Lilly is there in my head. *I don't like this, O. Bionic eye, that's halfway to becoming Paul.*

For days I have worked so hard not to think, to keep her out of my thoughts as best I can, but I can picture her now and I can almost smell her she seems so close. The eruption of grief inside me is nearly overwhelming.

Don't think about that, I tell myself. *She's gone. Dead. I am doing what it takes.*

This is what it takes.

And yet I can just imagine what Lilly would say to that. *That's probably what Paul tells himself.*

Maybe.

I blink, and here in the silence of the ship, I hear a little hiss. There is a cool sensation, and a momentary blur in my vision.

"Did you feel that?" Serena asks, touching the pad.

"I've only worked with this calibration software a couple times, but I think I just synced the tear ducts with your blinking musculature."

I blink a few more times and things clear up. I run a finger below my eye, and find a stray drop leaking down, like a tear. I look at the liquid and see that it's slightly pink.

"There are antibacterials in the initial coatings," says Serena when she sees me noticing this. "It will clear up after a day or two." She puts down the pad. "And how is that wrist?"

I grit my teeth and try moving. There is stiffness, but the wrist moves like it's supposed to. There is a slight sound like rolling when it does.

"Some of the wrist bones were crushed," explains Serena. "Dr. Viram replaced them with titanium bearings. Pretty elite treatment. Roll on your side."

Serena peels a bandage away from the side of my left thigh. "This looks good," she says. "Want to see?"

"Sure."

She holds out a mirror and I can see the thin seam of clear plastic that runs down my thigh. It looks like an old scar. Just below it, there is a coin-size mole that also wasn't there before. I can feel the dull pain all around the area.

"If anyone asks, you can say you had one of the degenerative joint infections as a kid and had surgery."

Serena starts pulling off her gloves. "Well, I think you are good to go if you want to get dressed."

When I first slide down off the bed, my thigh burns, and balance is tricky with the still-new vision. The bionic eye has a small focal point square in the center of it. The eye is supposed to sync perfectly with the other, but if there is ever a delay or malfunction, I can press the inner right edge of the eyeball with my fingernail and this will manually focus. It's working fine now, but the square is a constant reminder: no matter where I look, I see what I've become.

Serena works at a far cot while I dress. One of the *Solara*'s crew took a stray bullet at the Flotilla.

"I'm going to go up on deck," I say.

"Okay." Serena sanitizes her hands with foam and comes over. "Owen, I . . ." Her eyes start to well up, and she wraps me in a hug. "You're very brave. I am glad to have known you."

This should probably make me feel scared. Maybe it does, but more than anything, I feel a cold wash of guilt, for reasons no one can know. I excuse myself as quickly as I can.

The *Solara* docks at a tiny shanty village. It is evening, nearly seven, and the sun is blood orange and setting. The air is still unmercifully hot and baked.

Robard and I descend the gangway over brown, polluted water, flanked by four soldiers. A band of five heavily armed men waits for us. They have dark skin and ratty NoRad clothes. The rest of the village's residents stay out of sight.

"Stay alert," Robard says under his breath. "They are Nomad Alliance but also probably pirates, and they may smell a nice bounty for delivering us to Eden."

We stop before the group, their weapons on their shoulders but their hands near triggers. Robard speaks in what I think is French, and the group's leader responds. He motions to a pair of sailcarts up the rise at the edge of town, like little sailboats on wheels, their masts catching the last pink rays of sun.

The conversation rises in volume. The group's leader points at Robard repeatedly and says something that sounds like *double*.

Robard grows agitated.

The group leader shakes his head. *"Cette mission est trop dangereuse,"* he says.

"We had a deal," Robard says in English.

I can feel my pulse speeding up as their voices shade toward anger.

The group leader shouts now, and guns come off shoulders.

Robard grows louder. He turns to me and our soldiers. "He doesn't understand what's at stake here."

The group leader shouts again, and starts backing up.

Robard throws up his hands, speaking forcefully, and

the group leader whips a pistol from his belt.

"C'est fini!" he shouts, waving the gun at us.

Just then, one of the soldiers looks up and his eyes go wide. He shouts to the leader in a panicked tone. *"Général! Un fantôme!"* They all turn.

I look over my shoulder and see the pale white light.

Rana has arrived early.

She lands beside me and I am glad to feel her glow on my skin, to see her hollow eyes and downturned mouth. She still carries the black bag with her—*Lilly's*—skull inside.

To all the soldiers around us—including the *Solara's* crew and Robard himself—though, Rana's appearance is otherworldy, impossible, terrifying. Not to mention that she has drawn her twin blades and holds them ready to use.

I'd almost forgotten that other than me, this is still a planet where no one knows of such things as crystal skulls, ancient Atlanteans, or dead girls who linger.

"This is my friend I was telling you about," I say mildly to Robard.

He regards me with wide eyes that flick to Rana and back, and then nods slightly. I realize that I have become something foreign to him now. And when Rana speaks: *"Y at-il un problème?"*

One of the soldiers actually runs.

The others train their guns, but the tips shake.

"Tell them to take me where I need to go," I say to Robard, and after he translates, I add: "And tell them afterward to spread the word: beware the boy who walks with the ancients."

We load into the two sailcarts. Rana and I sit in the back, and everyone leaves space around us. The carts gather wind and shoot off across the hardpan, single headlights spearing out from each, their wheels bouncing off the rocks. As we gather speed, their windward sides lift off the ground, and we skim on two wheels.

The breeze grows cool and refreshing as the heat leaves the world. My bionic eye starts to stick, maybe drying out, and I press my finger against the acrylic surface, wiggling it until some tears leak out. I already hate the thing, but whatever.

Robard talks with the other leader as we travel. They all glance at us from time to time.

"Good timing," I say to Rana, leaning close to speak over the wind. It is weird being near her surface, because she gives off no heat, has no smell. Tight corners cause us to lean into each other, and she dissolves partly into me, or me into her, depending on the angle, and there is a cold tingling when it happens that feels strange, and yet I've started to find it comforting.

"I thought so," she says. She looks at me. It is hard to tell with her eyeless gaze but I think she is studying my eyes.

"How do they look?" I ask.

"Like you have a real eye and a fake eye," she says.

"Great."

"No one will look at you from as close as I do. But the colors are slightly different."

I never would have let you do that, Lilly's voice echoes in my head.

I push it away.

Still, I find Rana looking at me. "What?"

"What is it like, to have parts of you be machine?"

"It's different." I feel myself tensing at this question. "But not really. Why do you ask?"

"I just wonder how it changes you."

"You sound like—" I almost say she sounds like Lilly. "You sound like you don't approve of this plan."

"I understand it, probably better than you do."

"What's that supposed to mean?"

"We shall see."

"Fine then." I hate how sulky I sound, and so I concentrate on watching the shadowy desert world slide by.

We cross the dark plains for five hours. Finally we stop on the shore of a large body of water. Its coast is devoid of any plant life. A dull yellow glow lights the horizon.

"This is it," Robard says to me. "We can't go any closer or we'll trip their sensors." He hops out of the sailcart.

I join him at the lake edge but then recoil. The water gives off a scent of rot and feces and decay so strong it feels like my nose is burning. Without the humming of the sails, I can now hear an incessant buzzing of insects, and flies start to slap off my face and head.

"What is this?" I ask.

"Sewage runoff from EdenEast," says Robard, wincing. "No need to treat the sewage when there's no one around." He points around the coastline a little ways to where a line of lights leads up a gentle rise. The lights outline a cement river, more like a trough. "Follow that trail of sewage, straight to Eden."

I pull my LoRad jacket up over my nose. "Okay."

"And you have a plan for getting in . . . ," Robard says skeptically.

"We do," Rana replies for me.

Robard can't hide the tremor that passes over his face when she speaks. "Are you"—he seems to be summoning his courage—"an Atlantean?"

"She is," I say, "and we'll be okay. Robard, thank you for helping me."

"Owen . . ." Robard wraps me in a big hug that smells of dust and leather. Then he holds me at arm's length. "You're our best hope, and so brave. When this is over, we will sing your name so that all future generations remember you."

My heart races at this, the fear, the guilt, the hollow,

overwhelming feeling. If only he knew the truth. But instead I say: "If I succeed . . ."

"*When* you succeed." Robard slaps my back and steps away. "We will watch the skies."

The carts turn and catch a breeze, their sails humming, wheels clattering, and they shoot away and are soon lost to darkness.

"You scared them," I say to Rana.

"Not the effect I used to enjoy having on boys," she replies, "but, yes, making them quake in fear isn't so bad."

We start around the edge of the sewage lake. My boots smack in the sticky mud, and I take the smallest breaths I can. The smell and the flies abate a little when we reach the concrete river, but the gurgling sound of moving sludge keeps me on the edge of vomiting.

We walk beside the river of waste for twenty minutes and finally crest a rise of land.

Before us is a skyline of wonders.

The great pyramids are a few kilometers ahead, standing silent and majestic, thousands of years old. They are lit by the curved rows of white lights on the enormous dome of EdenEast, not far beyond that. It dwarfs them in size.

The dome makes a low, constant hum, all the electricity coursing through it.

We follow the sewage a little farther, then cross a steel

bridge. On the other side, we finally start away from the stench and sound.

Rana points to the tallest of a trio of pyramids. "Giza. I must show you that view."

It takes us another hour to reach it, the pyramids slowly growing in the sky, yet the dome growing even more. Here and there, we pass piles of carved stone and the broken backs of obelisks. "There were streets here once," says Rana. "It neared Atlante in its greatness."

We reach the great pyramid of Giza and gaze up its immense side. "It's okay if we skip the view," I say to Rana. My body hurts all over, already sore from the surgeries, now from the long walk on top of that.

"We can't," says Rana, "it's lovely. Also, that is our way in."

"Into Eden? How do you mean?"

"You shall see."

She begins to float up the steps of rock. I start climbing, hauling myself from one level to the next.

"Of all the civilizations," Rana says as we climb, "that slowly grew back from the destruction wrought by the Paintbrush, the Egyptians came the closest to that magic, the wonder of my world. They had help, though."

"What does that mean?" I ask, breathless from the climb.

"I will show you."

It is a half hour of scrambling, scraping, and slipping

in the dark on the shadow side of the great pyramid. My recently repaired wrist aches by the time we finally reach the top, and the knees of my pants are shredded. Sweat stings one eye but not the other. I find Rana sitting peacefully on the weatherworn tip. I collapse beside her, breathless.

"Was that really necessary?" I ask.

"Yes. See the stars?" Instead of pointing up, she points down.

I turn and balance myself beside her, trying not to think about the long drop in all directions, and when I look ahead, still breathing hard, I do see them. A desert of stars, glittering and dancing on the ground below us.

It's the solar panels, I realize after a moment, but that doesn't lessen the effect: the rings and rings of mirrors that surround EdenEast all reflect the stars above, and it is as if we are sitting above the universe, looking down into it, or, if you position your eyes just right, like we are floating in space with stars above and below. There are moments when only the tiny focus square in my right eye reminds me that I am still on earth.

"Okay," I say, "this is cool."

And I realize that this is the first time since Lilly died that I have felt inspired by anything, felt any sensation at all other than a dark nothingness.

That this view is inspired by the creations of Eden, of Paul, means something I can barely fathom. The solar-panel sea of space is as wonderful as any of the glimpses of beauty I have had on this journey. And it is made wonderful, too, by the presence of Rana because she thinks it beautiful, which also means something. I feel suddenly terrified that I have been in danger of losing what it is to be alive. And—oh no, oh no—I feel something certain now in the way my heart is racing, not just from the climb anymore.

"Tell me," says Rana.

"Tell you what?"

"Why you're shaking."

"It's cold," I say. "And this is a good view."

"Don't lie to me," says Rana. "We agreed I would be the only one you didn't lie to."

I nod. "Okay. I just realized how much I don't want to die."

"Of course not."

"But I might. I just spent two days planning for it."

Because this is the reason why Robard and the Nomads helped prepare me to get inside EdenEast, to infiltrate the selectees . . . so that I can get to Paul and the Terra, and then . . .

There will be no way to get the Terra off *Egress*. But the cube itself is indestructible. And a space station is not.

We can return the Terra to the earth by bringing the station down.

The scar on my thigh: an untraceable oxygen detonator, stitched into the muscle. It is only a few centimeters long. Space stations are fragile things. And the bomb, despite its size, is extremely powerful.

The plan does not go further than that, because it does not need to.

The plan does not include survival. Rana has known of such plans.

There is no other way. The earth is dying. And the more that chaos reigns, the more distracted the nations get. And no one knows the truth. It is up to me.

A martyr. A hero. That is what I would be to them. But inside all I feel is terrified and empty. That is not why I am doing what I am doing.

"Robard says they'll write songs about me," I say.

"I had a song written about me, once," says Rana, "by a Germanic druid mystic. It was unbearable."

I laugh, but the feeling gets worse, this tightness. I do not want to die, I do not want songs written about me, I don't even want to save the planet or anything. There is nothing for me here, I don't care, I barely want to exist, and I know these are all contradictions. . . .

I feel the tears welling up on one side, and a strange blocked pressure on the other. The bionic eye does not register emotion. It's made to be more efficient than that. I squeeze at the skin on the inside of my eye socket and a squirt of fluid shoots out. Oh, what have I become . . .

"I promised myself I wouldn't feel these things anymore," I say to Rana. "Wouldn't *feel* anymore." The tears come harder now.

"I know you did," says Rana.

"I don't want grief, I don't want sorrow, I don't want Elissa or my family or my dead friends. I just want . . ."

I just want . . .

Rana slides her hand inside my shoulder, her fingers mingling with my muscles and bone, and rubs. The buzzing sensation soothes me. "It's going to be okay."

"How is that possible?"

"Because we have a plan," Rana says. "And it's time to go."

And then she sinks into the stone we are sitting on.

I look around, and nearly lose my balance as I try to find her, but her light is gone.

Then the stones begin to rumble, and a section of the stone grinds open in a cloud of dust. As a rectangle of darkness opens up, a thick metal ring rises from the side of the opening.

Rana floats up out of it. "This way."

20

I LOOK FROM THE RING TO THE DOOR. "THIS wasn't the normal entrance. That ring would be for tying off a ship."

"Yes. Now, let's go. The stairs have crumbled in spots, so watch your step."

I start down the stairs, and Rana turns a copper wheel that makes the ring lower and the door rumble closed. We descend by her pale light, a steep staircase in a passage so narrow I have to turn my shoulders and duck my head to fit. Down and down we go, the staircase making hairpin turns. The air is dank and close and chalky, and I am sure we have descended as far as the actual pyramid's height, but we keep going down farther and farther. The air begins to cool, to feel like underground.

"Shouldn't there be pharaohs' tombs?" I ask.

"We are well below those now. They came much later. This tunnel was built during the original construction. A temple before the pyramid. Long before."

The lower we go, the better condition the stairs are in, and the hall begins to widen, too. Finally, it flattens and the passage opens into a vast darkness. Rana moves her hand to the wall and illuminates a line of torches in copper sleeves. Below these are holes in the stone. There is a sharp smell of oil. I pull one of the torches from its holder and slip the top, a bundle of tightly strapped reeds, into the hole. It emerges soaked. Rana claps her hands near it, and a spark ignites the torch in greenish-gold light.

We cross a polished marble floor. My torch begins to illuminate the bases of thick columns on either side and in front of us, looming shapes. Giant, arcing sweeps of wood and copper. The hulls of ships, Atlantean ships perched on heavy wooden stands with enormous stone wheels. We pass one, two, and by the fifth I realize this is a fleet, a fleet of Atlantean transport ships that would have held hundreds of people.

"The biggest groups of Atlantean refugees settled here," says Rana, "in what would later grow into Memphis, the first of the major ancient Egyptian cities."

"So, these ships were used to build the pyramids," I say.

"How else could they build something so tall?" Rana asks.

"People in my time think it was aliens."

Rana points ahead. "Beyond these ships there are passages. Paul and the Eden archaeological teams discovered these not long after finding Polara and our bodies. They also found a great map room in this complex. That unlocked the location of the other major Atlantean sites around the globe, and allowed them to begin their search for the Three."

"Why didn't they just go straight to Atlante and search for the Paintbrush?" I ask.

"Our people made sure to erase the location of Atlante from the collection. The city had been destroyed and covered in ice anyway, so navigators of the era didn't include it in their maps."

We are passing under the largest craft yet. Its belly is flat, different from all the rest in that it is coated in small squares. I reach up and run my fingers over them. They are smooth and look like ceramic, like perfectly glazed pottery.

"This is different," I say. The tiles have burn marks here and there. Scorched sections as if they have encountered incredible fires.

"Wait," Rana hisses. I stop, and I hear it, too. A faint, clanking sound. Once . . .

Now again.

Rana gazes up at the tiled ship. The sound reverberates through the hall. And now a twisting of metal.

A flicker of white light.

"I should have known," says Rana.

"Known what?" I ask.

She doesn't answer and I follow her as she floats under the ship, toward its front. A copper ladder hangs down near the bow. I climb up, Rana floating beside me, and find a heavy metal door, half-open. The whole ship is made of copper plates, the seams hammered together. It looks as much like an old submarine as an Atlantean craft. There are no spots for masts on its oblong body. Unlike any other ship we've seen, this one seems to be enclosed, the aeronaut's controls somewhere inside. The copper has black burn marks, too.

And there is something inside. A flickering light, weak, like a flashlight or . . .

Rana slides through the door.

I follow and step into the low-ceilinged compartment, its walls lined with thin girders. The floor is made of panels of hammered bronze, and there are rows of high-backed wooden chairs. It looks like an ancient airliner, except each chair has a crystal globe suspended above it. The globes are half-open as if they were supposed to be helmets. Fabric tubes run from their tops into the floor.

Rana stands in a doorway at the front of this cabin. I step quietly to join her.

I find myself looking into a cockpit, strung with ropes and levers, encased within a half-sphere crystal windshield, with two chairs that each face pedal rudders and copper wheels.

Someone is sitting in one of the chairs, glowing deathly white.

Rana makes her crack-in-the-door sigh.

"Lük," she says.

The boy looks up with hollow black eyes. He, too, wears white and flickers as if his skin is just a light overlay on his bones. "Rana." Their voices are a match of sad, hollow tones.

He looks me up and down, his face expressionless, and I wonder if he feels like I did when I saw him in the skull, if he thinks we look familiar. But after a moment, he only turns back to what he was doing.

He holds a modern-looking wrench and is tightening what is also a modern-looking bolt on the wheel in front of him.

"Is this where you have been," Rana asks, "all these years?" She sounds as sad as she has ever sounded.

Lük twists at the bolt. "Do you know what they were trying to do here?" he asks, his voice thin and windy. "The last descendants of the masters, who remembered the old ways?"

I look back at the chairs and consider the ship we flew to Antarctica. I look at the helmets, remember the burn marks on the bottom tiles. . . .

"This is a spaceship," I say. "Isn't it?"

Lük regards me again. "You are not of the Three."

"But he has communed with your skull," Rana snaps in my defense.

Lük keeps working. "Then what is he?"

"He is the one chosen by the Terra to save her."

I do not like hearing this, being reminded of some noble mission, nor the feeling of guilt it inspires. And I do not like that Rana glances over at me, because I wonder if she is judging my current plan.

Lük finishes the bolt, then works the lever beside it. "Yes, it's a spaceship. The masters' descendants watched the ruin of their world and wanted to go to another, to start over."

"History doesn't much change," I say, "does it?"

"It shouldn't surprise us," says Rana. "Once the Terra was lost, humanity began to look away rather than within to find a better world."

"Does this thing work?" I ask.

"It seems that they did fly it, based on the burn marks," says Lük. "But either it became too damaged or over time they lost their knowledge of how to use it. I don't know what they were up to."

"And you think you can fix it," Rana guesses.

"I do," replies Lük. They sound like the ghost version of an old married couple. "I've been working on it for a while and studying the advancements of space travel in the modern world."

"You know it has been five thousand years since we were here in ancient Egypt together."

"Has it?" says Lük. "I thought maybe two or three. I haven't been keeping track."

Rana's tone thins. "Did you ever think to come find me?"

Lük finally looks up at her. "Yes. Every day. But what good would it have done? So much of us was lost to the skulls, and this lingering, it seemed like it was worse when we were together."

Rana sighs. "Well, yes. It did."

Lük turns back to his work. When he moves the lever, there are clicks from the floor beneath us. "Yes," he says to himself, satisfied.

"Does that mean the ship will work?" I ask. It suddenly occurs to me that a spaceship would make other plans possible. I wouldn't have to follow this course I'd set out on. . . .

"Almost. There are a few more things to do," says Lük. He puts the wrench down in a bag on the floor. I can see that he has a collection of modern tools there, and now he's picking up a blowtorch.

"How long will it take you?" I ask him.

"Not long. These latest corrections have been quick. Maybe just a few more decades."

"Oh," I say. Never mind. It makes things simpler, of course, but I still feel air escaping me. A little part of me still wishes for the same thing Seven did: a third option. Oh well.

"Boys and their toys," Rana says.

"Why are you here?" Lük asks, still working.

"The world is ending," says Rana. "The Heart of the Terra has been found and taken. The Three have failed."

Lük pauses. "That explains why those Eden soldiers haven't been down here in so long. Well, it was always a risky plan." He looks to Rana. "We knew that."

"We did. We have a new plan, now. Will you come with us?"

Lük surveys the controls. "I have a little more to do here," he says.

Rana doesn't answer for a moment. I can feel her frustration like gathering lightning, but all she says is, "Suit yourself. Be well, Lük."

She begins to move away and I follow. We are back at the door when Lük calls, "Find me when you're back?"

Rana's last words to him are as brittle as a desert wind. "We're not coming back."

I take one last look at the cabin of the vessel, trying to imagine the ancients taking their seats, the masters reaching for the stars.

The cycles repeating.

I climb down the ladder. Rana is silent beside me as we pass two more smaller craft.

Suddenly she hisses like boiling water and shoots

ahead, becoming a lethal beam of energy and she blasts through a small craft at the end of the row, shattering it into splinters of wood and metal in a tremendous explosion. The sound ricochets through the wide hall.

I pick my way through the wreckage and find her on the other side, kneeling on the floor.

"Feel better?" I ask her.

"I am sick of all the melancholy," says Rana. "Sick of these end of days."

"It seems like you're also maybe mad at Lük."

"To be mad at him, I would have to still love him, but I don't. I'm not whole." She tugs the black skull bag as she says this. "Seeing him just makes me feel more empty."

I rub my hand into the white of her shoulder. "I'm sorry."

She doesn't reply. We stay there for a moment.

Until something rumbles the floor, the entire cavern. Dust sifts down from the ceiling.

"What was that?" I wonder.

"I don't think that's a normal sound for an Eden," says Rana. "This way."

We reach the far side of the wide cavern and here is a modern steel door embedded in the ancient stone wall. Light seeps beneath it. I try the smooth handle, but it is locked. I study the door in Rana's faint light and find a red button beneath the handle. I press it.

"Emergency override," an electronic male voice says. "Please show identification."

A small circle in the middle of the door lights up green. The retina scanner.

I glance at Rana. "Well, here we go."

I put my bionic eye to the light.

21

THE GREEN SPEARS INTO MY VISION, BUT INSTEAD
of seeing spots or greenish blobs I see a kind of static
white that fractures into pixels. The light hums, moving
up and down and then left and right and then winks out.
I blink at the distortion, and in the moment of silence my
heart begins to race. Each step now feels almost unbearable, like the journey may end at any moment.

Somewhere far above, there is another explosion.

"Identity verified, Eden citizen: David Marks, age
eighteen, Eden community participant level one-A."

I exhale hard. Robard's people did it. They probably
made me eighteen so I could travel as a selectee alone.

The door doesn't open right away, though, and I am
just beginning to doubt, when there is a shrill beep and
the handle turns. We step back as the door hisses open.
A short woman in a white lab coat stands on the other
side, wearing thin-framed glasses, her hair back. Behind
her is a bright, clean lab of metal tables holding ancient

tablets and artifacts, computer screens angling down from the ceiling, workstations with other white-coated technicians tapping busily—

But also red lights flashing everywhere.

The woman looks at me bewilderedly. Out of the corner of my eye I notice Rana's glow is gone, and I feel a sense of expanding and tingling all over. She has slipped inside me and out of sight.

"I'll travel with you like this," she says, her voice somewhere near my ear. "Hold my bag." I feel the skull bag's strap slipping onto my shoulder.

"Who are you?" the woman asks. She looks around me. "How did you get in here"—she checks the pad in her hand—"David?"

"I, um, got lost." This feels like an impossibly lame excuse.

And the woman doesn't buy it, but there is another rumble from above; and as dust rains from the stone walls around me, one of the computer screens crashes to the tile floor of the lab, smashing and making the woman and everyone else jump. She looks frantically around the room. Other technicians are hurrying toward the door on the far side. Some are tucking computer drives under their arms.

She glances back at me. "Whatever—you're on your own." She runs for the door.

"Go," says Rana.

I jog after her, through the lab so similar to the one beneath the Aquinara in EdenWest. We hurry out into a long white hall with flashing red lights. Other doors are popping open and workers are all running in the direction of an exit sign.

"What's happening?" I ask a young man who happens to catch my eye.

"It's crazy. Some kind of revolt," he says breathlessly. "Something about unfair treatment? I don't know—I thought the suicides last night were the worst of it. Those people leaping off buildings, but this is just getting insane."

"The loss of the Terra," Rana says, and I know this but I am not going to think about that. Just keep moving.

Except something out of the corner of my eye makes me stop. We're just passing double doors that hang open, and I see a large space of carved stone inside. A technician darts out, slamming into my shoulder without an apology.

I step through the doors and find myself in an ancient dome-shaped room. It's similar to the navigation room beneath EdenWest, with tiled walls that show oceans and islands that were a mystery to me then but I know now: scenes from Atlante. But this room doesn't have an obsidian star ball on a pedestal. It has many pedestals, all arranged on circular copper tracks in concentric circles.

And each pedestal holds a stone ball, of varying sizes,

carved with stripes, with mountains and canyons. Some have rings.

The planets.

"This is a model of the solar system," I say.

"We knew of the planets," says Rana. "Just some of the knowledge that was lost in the fall, not to be found for thousands of years."

"Yeah, but, these maps make it look like . . . like someone saw them. Like the masters actually got up there in that ship."

"I don't know," says Rana.

There are more details around the room: maps that look like planet surfaces, sketches of more temples and crafts like nothing we've seen so far. But there is no time to examine it all. There is a huge thump of air and a crash. An alarm begins to sound. The lights go out, then blink back on in red emergency lighting only.

"I think now is not the time to find out," she adds.

"Okay . . ." I back out but can't help lingering on this model of the solar system, and the carvings on the ceiling that look like clouds, or galaxies, nebulae. . . .

An alarm begins to sound and the electronic male voice speaks again. "EVACUATE THE FACILITY IMMEDIATELY. SECURITY LOCKDOWN IN ONE MINUTE."

We move back into the hall, empty now, papers fluttering in the wakes of the evacuees. I run toward an exit sign and it leads to an elevator.

As we near, flickering lights and a blast of sparks indicate that the elevator is not going to work. It's lying tilted in its shaft, smashed glass everywhere, and there are silhouettes inside, unmoving.

"Stairs," says Rana.

I turn and push open a door and begin racing up metal switchbacks.

"SECURITY LOCKDOWN WILL BE IMPLEMENTED IN TWENTY SECONDS."

There are no doors at each landing, just more stairs.

"TEN SECONDS."

My heart is pounding against my ribs and my legs burning when I finally reach the top flight and a door. I slap the handle.

Locked.

"SEVEN . . . SIX . . ."

I find a red button, press it, and another retinal camera lights up on the door.

"FOUR . . ."

I put my eye to it. The light blinds me again.

"TWO . . ."

It flicks off.

"ONE . . ."

Come on—

"SECURITY LOCKDOWN IMPLEMENTED. RATIONS ARE STORED IN THE SUBBASEMENT LOCKERS."

"No!" I slam the door with my hands.

"Identity verified," the door says, its voice calm by contrast. "Eden citizen: David Marks, age eighteen, Eden community participant level one-A. Please note: All one-A personnel are requested to make their way to the East Terminal exit for immediate transit."

"That's got to be the selectees," I say, and pound on the door again. This can't be happening. I can't miss the exodus after all this.

I hit the door again and again until my hands ache. When I stop, I hear shouts, and now gunfire outside.

"Maybe we should look for another way," Rana suggests.

I glance back down the stairs. "It's too far and there isn't time!" I slap the door again.

This time, something hits back from the other side.

"In here!" I shout.

A muffled voice replies, "Stand back!"

I move away and there is a hiss, and now sparks jump through the seam beside the door handle. There is a glow of melting metal and then a snap. A heavy thud and the door pops open. A black-clad Eden soldier stands before me, gold visor down. He holds a pulse rifle in one hand and a subnet phone in the other.

"Identification," he barks at me.

I step toward him. "My eye?"

"No, participant level one-A confirmation. That's

what brought me here." He holds out the phone, and I realize he means the bar code.

With a wave of nerves, I hold out my right pinkie, hoping the soldier won't see the stitches, hoping the bar code will actually work. A red light beams from his phone, and he moves it slowly over my finger.

There is a beep. The soldier reads the phone.

"Mrs. Reeves," he says, but then he realizes I'm not a woman. "Wait, that can't be right."

"It's Marks," I say. "You don't have me?" I try to sound annoyed by this.

Something cracks and splinters in the nearby streets and there are screams.

The soldier glances at his phone again and then shoves it in his pocket. "Network is going haywire. Sir, you need to get to the east exit immediately. I'll escort you there for your safety." He motions to a small electric motorcycle.

I step out and see that we are in an alleyway between buildings in the EdenEast city. We get on, and the soldier speeds out onto a larger road. The street is largely deserted, littered with debris, and many windows are smashed.

"Most of the rioters have moved toward government buildings," says the soldier.

"What are they protesting?"

"Someone leaked the dome integrity data," says the

soldier. "A senior official, just before he leaped off the Extension Services building last night. Selectee lists were publicized this morning. Mobs have been on a witch hunt for officials or selectees. We've gotten most of you out, but not all. You're lucky. I was on my last sweep."

Lucky isn't a word I'd choose for my history, but so far this plan is breaking right.

As we move, I consider how weird it is to be back in Eden. I look up at the light blue TruSky, the diffused glow of SafeSun through SimClouds and feel that light, humid air, so delicate compared to the harsh deserts, steamy jungles, and biting cold I have been in since. And the smell, so pleasant, tinged with flowers. Being here now, after everything since EdenWest, I feel like I get it, I so get why all these people chose this, why you'd lock yourself away in one of these domes rather than face reality . . .

But it's getting real in here now.

Something explodes a block over, and as we speed through an intersection I see figures running furiously amid clouds of smoke and shouting.

The soldier skids to a stop. Up ahead, a crowd is milling. A woman and a man are huddled up in the curving second floor window of a luxury apartment complex.

"You're no better than the rest of us!" someone shouts to a chorus of support.

A rock flies through the air and smashes the window.

"We'll go this way." The soldier skids out and takes a side street for two blocks, then turns onto the main avenue through town, the twisting SensaStreet that is supposed to be pedestrian only.

"Good morning, Mr. Marks," the SensaStreet says to me in a series of overlapping voices that filter up from the glowing hexagonal panels. "Please update your preferences by purchasing your favorite breakfast sandwich! It will be ready at the next intersection."

The voices speak in intervals, one blending into another.

"Mr. Marks, we don't know your shirt size. Let us know so we can pick out the coolest new T-shirts for all your summer adventures!"

"Mr. Marks, do you like tacos?"

There is a flash and the voices whine to a high pitch and die out. The SensaStreet begins to go dark and ahead I see a crowd cheering this result as two men swing axes at an open power compartment on the side of the street.

"Animals," the soldier mutters.

But I have to wonder: Who are the animals, those that are coming together to cheer, or those fleeing for the exits?

The soldier veers right and into an alley between curvy plastic-looking buildings. Gunfire rattles. It sounds like it is coming from all directions.

We emerge from the alley, and ahead I see the wall

of the dome and in front of that a line of soldiers along a barricade of carts. Two hover copters buzz overhead. The soldiers in them are firing stun bursts into a crowd. On the ground, the soldiers push back with tall plastic shields.

As we speed toward the barricade, two soldiers clear the way with long stun bursts from their pulse rifles that sends people staggering and convulsing, doubling over and vomiting. We splash through one of the brown pools.

We race through the gap, and the soldier stops on the other side of the barricade. Without the sound of the bike, the shouts and screams of the crowd are over-whelming.

"This way, Mr. Marks." The soldier leads me toward a frightened huddle of Eden citizens who are in line at a little checkpoint guard stand. Beyond that, people are heading toward a large door that leads outside into the searing sun.

"Okay, just stand in line here," says the soldier, "and you'll be on your way, sir."

"Thanks," I join the line, heart racing, and try not to listen to the screams and accusations of the crowd, try not to think of how Owen from Yellowstone Hub was always on that side of the barricade, not this one.

I step up behind a family of three: mom, dad, and daughter. They watch nervously over their shoulders as the rioting people pulse and seethe, the Eden forces shocking them back.

"It's not fair!" someone screams.

"Take us all! You can't leave!"

"Penny," the father in front of me calls to his daughter, snapping her out of a nervous trance, "don't listen to them."

"Okay," she replies, like that won't be possible.

Everyone in this line carries a small, black shoulder bag with the EdenCorp logo on it. Rana's skull bag is similar enough that in this chaos, the guards are unlikely to notice.

We move slowly past the checkpoint, a soldier there scanning our finger bar codes, and I can't help but watch the angry mob receding behind me and feel guilty that here I am, one of the incredibly few who is getting to leave. And these people don't even know how bad it's going to get, how dark this world will likely grow without its heart. . . .

"Welcome, Charmaine, Walter," the soldier with the scanner says as he checks the fingers of the parents in front of me. Then he checks Penny. "Hey there, little lady. Ready for a really fun ride?"

Penny just nods, looking pale, terrified.

It is my turn and I keep my head down. "Welcome, Mrs. . . . well, that must be a glitch." The soldier peers at me. I wait for him to tell me to get out of the line. Finally, he says, "You traveling alone?"

"Yeah." I try to sound nonchalant.

"Let me check your retina for verification." He holds a pen-size light to my eye, then checks his phone. "Okay, yes, Mr. Marks, here you are. Welcome aboard."

I pass him and continue along behind Charmaine and Walter and Penny as we are marched quickly toward the double doors and the brilliant sun. We are just about there when something booms and a blast of air nearly knocks us all over. I look back to see smoke rising from the crowd, and I can hear desperate wailing.

"Just cover your ears, honey," says Walter.

"I'll cover Standish's ears, Daddy. They're smaller," she says, and puts her hands over the head of the pink bear she carries.

We step out into the early morning, the sun just up and skimming across the ground right at us. My bionic eye hums as it tries to focus.

Ahead, the thread of a space elevator shimmers, extending up into the blue as if it never ends. A pod awaits, larger than the one Paul used in Antarctica, doors open.

"This is so exciting," I hear Walter saying.

"Let's just hurry," Charmaine says over gun cracks as she rubs Penny's shoulders.

Penny cranes to look back at the dome. "But I don't want to leave," she whimpers. "Daddy, I don't want to go."

"It's okay," says Charmaine, but she is crying, too.

"We get to be very happy, even though this is sad."

I try not to listen. They haven't lived outside the Eden bubble. I want to hate them, but I'd also like to be a boy with parents, taking a trip from one safe place to another, with the promise of more easy days.

Or, depending on how my plan goes, the promise of imminent death.

Penny hasn't done anything wrong, I think.

Neither had Elissa. This thought fills me with a rich bitterness. I try to just close my mind.

We reach the metal steps, and as we do, there is a huge explosion and smoke billows out of the doors to EdenEast. A mob surges through a jagged hole in the wall, sprinting toward us.

"Go!" the soldiers shout. They push us forward, herding us into the pod.

And I take my last step on planet earth.

22

A PLEASANT FEMALE VOICE INSTRUCTS US TO EACH take one of the restraining belts that hang from the ceiling and clip it around our waists.

The doors slide closed and the sounds of the rioting are extinguished. Just outside, soldiers are holding back the mob, and now that we can no longer hear them, they become just a curiosity seen through the small windows in the door.

After a moment of heavy breaths and whispers, the selectees begin to relax and sigh with relief and turn their attention to the wide screen that at the moment displays a view of the rocks just beneath the pod. They anticipate that this screen will provide *quite a show* once we get started.

"It would be nice if there were beverages," a woman comments, fanning herself.

It's like for them, we're boarding the elevator onto one of the old mega cruise ships that circled the globe pre-Rise, like we're heading up to the promenade deck, to drink from blinking glasses or eat a seven-course dinner.

"I wonder what will happen to the poor people in there," another woman says. "The Changs were nice people," she comments to her husband.

He shrugs. "What can be done," he says, but it's not a question.

"Please prepare for immediate departure," the female voice says. "Your future is just moments away."

The selectees' chatter rises enthusiastically. One man flicks on his phone. "The fitness centers are supposed to be top-notch," he says to the man beside him. "Apparently you can get great muscle isolation in zero gravity."

I listen to this, feeling numb.

"These are the chosen people of our race?" Rana wonders in my ear.

Charmaine adjusts the sweater around her shoulders, like there might be a chill when we get up there.

Penny, meanwhile, clutches Standish tightly to her chest and watches the people around her with worried eyes, almost as if she knows this isn't right. As if she's wondering what she's gotten herself into.

I rub the side of my leg, the hard impression there. Try not to think.

There is a beep, and the female voice counts down: "Three . . . two . . . one. . . ." Immediately, the pod begins to hurtle skyward at full speed. It feels like we are being shoved into the floor, and we are lucky to have the restraints.

Everyone adjusts to the incredible force of the ascent and I watch the video screen showing the view beneath us: of the desert and EdenEast and the pyramids all shrinking. And then the brown bed of the Nile, the sickly green Mediterranean Sea, the mountain ranges, the continents, the deserts of Europe, and the savannas of Russia. I see the greening steppe of Northern Europe, now distantly the lush, forested mountains of Greenland and the emerald coasts of the Arctic, the glitter of Northern Federation cities, just brushed by dawn light.

"Thank god we're finally off that hellhole," Charmaine says to Walter.

"Good-bye, Eden," says Penny quietly.

Hellhole. But I think the farther we get, the more beautiful the earth becomes, the more jewellike and painted and wondrous. From up here you can't see the trash, and the brown smog of fires and toxins give the world a sepia tone like that of old maps. There are oceans to be sailed, deserts to be crossed, northern forests to be explored, and all of it looks romantic and none as lost as it felt to be there.

But it is lost to me now. And again I have to press down on that terrible feeling of sadness, of isolation. Can I really be making the right choice? But then I remember that, yes, there is only one thing left for me. And this is it.

The planet bows out in an elegant curve beneath us, like looking into the largest eye, with a sky-blue iris— *Lilly*—threaded with browns and hazels and emeralds.

Then suddenly, without warning, the hum of the elevator ceases completely.

We have crossed the skin of the atmosphere. Into space.

Off world.

Everyone's voices hush.

Still we travel, up and up, the continents losing their minor features, becoming broad swaths, the clouds looking like they are painted, the planet looking like a glossy marble, until finally we begin to slow. The video screens switch and now we see the view above us, the thread ascending to the belly of a spindly spaceship.

At first it looks awkward and small, fragile, like something a child could drop and smash, but as we close, we can see the size of it, at least two kilometers long, maybe more, made of three main sections. The front is a short series of square compartments that branch in a T-shape. It is dwarfed by the massive central cylinder, which spins slowly. It is so enormous that as we approach we nearly lose the sense of its curve. Hundreds of small pods and other cylinders stick off it; and in the center, it is ringed by giant antennae. I think they look like masts. Behind the main cylinder there is a long, skinny section like a tail, and then a cluster of glowing egg-shaped pods. The engines.

"Ladies and gentlemen and children, welcome to *Egress*. Please remain affixed to your restraints while docking commences. Do not attempt to exit the elevator until the green signal lights and the doors open. Thank you for your patience. We look forward to beginning a new dawn with you."

"Here we are," I whisper so only Rana can hear me.

I can't help myself from starting to shake. We are getting close to the moment.

The pod stops and after a series of hisses and mechanical whirs, the voice announces, "Airlock secure." A bell sound chimes and the green light comes on. Everyone begins to unfasten the restraints.

The doors slide open.

"Welcome, ladies and gentlemen, right this way," says a tall, elegant woman with deep brown skin and green hair. She wears a black skirt and blouse, and we see other workers who are nicely dressed as well, darting around the clean white halls.

"This feels very elegant," says Charmaine approvingly.

"She makes me want to destroy something," Rana whispers.

We are led from the pod down a series of carpeted

halls with glass walls. To either side, men and women sit at high-tech consoles, working diligently.

"You've all been assigned staterooms, but first we'd like to give you a brief orientation."

Glass doors hiss open and we emerge into the central cylindrical core of *Egress*. It is a dizzying sight. A uniform grid of low buildings and walkways spreads before us, accented here and there by small grassy spaces. It is level in front of us, but then this scenery stretches up and completely around the curve of the cylinder. Looking up, we see upside-down buildings and people walking on paths they should fall from, but they don't.

"Mommy, are we going to fall if we go up there?" Penny asks.

"No, sweetie."

"The view is disorienting at first," says our hostess, "but the ship's rotation creates gravity and the effect is such that wherever you are standing will feel like right-side-up, solid ground."

The hostess leads us toward the center of the cylinder, which is maybe a kilometer long inside and half as wide. There are banks of SafeSun lamps at intervals, and a hazy sense of sky, but always overhead there is some part of the landscape spinning by.

In the very center of the cylinder there is a spindly metal structure that connects to the near and far end and also to four equidistant points on the rotating wall. I can see open-air elevators carrying people up and down and side to side.

That is the spot. I rub my leg. Breathe hard.

"You can do it," says Rana. "Do you want me to open your compartment?"

Everything about the question is weird but then I realize that I have pants over the wound on my thigh and I'm surrounded by people.

"Yes." It's a good thing I only have to whisper, because my mouth is dry.

This is it. Only minutes left now.

I feel Rana's hand slip out of me and tingle down my side to the dark mole below that line of plastic stitches. Her long fingernail peels up the mole, which is not a mole at all but a camouflaged tab. She pulls it up, and the tab works like a zipper. The plastic stitches come apart like teeth, revealing a thin pocket in my skin. It feels like I am being opened up, like I am a machine. Once the zipper is open, her fingers probe inside and begin to slide out the carbon cylinder that is embedded there. It is six inches long, and I feel a strange tugging sensation beneath my skin as it pulls free.

"Ready," she says.

It is time.

The hostess is going on about the features of *Egress*, where the dining rooms are and how the three-sixty pool works, all about grav yoga and how the engines function, but I am not hearing it.

My heart pounds.

My legs feel weak and my arms tingle. This is it. This is it, this is it . . .

And I press down on all the stormy feelings, the guilt and worry and shame and also hope because this is what I'm doing, *this* is what I want.

I will no longer be someone's tool, someone's instrument.

I will no longer serve powers that cannot help me, that could not keep the only thing I loved, the only thing I had left, alive.

I won't be someone's hero. Or their martyr. I won't be their anything. I will do what I need to do.

This is what I have been telling myself, in secret, since I was pulled from the ice.

This is my secret plan.

It is not what the Nomads think it is.

I'm sorry, Robard, Serena, but I will not die for some cause. I will not strip away myself after all that's been taken from me.

We board an open-air elevator and it takes us up, up into the space in the center of *Egress*, where my weapon will have access to the most oxygen possible.

Where it could tear this ship apart.

And it will if it has to.

But that is not my plan. I do not want to die.

No more dying.

"Go," says Rana.

She understands. She is the only one. She knows what it is like to live without love and that is all that matters.

So I am doing something I have told no one but her. This, right here, right now, is where I launch my own plan.

My fingers are slick with sweat, but I have positioned myself at the railing of the elevator and I reach down and take the oxygen detonator, still warm from my insides, out of Rana's misty fingers.

"PAUL!" I shout as loud as I can. Everyone turns.

"Excuse me, sir—" the hostess begins.

I hold the detonator up over my head, between my two hands.

"PAUL!" I shout again. I know there are surveillance cameras—this is an Eden, after all.

"What are you doing, kid?" a large man calls to me, and I can feel all the eyes in the elevator sizing me up, figuring out if they can take me.

"It's an oxygen detonator!" I shout, my mouth dry and my voice threadbare. I know I sound crazy, all my pent-up hatred for Paul seething out of me. "All I have to do is snap it and it will incinerate all the oxygen in this ship, and this whole place will blow!"

"What is he saying, Mommy?" Penny whines. "What is that bad boy saying?"

"That is a very risky plan, Owen." Paul's voice. Coming from the intercom system, echoing in the vast space. "One that you won't survive."

"I know!" I shout, trying to hide how much I'm shaking.

Silence. I feel like I can hear Paul thinking. Everyone on the elevator is frozen in terror.

"It's nice to see you again, by the way," he finally says. "Well, if you're going to do it, why haven't you done it already? You've lost your element of surprise."

And now I have to say it. And maybe I am betraying a whole planet. Or maybe, despite my hatred and rage, I am just doing what Paul asked for way back at the beginning. In the temple beneath Eden, he asked me to join him, and I said no. Because I thought I knew better. And because I wanted to see who he really was, and I wanted to have my honor. And yet ever since that moment, I've lost more than I've won, and Paul has punished me again and again. Maybe he has won. Caring about that doesn't matter. All that matters is now.

"I want to make a deal!" I shout.

"Really?" Paul sounds intrigued. "Well, by all means . . ."

"I won't blow up the ship, and I'll stay here and help you. I can talk to the Terra. She speaks to me. She chose me to save her."

"Yes," says Paul, "I suspected as much."

"But I won't save her!" I shout. "I won't save anyone. I'll stay here and talk to the Terra for you, and help you understand her."

A long silence.

"Well, you certainly have my attention. But what's the catch, Owen? What do I need to do for you?"

My body is shaking all over like my nerves are short-circuiting. Swallowing is hard, and I can feel the tears forming, but I force myself to press on. "I know what the Terra's energy can do," I say. "And all I ask is that you save one person for me."

I don't know if this feels right anymore, but nothing does. I am either betraying everyone I've known on earth or I'm going to die, and in neither of those circumstances will I be happy, without . . .

"Bring Lilly back."

As I say it, a sob overwhelms me. I hate that I look so weak, or maybe, based on the faces around me, I look insane. It doesn't matter.

"Bring her back for me," I say, "and I'm yours. Otherwise, I've got nothing to live for."

The longest silence yet.

"Where is her body?"

"Safe in a cave, near where we last met."

Rana rescued Lilly from her coffin, the one I built to float longer, rescued her body and put it in a small cave in the mountains, then sealed the entrance. That was the first part of our secret plan.

There are murmurs among the people around me. Frightened looks.

It is all I can do to keep holding up the detonator as Paul considers my offer.

"Owen," he says finally, and I can hear how his voice is shaped by a grin. "We have a deal."

23

IT IS A BEAUTIFUL ROOM. THE NICEST ROOM I HAVE
ever stayed in. The walls are clean and lined with draw-
ers. Inside are clothes, casual wear, shorts and sneakers,
a pressure suit and a helmet. A window looks out on the
stars, our view slowly spinning.

"It's kind of like the view from Giza," says Rana,
"only without the imagining."

I don't know whether she means that as better or
worse. I don't ask. Looking at the stars, I think of Lilly.
Wouldn't that be amazing? To see something like that,
she said of Orion's shoulder. She wished to travel in
space, to see the stars. . . . It hurts to think about, but
I remind myself, *She will get to see them, soon enough.*

The light in the room is always golden, like late afternoon. The bathroom shower literally rains on you from a
hundred points in the ceiling. And smells like pine trees.
The bed feels like floating, the sheets silky and cool.

But I have barely slept.

When I did, I found myself running from frozen Cryos that were lurching toward me over ice fields, as a legless version of Robard, stuck in the ice, called me a traitor. Told me I had sold my soul. So when I snapped awake, out of breath, I turned on the lights and stayed up.

I have watched videos detailing all the amenities that await us at EdenHome. It's small and spartan compared to an Eden on earth, and it makes me wonder why Paul didn't choose to bring the Paintbrush along for the journey. That would have at least made sense with what he once told me, about perfecting the technology.

"Good morning," the pleasant, honey-toned female voice says over the ship-wide communication. The clock reads seven a.m., but outside the darkness hasn't changed. It's no help when earth is visible, as we're zooming around it in orbit, seeing day become night become day again, almost as if time is in fast-forward.

Everyone is dying down there. I fight the thought. *But she will live.*

"Today we will be welcoming the final selectees from EdenNorth," the voice continues. "Unfortunately, selectees from EdenWest will not be joining us, due to an internal conflict. That said, we are still on schedule to begin the journey to EdenHome. The trip will take approximately seven weeks, given our current uranium fuel supply.

"Now, I know that is longer than our original

timeline, but given the deteriorating situation on earth, we feel it is best to leave now, which means we need to take it a little slower to conserve fuel. And remember, the board of directors will be waiting to greet you with a party that they promise will be the finest that Mars has ever seen." She chuckles at this.

"Please let me kill her," says Rana. She sits beside me on the bed, both of us with our hands in our laps.

"Once we are under way, we will begin calling you all to *Egress*'s version of extension services, where you will begin your exclusive Eternity treatments. In the meantime, relax and enjoy all that the ship has to offer. Have a pleasant day," the voice concludes.

"When are you going to go look around?" I ask Rana. "You don't have to stay with me."

"I want to be sure you are safe. I don't trust Paul. Do you?"

"No. Though, I'm not sure it matters now." I made my choice, I think, and this thought chills me. Did I really choose this? I look at the lovely room. I think of Lilly getting a room like this. I think of the alternatives on earth.

There are no other alternatives for her, I remind myself.

A beep sounds and the door begins to slide open.

Rana slips into me.

It is Paul. "Well. Good morning," he says mildly.

He stands there and he is just Paul: a middle-aged man in khakis and a shirt and tightly knotted tie. He wears the dark sunglasses to hide the eyes I now half share, but other than those, he is just a man; and seeing him here in this normal light, not in some underground chamber, makes it almost hard to believe that he is the same monster we were running from for weeks.

But is calling him a monster even fair? He's saving all these people, and these people will have children and the human race will go on, improved by the Terra's power. All he did was take matters into his own hands. Except there are many more people, both living and dead and suffering now, who will lose their chance to survive because of his actions.

"Did you rest?" Paul asks.

"Yeah," I lie.

"I have to say, Owen, I did not expect this." He sighs. "You know, I still regret not just talking to you at the moment you arrived at Camp Eden. Or even when I woke you from cryo. Had I made the full reality of your situation clear from the start, we could have gotten to this point with so much less difficulty."

"Difficulty like leaving me for dead in the ice?" I know I sound sulky but I don't care. Seeing Paul reminds me that the pit of hatred I feel for him is still there. His casual assumption that I would ever have chosen to go with him while I had any other choice only reinforces it. Except I have to wonder if maybe he's right. Would I have been strong enough to resist him, to run, to at least try, before I'd found Lilly and Leech and Seven and the rest?

But I remind myself that it doesn't matter now. They're gone and I've made my deal. And yet all this makes me feel like I am made of lead.

"Actually," says Paul, "I always thought you'd survive that. Despite my best efforts, you've had a way of persevering. I'd mostly given up, but I always suspected that you and I would have another chapter together."

I don't respond.

"And I suppose the difficulties were necessary to finally get us on the same page. Anyway . . . ready to go see her?"

I force down my nerves. "Yes." I get up and grab the skull bag, which Rana insists that I bring everywhere I go. I think she feels more whole with it around, even though she can't be inside it.

"Why do you still have that?" Paul asks. "I think we're a bit past those old notions of the Three."

"I like it," I say.

"Suit yourself."

We walk down a dark-carpeted hall of numbered doors: more staterooms like mine. *Egress* has rooms for a thousand selectees and support staff. Every few doors, a panel of the wall is accented by a waterfall of mist, or a tasteful reproduction of a famous work of art.

"We're going to be a lot lighter with the news out of EdenWest," says Paul. When I don't say anything he adds, "but that also means we can travel faster. I heard it was Nomads who launched the attack there and leaked the information. Are they the ones who helped you get in here?"

"Yes."

"And they thought you were going to blow this place up."

"Yeah." Saying it reminds me of the dream, of a maimed Robard shouting to me.

"That's going to be a major disappointment for them," says Paul.

"They're going to die," I say quietly.

"Of course, someday," says Paul, "but that's no longer our concern."

"No, I mean soon. Don't you know that?" I wonder why I am bothering to tell him this, but I feel it coming out anyway. "Taking the Heart of the Terra from earth is going to make life die out there. It's like . . ."

"Ah, like a Heliad-seven ceremony on a planet-wide scale," Paul says, his tone awed. "Well, in that case, live bright!" He smiles. But I don't find it funny. "Sorry," he says, "that probably cuts close to the bone. Oh my, I should avoid puns, shouldn't I?"

"Please," Rana whispers. "I could rip out his intestines."

I wish I could let her. Smug, victorious Paul is even worse than the old ruthless version.

"Well," Paul continues, serious. "She told you this, I gather? The Terra?"

"Yes."

"It does explain all the violence these last couple days. Mankind showing its true nature, I guess."

"More like its incomplete nature," I say.

Paul raises an eyebrow at me. "Ah, more secrets that you know. I can't wait to hear them. All the same, you are still here. You still chose to be part of this over staying behind."

I just keep walking.

We emerge in the hazy sun of the living area, and take an open elevator and then a walkway. People pass us, a few saying good morning to Paul, most not even knowing who he is. Here and there, some recognize me from yesterday, and look at me perplexed.

As we go, I feel my whole body clenching tighter. I have to consciously open my jaw to get it to relax. Seeing her . . .

I try to get my mind off it and look at the sunny habitat spinning slowly around us. We pass over a small park. Parents are playing with their kids on grav swings.

"These must have been expensive tickets," I say.

"About half of the selectees were chosen based on experience and value," says Paul. "And, yes, the rest did pay just an unbelievable sum, but, after all, building something like this isn't cheap. Not surprisingly, people were willing to pay nearly everything they had for what we offer."

"Living on a desert planet doesn't sound like a huge improvement," I say.

"Oh." Paul claps me on the back, which makes me flinch and makes Rana growl. "You mean Mars?"

"Yeah, isn't that where you're going?"

Paul smiles and stops at a screen that's perched on the walkway railing. It shows a list of activities for the next twenty-four-hour period. "Let me show you something." He taps the corner and types a password quickly into a command box. The screen flashes to a set of folders. Paul's fingers dance around, and then a picture appears. It shows the barren, rust-colored surface of Mars. And a small, steel-looking dome, like a mini-Eden.

"EdenHome," says Paul. "There's a volcano nearby called Elysium Mons, with a curious set of caverns. Guess what we found there."

I don't reply and he taps again. A red-walled cavern. Inside, a structure of metal and glass.

Another Paintbrush of the Gods.

"That's on Mars?" I ask.

"Amazing, isn't it?" says Paul. "The Atlanteans were unbelievable. They traveled the solar system, looking for a place to be reborn. They chose Mars. But even though they built this, they could never find the Heart of the Terra again. We found their maps. We found this place, and we thought, what a perfect way to save the human race, to follow in the masters' footsteps, to recapture our alien roots."

"The Atlanteans were aliens?"

"No, I mean, we all were, in a sense," says Paul. "Life didn't begin on earth, Owen. Our ancestors are microbes that traveled by comets, frozen refugees from earlier solar systems, dating all the way back to the big bang. Earth is four and a half billion years old, but the universe is nearly fourteen. And over all that time, life has made its way from one galaxy to the next, across the universe. We all come from cryo, if you look back far enough."

"Wow," I say flatly.

"Anyway . . ." Paul taps the screen and the image disappears. "That was our plan, when we discovered the maps under Giza and their relic spaceship. We thought we'd find the Heart of the Terra and take it to Mars to use with the new Paintbrush. But, after enough research on the Sentinel we'd found in Greenland, and on the test subjects in my lab in EdenWest, I realized what the true power of the Heart of the Terra really is."

"Eternal life," I said.

"Exactly, and we thought: Why settle for Mars and some dangerous terraforming project? Why settle for this *galaxy*? With the power of the Terra, we have all the time we need. We have more uranium mining and water converting to do at EdenHome, but after that . . ."

We reach the end of the walkway and pass through a wide door into a curved hall that leads to the front section of the ship. Windows to either side look out on the black and glittering space.

Paul extends his arms. "We're going to the stars, Owen. We'll find a real Eden, one we don't have to engineer, and we'll start over. How exciting is that? We've realized the greatest quest the world has ever known. The desire to extend life is what brought the first humans out of the trees, led to the first weapons, villages, cities, and religions. And now we have conquered death, and we're ready to begin the next phase of life's journey across the stars. We're the gods now, Owen. And that includes you. We'll travel through the darkness to a new dawn."

"Yeah," I say. I want to tell him how much he sounds like Master Solan. And there is still that innocent part of me that finds what he's saying interesting, but I also have that same feeling of not wanting him to have the satisfaction of knowing. "And Lilly will be there," I say, just to remind him.

"Of course. Both of you."

We pass through multiple locked doors, past two teams of security guards, and enter a lab beyond that.

We arrive in a dark control room, full of consoles. A

wide window looks into a round room of blinding light. I feel my eye whirring to adjust. The Heart of the Terra is inside, held between two steel columns. The Terra sits as she did in my view from Atlantis, legs crossed, eyes closed.

"Erica, Damon, how are we today?" Paul asks.

Two young technicians are busy at the consoles. "Just about to try taking a sample," Damon replies.

"Excellent," says Paul. "Let's do that. This is Owen. I know you've heard a great deal about him. He's going to be helping us to unlock the Terra's secrets, show us all it has to offer."

"She's not an 'it,'" I say.

"Fair enough. 'She' . . ."

A large robotic arm appears, sweeping toward the Terra. It has a long metal needle at its end and rotates so that this points at the small opening in the side of the crystal cage, the copper-rimmed hole where the masters once took the Terra's blood.

I feel Paul looking at me. "Is this right?" he says.

"Yes," I say.

The needle slides into the cage. It pricks the Terra's shoulder and her eyes pop open and the cage glows white-hot.

The glass in front of us darkens for our safety. I look away, but I feel her staring at me.

"Running the secondary cooling system," says Erica.

"What were they like?" Paul asks. "The masters, I mean."

"I don't know," I say. "Powerful, believed in what they were doing, wore robes."

"So you've seen them."

"I've been there."

I can feel Paul's gaze on me, until a shrill beeping distracts him.

Liquid light is leaving the cage, traveling through a clear tube.

"You'll have to tell me more sometime," says Paul.

The needle slides back out of the cage and the Terra's eyes close.

Paul pats me on the shoulder. I want to flinch, and wonder how I'm going to survive this proximity to him for . . . centuries? Even just a few minutes feels too long. "Come on," he says. "Let's go visit. I'm sure you two have loads to catch up on."

"Where's Lilly?" I ask.

"Right," says Paul. "Damon, do we have a feed from the extraction team?"

"Yes, one sec . . ." Damon types rapidly, and then a video screen overlays the window. There are six Eden soldiers standing in the space elevator pod. "We'll be coming up on the target point in about forty minutes," Damon reports.

"Good. So," Paul says to me, "it won't be long now.

I know you have little reason to trust me, Owen, but please have no doubt that I will bring you Lilly as you wish. You have earned it, to say the least. And hopefully, over time, I can earn back your trust."

I just shrug, knowing I seem sulky, but again I have nothing to say to him.

"Erica, please open the door."

A thick door hisses open and we step into a small waiting area. The door closes and locks and then the inner door slides open.

We enter the white room. The Terra is in the center. The walls are smooth and clean. It reminds me of Vista. The large robotic arm is attached to the wall by the window of the control room.

As soon as the door clicks shut behind us, Paul says, "Now, Owen, listen, there's one thing I want to clear up first. And don't worry, I understand, believe me I do."

"What?"

"We have one other prized possession here with us." Paul motions to Erica and Damon through the window.

A small, circular panel slides open in the floor. A crystal skull rises from it on a steel stand. The sight of it reminds me of the others so callously killed, of Evan and Mateu and Anna and Colleen and others I never even knew. The skull gleams, and begins to light in my presence.

Come home, Kael.

"I'm hoping that you can tell me more about it. I

mean, its purpose is finished, but the technology . . ." Paul inhales deeply. "So fascinating." He turns, motioning with his hand again. "And," he says, "we have the complete set."

Now a portion of the wall slides open and with a hiss of steam, two tall clear cylindrical containers slide out. One is empty, but the other is lit in black light, and in the purplish glow I see a wispy form, ghostlike with black eyes.

"Kael," says Rana.

The dead boy looks at us vacantly, and then his mouth moves but we cannot hear him. And yet, that empty container beside him . . .

A burst of electricity leaps from the robotic arm and slams into me before I can even turn. I am thrown to the ground, tingling all over, pain in my head and teeth and joints.

"It's okay," says Paul. "I'm sorry about that."

But it's not okay. I feel a vacant sensation.

"Owen!"

I look up and Rana has been separated from me. She is hissing in pain, trapped in the electric beam from the arm.

The front of the empty container beside Kael's pops open and the robotic arm moves Rana across the room and into it. The door slams shut.

Rana beats at the glass, shouting viciously, but there

is no sound. She and Kael are like experiments trapped side by side in giant test tubes.

I turn to Paul, ready to scream.

"What?" says Paul. "What kind of frank relationship can we have if you're hiding an Atlantean Sentinel? Which, by the way, is another marvel."

I want to ask him how he knew, but I won't give him the satisfaction of explaining it. "She wasn't going to do anything," I say. "She just wanted to come along and be sure I was safe. I was going to tell you about her once I knew you had Lilly. Once I knew I could trust you."

Paul considers this. "Well, I understand your reasoning, of course."

"Let her out."

Paul's lips purse. "Owen, I saw what she did to my men in the Andes. She could tear this ship apart if she wanted. Now, you can visit her anytime. I won't harm her. She's far too interesting." He looks at the cylinders. "If only we had all three."

I look back at Rana, burning inside, not knowing what to do with the rage I am feeling, yet another loss I can't control.

Paul turns toward the Terra. "Well, looks like someone knows you're here and has decided to wake up."

The Terra's eyes are open. She stares at me, and I can barely meet her gaze, knowing that I have betrayed her, if that's even what I've done.

Owen.

As she speaks I feel a strange sensation of warmth, but it's not coming from the Terra. It's from behind me. From my back . . . from Rana's skull.

You are here, the Terra says, *but . . .*

I can feel her reading my thoughts and I feel the floor dropping out of my insides, the flood of guilt. I have chosen wrong, I have not been true, I have let her down, I—

I understand the choice you have made, she says.

I'm sorry, I think to her. *It was the only way to—*

But I am not the only one with an opinion.

I feel the wind just as I am hearing the words.

Qii-Farr-eeschhh . . .

That voice is a whisper of swirling air and it is not the Terra. It is not in my head. It's . . .

"What is that?" Paul asks, his voice rising over the swelling wind in the room. His eyes flash to my back, and I turn to see that Rana's skull has lit up. So has Kael's, so has the Terra, and everything is erasing itself in brilliant white.

"What's happening?" Paul shouts. "Owen, what are you doing?"

"I'm not!" I shout.

Interesting. The Terra looks at Rana and then back to me. *Very interesting.*

"What?" I call over the wind.

Qii-Farr-eeschhh . . .

But that voice. I know it, but it can't be . . .

"Adjust the containment fields!" Paul shouts to his technicians. He reaches for my hand—

But his fingers slip through my skin as if I am not completely there, and I feel myself leaving, being sucked away from the world and into white light.

There is wind like I have known twice before. And in a flash, I am inside the skull. Not Kael's.

Rana's. Summoned here by . . .

My eyes can barely adjust to the dim light, but I can make out enough to see that someone is right in front of me: long, dark hair . . . Rana. No. The Terra. No—

"Lilly."

Her sky-blue eyes bore into me. And she looks—

Furious. "What the HELL?!" she shouts, and she shoves me in the chest with both hands.

24

THERE IS NO TIME INSIDE THE CRYSTAL SKULL. There is before, and there will be after, but within the crystal electric medium there is only a sense of now and that all things are and have been and will be.

I trip over something and fall to the ground on my elbows.

Lilly glares down at me. Lilly is here. In Rana's skull but this is not Rana's place, not the temple where I met her in Tulana on the coast.

This is somewhere I know much better than that. A place I've spent many hours remembering while roaming the borderland of sleep.

I tripped over the large stump of a birch tree. Above, stars glimmer through a gap in the pines, but they are too gauzy to be the real stars. The sky has a satin quality of humid air. Not the steam of the Desenna jungle. This is climate control and SimStars.

Three candles flicker in tin cans on a slab of rock

surrounded by tall, matted grass. The lapping of water nearby.

This is Tiger Lilly Island, Lilly's place. Somehow, we are there.

Through the white realm. I see that the Terra is here, too, and so is Rana. They float together at the edge of the clearing, like a ghost jury.

All of this I see just in my peripheral vision because I am staring at Lilly, who is standing over me in candle-light and I nearly can't breathe to see her again. Even though I have mourned her and tried to remember every inch of her in my mind over and over, I know now that I was wrong. Oh, how I was so wrong and not even close, not even close because she is so much more wonderful than that—

But also, at the moment, she is seething with anger.

"What are you doing talking to HIM?" she shouts, throwing a hand over her shoulder. We both look in that direction, but the lab is gone.

"You can see outside the skull?" I say dumbly.

"Not really," Lilly snaps. "I can sense the Qi and An, though, and I can tell what's happening well enough to know you're, like, making deals with Paul! Why would you do that? And what is that place you're in?"

"Lilly, hold on!" I finally overcome the shock and lurch to my feet and grab her before she can resist or hit me again—you never know when she is this angry. . . .

Was, I have to remind myself. For a second, reality wavers and I have to remember that I am not waking up from a nightmare. We are not back on Tiger Lilly Island the night she smushed brownies in my mouth. We are not waking up later in that dark after a twisted and terrible dream.

It all happened.

Even as I am wrapping my arms around her as fully and tightly as I can and I am feeling her warmth and her breath on my neck, I am also turning to look at Rana.

You did this, I think to her because it seems that Rana and the Terra are only here for me, that Lilly is not aware of them.

Rana, down on the floor of the ice cave with the skull.

I performed the preservation ritual before she died, she says.

You uploaded her into your skull.

Yes, to save her for you. At the time, it seemed like the only way.

Why didn't you tell me?

Because this isn't completely her. It's like me. A split. You needed to say good-bye to the real Lilly. I was going to tell you after that, but then you had this plan. If Paul brings her body up here, she and her skull essence will be reunited. I wasn't going to tell you about this ghost of her unless that plan didn't work. But I didn't realize she could sense what was going on outside. And I didn't know she could draw you into the skull.

She didn't do that, says the Terra, *I did. Lilly was calling out to you, but only I could hear it. So I made this connection.*

The perfect night flashes for a moment, like a burst of lightning.

But I cannot hold us here for long, says the Terra. *Paul will be able to disrupt the frequency of this skull connection with his machines.*

"Owen." Lilly's voice is quiet now. We are hugging with no space between us, and yet, while I am heaving with fast breaths, Lilly doesn't move. No rise and fall of her chest, no ribs aligning, no hearts thumping code to one another. She is just still, like a photograph or a statue.

"I died," says Lilly softly in my ear, "didn't I?"

I feel the draining inside me all over again and it is all I can do to stay on my feet. I hold her as tight as I can, this heatless version of her, but she still feels real, Lilly arms and Lilly hair and Lilly eyelashes against my cheek, but . . .

"Yeah," I say. "You died in the ice, in Antarctica. . . ." The memories flood back and I can't believe I have been making deals with the person who aimed a gun at Lilly's head and pulled the trigger and sent a bullet through her brain. That man . . .

The darkness flashes again, a glimpse back into the lab.

"Dead," says Lilly. "I figured. And what about you?"

"I survived, barely. The Sentinel in the Andes, Rana, she uploaded you into this skull, though I'm not sure why you're on this island."

Lilly glances around. "I think it's the last place I was thinking about, kinda like a cryo dream, and it stuck. I always felt safe here, more than anywhere else. I remember I was dreaming of being here, and there was a bright light and cold, the ice, but the light must have been the skull sucking me up. Oh god, Owen . . ."

She starts to cry on my shoulder, only there are no actual tears here.

"It's okay," I say. "Lilly, I love you"—ninth time—"and you're going to be okay soon. I'm going to fix this. You won't be in here much longer."

Lilly's face rubs up my neck, across my cheek. She kisses me quickly and pulls back. "Really? How is that possible?"

Her eyes are more than I can handle. I have to look away. But maybe it's because I am worried about how she's going to react to what I say next. I have been imagining her eyes opening, the spark of animation returning to her face, her joy at being alive again. It has been the image that has kept me going for days. And then, once she was back, I would explain the choices I had to make, but here . . .

"Owen, what is it? What's going on?"

The lab flashes again.

I have to spit it out. "The Heart of the Terra has the power of eternal life, of resurrection. It can bring you back."

Lilly's lips purse. "Okay, but . . . that lab you're in, with the Terra in a box. And *him*. How are you going to free her to do that? What's the plan? Are those Sentinels going to help?"

"I, um . . ." My heart races. I can feel the danger in what I'm about to say. "We don't have to free her to save you. We can use a sample of her energy—"

Lilly's face contorts. "A sample? What, is she a lab rat now, too?"

"Well, no, but . . ."

"Typical Paul," mutters Lilly, "locking up everything he can . . . Okay, but how do we free her when I'm back? How are you going to revive me without Paul knowing?"

With each of Lilly's questions, I feel myself twisting into a knot inside. "No, Lilly, listen. Paul . . . he *knows*. His men are the ones going to get your body. He's helping me to save you." These words don't sound as convincing when I say them to Lilly. I worry that they sound like a betrayal.

Sure enough, storm clouds blow across Lilly's eyes.

"Paul. Helping us. And why would he do that? Why would *we* do that?"

And now I have to tell her. "Because I told him I'd help him. I can communicate with the Terra and so I said I would help him if he agreed to bring you back. It's the only way."

I reach out to touch her arm, but she pulls away and glares at me like I am something radioactive.

"Owen, what are you saying? How can you help him? He's tortured you, murdered our friends, murdered *me*! And how many other people?"

"I didn't have any other choice," I say, pleading but now hating hearing my own words, because now I am seeing them through Lilly's eyes and realizing, oh no . . . have I been a fool? But, no, I haven't. "What else was I supposed to do?" I say, nearly shouting. "He had the Heart of the Terra. *Egress* is a space station. I could have blown it up, but if I did . . . you'd never be able to come back. You *died*, Lilly."

Lilly won't look at me. Her face flickers in the candle-light. She speaks slowly. "And when I come back . . . if I come back . . . what then?"

"Well, we . . ." It is all sounding so wrong but I try to spit it out. "I mean, first of all, you can be alive. And then, we'll get to travel in space like you dreamed about! You said you would have given anything for that chance."

Lilly breathes in slowly. "What about the rest of the

world? I can sense its pain, like everyone is crying at once. The Terra's been taken. . . ." A shudder runs through her. "No one can hear its music," she says, horrified, "even the little bit that was still in the world. That was the last bit that was holding us together, keeping humanity from dying out. It will be the end."

"Well," I stammer, "yeah, but . . . not for us. We'll be okay."

Lilly's eyes return in a lethal glare. "How can you say that?"

"Because!" I shout. "There was never going to be a perfect beach, a clean ocean for us to live beside, me catching you fish or whatever. There was never going to be an Eden or somewhere for us to be! Those were just stupid dreams. Our whole quest was doomed, and you died! You died. But now we can actually have that thing we always imagined—"

"We?" Lilly throws up her hands. "I never imagined *this*! I never thought we'd be talking about sacrificing the fate of the earth!"

Her words are making my brain feel blank, stuck spinning. "But," I say, and I know how desperate I sound, "we'll be together. We'll be safe. Isn't that all that matters?"

Lilly stares at me hard. I have no idea what she'll say. Then her eyes shake and she steps in and hugs me again. "I can't imagine what it would be like to lose you. To watch you die, to . . ."

"To build you a coffin," I say, my legs threatening to buckle beneath me as the words come out, "To push you out to sea."

"Oh, Owen . . . I couldn't have done that."

"Yes, you could have," I say into her hair. "You're stronger, Lilly, and I need you. You're the only thing that matters in this world to me."

Lilly shakes her head. "But I'm not. I can't be."

"What do you mean? You are."

Lilly steps away again. She stares down into the candlelight and then holds her hand above the flames. "I'm kind of transparent," she says quietly.

"Not for long," I say.

"Stop!" Lilly presses her temples. "Just . . . stop. O . . ." She sighs. "I know where you're coming from, but . . . we can't do this. It's wrong. We can't put ourselves before the whole planet."

Her words are burning me up, maybe because I should have known. Of course this is what she'd say. And yet, these noble thoughts of hers, where had they gotten us? "What's wrong," I say, "with thinking about us, for once? No one else ever has. No one's ever cared except to use us as pawns. What's wrong with putting me first?"

"You?"

"I mean us!"

"And what about everyone we were fighting for, who

lived on in our mission? What about Carey?"

"They're dead!" I shout. "You're DEAD! But I can bring you back! Everyone else is gone forever, but not you. This is our only chance to be together! Isn't that worth it?"

But even as I am saying this, I have this terrible feeling that I know what Lilly will say. She wouldn't have had this choice if she'd already been back, but . . . who am I to take her choice away? It isn't fair, and I knew that, didn't I? Maybe that's why I tried not to think about it, about her.

Lilly wipes at her eyes again. Looks to the sky, around her little island, her virtual tomb . . . "No," she says finally. "I love you, Owen, but I can't live with this. You can't live with it because I can't, we can't live with this choice. It's too . . . wrong."

"Says who?"

"Says, I don't know, me? My brother, my parents, they all died for me to be in Eden! In a way, they all died for me to have this chance. Carey died to show you Paul's lies. Even Seven died to save us from Victoria! This may not have been our choice, being Atlanteans and all, but that doesn't change the fact that we are the only ones now who can do what needs to be done."

"*You* can't," I say. "You're dead."

"God, I know! Believe me, I know. I've had plenty of time to think about that, stuck on this island inside a skull. I'll never see a sunrise again, never watch the beauty of trash falling from the skies, never fly with you again, never joke about bow tie–shaped cookies with blue frosting. . . ."

Of all this, the mention of our old game nearly kills me. "Geronimos," I say quietly.

Lilly smiles tragically. "That name never made any sense."

"Lilly . . ."

She throws up her hands. "I can't stop you from bringing me back. I'm a bunch of electrical impulses inside a glass head. But . . . if you do, Owen . . ." She stares into me. "I will hate you."

"Lilly, don't say that—"

"No, Owen, I will! Oh man, I will hate you and I'll never forgive you, and I will never want to be with you, and I'll be a maniac and I'll do everything in my power to destroy what Paul has done. He'll probably shoot me again within minutes." She puts two fingers to her forehead. "I remember a big bright pain . . ."

Everything is draining out of me. "Why are you saying this?"

"Because that's what you should want, too!" she shouts. "I know it hasn't been fair. None of this has been fair, but that doesn't change who we can be."

"But, Lilly, I don't care who we can be. I just want you."

"You have me." She steps close again, and puts her palm on my chest and her other hand behind my head, fingers ruffling my hair.

Fake fingers.

Fake hair.

But still . . . "You'll always have me. You can visit me in my fancy little skull. It sucks, but it is. And the only way I'll be happy in . . . here . . . is if I know that you tried to do what we believed in."

The words sink in. Sink in and wash away my intentions, my motivations, like what I thought were the deepest of convictions were just footprints on a beach.

The clean sands of Antarctica, where I pushed your coffin out to sea.

The words swirl and drain out, and more than anything, I feel like the world's biggest fool. How could I *not* have known she would feel this way? Maybe because I never thought about her. Well, I did, but only when I was thinking about me. About how I wanted her back, how I didn't feel like I owed the world any more of my blood and suffering. Maybe that's not surprising, given everything that's happened. But still.

Of course she was going to feel this way.

I thought it was a good idea, says Rana, *for what it's worth.*

I gaze at Lilly, the memory of her standing there. This isn't her. And even worse than when I pushed her out to sea, with a secret plan to stow her in ice, this . . .

This is the moment. She is really gone. Even if there is a body and a third option. There's no third option for Lilly. Maybe she's better than me. Maybe she's just stubborn and stupid.

But she's Lilly.

And who exactly am I?

Mendes's words echo in my mind: *In times like these, faith comes and goes. It's your soul you need to keep track of.* And in these choices, to save Lilly, to turn away from the Terra, from the planet, have I lost track?

Before the ice, what I wanted and what I believed in had been the same. Lilly, the mission, it was all united. And then torn apart. But by choosing what I wanted, what I felt like I needed, I forgot not just what I believed in, but what Lilly believed in, too.

Maybe this will always be a struggle. We will always want. We will always yearn and desire and crave and miss and feel empty when we can't have what we want, but to believe in something . . . is to know your soul.

I said once that I wanted to be true. All of this happened, even Lilly's death, after I said I wanted to see truth and said no to Paul. Where was that boy now? What had happened?

But I knew what had happened. Horrors. Things bigger than me that I could never totally understand. Loss, doubt, the world getting so big it folded in on itself and became something I could never fathom, something cruel and heartless and relentless and always sad. And yet, through all of that, there had been Lilly and me, an eye of the storm, the only good thing.

But hadn't I also believed in our mission? Yes. And how much of my belief had been my own, and how much had been because Lilly did, I will never know. Because it doesn't matter. There is only me now, and . . .

I have to believe enough for both of us.

And maybe that's not how a hero should work: maybe I've always been less than I should have been, less than everyone expected, and less than the world needed. Maybe this deal with Paul was just another pathetic act by the Turtle. Maybe the Terra was wrong about me. Maybe her next choice will be better. Because I'm *still* not sure I believe.

If I can't bring Lilly back, then she'll never know if I go to Mars. She'll never know if I stay on Egress. It won't matter.

I can do what I want and none of it will matter.

Except . . . it will.

Who am I kidding?

I do believe. It's just really hard.

I look to the Terra.

It's okay, she says, *if you want to go. It has never been the way of man to free me, but I still believe in you, Owen.*

No, I say. I'm ready, but I don't even know how to free you. How do we break open that crystal cage?

It is easy. All you h—

The Terra flickers out and the lab flashes back into being around us. There is a whining of electrical energy.

Then the darkness of the island returns. Pleasant fake insects buzzing.

Paul is breaking the field, says Rana.

Lilly has sat down on the grass and wrapped her blanket around her. "I'll be with you, Owen. Right here. Forever, now."

"That's never going to be enough," I say.

"I know."

I cannot hold us any longer, says the Terra.

The lab bleeds in on all sides.

"Lilly . . ." I suddenly want another hug, even if they are incomplete, only one of us breathing. I want to say more—

But then in a flash we are back.

I find myself on my knees on the lab floor. The Terra's eyes are closed again. Rana and Kael still silent and trapped.

Something's wrong, though. Through the window to the control room, a red light is flashing.

"The field is breached, sir," Damon reports.

"Good, now fire!" Paul shouts. He's beside me, gazing at a large holographic projection screen that has materialized in the air in front of us. It shows a map with the earth, the position of *Egress* in orbit, and something blinking also in red.

Something heading straight for us.

There is a faint rumble through the floor, and now onscreen, two dots speed away from *Egress* toward whatever is coming.

"Missiles have lock," Damon reports over the intercom.

I watch the dots close, nearing the incoming object . . . and then the two missile dots blink out.

"What happened?" Paul barks.

The incoming dot is still approaching. What is coming?

"Where did the missiles go?" Paul is as furious as I've ever seen him. "Somebody tell me something!"

Suddenly there is a huge crash from behind us.

"They missed," a voice hisses from right beside me. "But I didn't."

Out of the corner of my eye I see a light, and when I turn it has already blurred by, a streak of lightning, hurtling across the room and slamming into the glass containers in a spray of light and shards.

When the glow settles, the ghosts of Rana and Kael hover free.

They are joined by a third.

"Lük," Rana hisses, "what are you doing here?"

"I figured you needed a rescue," says Lük. "Don't you?"

"We do now," I say.

"Erica!" Paul shouts, pointing at the three. "Arm the electric—"

But Paul stops speaking and staggers, his head whipping back and his hands leaping to his neck . . .

To the ghostly edges of a triangular throwing blade embedded there.

"That's for fifty years in a test tube," says the shade of Kael.

And just like that, Paul falls to the floor beside me.

25

AT FIRST I CAN'T BELIEVE IT. PAUL, LYING THERE, blood spouting from the side of his neck. His fingers flick at the edges of the blade, twitching like the legs of a crushed spider. His body spasms, and he tries to get up.

I suddenly find myself feeling cheated, like I owed Lilly, owed myself and Elissa and Carey, owed them all vengeance against this monster, like I should have been the one; but once again, just like so many other times on this journey, I've never been able to be the killer. Never quite had it in me, just like Leech feared back in the desert, and it makes me feel weak, less worthy. Paul was *mine*, after all he did . . . and yet Paul had many enemies, a world of enemies, and I was only one of many with a score to settle.

"Nice shot," Rana says to Kael. And then to Lük, "How did you get here?"

"I flew the ship," he says.

"I thought it needed decades of work."

Lük seems to shrug. "It didn't seem like you had decades."

Rana smiles more than I've ever seen.

"It's a pretty good ride," says Lük, "bulky compared to my old craft, but not bad. It's waiting outside, but we should hurry."

I glance toward the control room window and see that Erica and Damon are gaping at us. Their mouths move, talking to one another, and then they turn and run. Just as they disappear, alarms begin to sound.

A choking sound makes me turn back to Paul, lying on the floor. He's slapped his sunglasses free and his electric blue irises flash in their seas of red. His pupils are whirring, opening and closing. "O-wen . . . ," he croaks. He's reaching for me. The pool of blood has spread beyond his head.

I want to say something to him. I want him to know . . . what? All I feel is blank seeing him like this. All the anger, all the betrayal, but in the end, Paul is just another frail body of blood and tissue, of electrical impulses, one that will have lived, and will die and will be gone, no worse or better a fate than the rest of us, despite all his efforts.

What comes out surprises me. "I'm sorry," I say.

"O . . . ," he croaks, his voice torn and blood soaked. He motions with his hand like I should come close. I find myself bending over him, taking one last look into his bionic eyes with one of my own, its focal point fixating on his. In spite of everything, some part of me wants to know his final words.

Instead, his hands seize me by the neck. He drags me down, flipping me over, and he slumps on top of me. I feel the gush of fluid from his neck hitting my chest. His eyes whir and his fingers press down. "I can't . . . die . . . ," he says in a haggard whisper. "You . . ."

He squeezes and I can't breathe, struggling but he's too heavy—

Suddenly his eyes brighten from blue to white. Sparks shoot and his eyes hiss and spin.

His whole body begins to glow, and though his mouth is still moving, no more sound comes out.

"You want to know what it feels like to be a god?" Rana hisses from inside him. "I will show you."

Paul grows brighter. His eyes go dark, but everything else is dissolving into light, his face and hair and shirt and tie, his hands that were on my neck, all become a ghostly shimmer and his face looks almost ecstatic, his mouth wide-open, before it is erased in light.

He rises off me, and Rana brightens more and Paul is lost to light, lost to energy, and his body disintegrates in glowing dust, like fireflies, all flying free.

And he is gone.

"Live bright," I whisper, and I watch the light swarm away. . . .

Actually, it all flows in the same direction. Toward the doors. And as it does, I become aware of a sucking sound and a breeze tugging me in that same direction.

"Attention, *Egress* citizens"—the pleasant female voice returns with no more urgency than ever—"please return immediately to your staterooms. All personnel in the forward labs please proceed with a code white. Repeat—"

Her last words are drowned out by a wicked shriek of twisting metal. And the sucking sound increases.

"Lük," Rana hisses, "how did you get in here?"

The control room glass cracks in a spiderweb pattern.

"Well," says Lük, glancing that way, "I didn't think there was time to sneak in, so I came through the wall."

Another groan of metal. The sucking breeze becoming a roaring wind.

"Warning to all forward lab personnel: code white. Hull breach," says the female voice. "Evacuate or report to life pods immediately. Forward lab will be ejected from *Egress* core in thirty seconds."

"You blew a hole in the wall," says Kael. "Subtle."

"But it's an easy way out," says Lük.

The control room glass bursts backward over the consoles, and a furious wind begins spiraling out of the lab, pulling me with it.

"Not for someone who needs air," Rana says, and Lük looks at me.

"Oh, right. Him."

Owen, quickly.

I turn to the Terra.

Free me, and I can protect you.

"Okay, how?" I have to shout over the wind and now it claws at my clothes and hair as I get to my feet. It increases so quickly that suddenly I am yanked backward, staggering against its force.

The question.

"I don't know—" I am dragged into the air, slamming against the robotic armature. "The question!"

The room begins to upend. No, it's gravity failing. The Terra's cube begins to float. Glass shards swirl around the room like an ice storm, and the wind becomes overwhelming and everything is moving toward the door. The walls buckle. Groan. Tear. Everything collapsing and pulling and I lose my footing and topple back over myself and see the white of the lab and then, far too close, the black of space. All the walls have ripped open, are peeling wider by the moment. In the last second, I reach for the bag with Lilly's skull, snaring it with my fingers as it bobs in the air. And then I am gaining speed, already feeling short of breath and cold. Colder than I have ever felt. Space.

It is going to happen in an instant. I grab for anything, but my hands only slap off other broken shrapnel. Everything spins. . . .

"Hang on, Owen." I feel a current enter me that resists the cold and the vacuum and it is Rana, filling me. "I can get you to the ship, I think."

We right, and I am gazing forward at a gaping hole in the ship's layers and the glitter of space beyond that. We shoot forward like a missile, along with the broken glass and chunks of machinery. Flashes as Lük and Kael blur past me.

Cold wraps around me and seems to squeeze, and at the same time my insides want to expand, my eyes to freeze, my breath to disappear, and I feel like I'll surely be crushed, but Rana's energy is there like a candle in a blizzard, keeping me with her.

And then we are out. Into space. Black in all directions except down. There is earth, the beautiful blue and green and brown, shrouded in wisps of clouds.

Ahead I see the Atlantean ship, hovering with a glow of blue fire beneath it. It is an impossible sight, an oblong shape of gleaming ancient metal reflecting the brilliant light of the sun. We are racing toward it, toward an open hatch in the back. Lük and Kael are already there waiting, phantom arms outstretched.

"Almost there," says Rana, and she reaches and finds Lük's hand, and he pulls us into a small chamber barely big enough for us all to stand in.

The Terra, I try to say, but there are no words in the vacuum.

Kael is pointing, too.

Rana and I turn to see the Terra's cage floating among the debris. Kael shoots out to it and puts his shoulder to it, pushing it in our direction.

As we watch, the entire front spindle of the *Egress* detaches, its compartments one by one going dark. There are little bursts here and there along its arms, survival pods, jettisoning. One is clipped by the tumbling carcass and explodes.

I see, too, starlike shapes spinning among the wreckage that I realize are people. Those who didn't make it to the pods in time.

Beyond them, *Egress* spins on, serene in the light of the sun, and I wonder what will become of those people, now, without their heart.

Lük pulls on Rana, and we float up to the ceiling as the cube lands in the compartment with us. Kael flies in and Lük shuts the door, twisting a lever in a circular motion. Then he pulls another lever, and there is a hissing sound, and a feeling of warmth.

The compartment is filling with air, and I feel my lungs wanting to work again. Lük opens an inner door and we float inside, Lük and Kael moving the Terra into the center of the cabin, between the ancient chairs.

"Okay," Lük says. "Time to head home." He shoots through the forward door and into a pilot's chair. Rana and Kael join him and I push off the wall, floating after them. Kael spins the wheel and pulls levers. There is a hum from beneath our feet and the craft shoots off, angling downward. The wide curve of the earth appears out the front windshield.

"Now we just have to hope these tiles still hold up to the heat of reentry," says Lük.

I look at Rana. "Thank you," I say. I float back, pulling Lilly's skull from the bag. I want to feel its smooth crystal in my hands. The skull grins back at me, dark, a cruel joke.

"I did not mean for her to speak to you like that," says Rana, "but it has maybe turned out better this way."

I nod but couldn't feel less sure. For a moment I feel a surge of anger at Lük for blowing the ship open to rescue us. If it wasn't for him . . . but the thoughts stop there. Lilly didn't want to be brought back. She would have hated me if I'd gone through with it. Living on *Egress* with a Lilly who hated me might have been a worse fate than whatever would happen now. Maybe.

"Lük, watch out!" Kael shouts.

Lük slams pedals and works the wheel and the ship spins. I am tossed against the ceiling as the first missile from *Egress* barely misses us.

"There are more!" says Rana, pointing out the crystal windshield. "Apparently the good people of *Egress* are not content to let their Terra go."

Two more streaks of light curve away from *Egress*.

"Okay . . ." Lük pushes a large main lever forward and up, while depressing floor pedals.

"It's too slow," says Kael as the missiles close.

I look at the second seat in the cockpit, at the second wheel. I grab the back of the ancient leather seat and slide myself in. "Maybe it needs a second pilot." I hand Rana the skull and affix a leather belt across my waist.

I feel a flood of relief as my fingers touch the wheel and my feet hit the pedals. Flying feels like some kind of home. I test the wheel in front of me. "I think it controls a lateral set of thrusters."

"That will help," says Lük.

"Hurry," Rana urges.

I see the closer missile bearing down on our port side, and I steer while pressing the rightmost of the two pedals at my feet.

We roll into a steep sideways dive and the missile sails by.

"Well done," says Lük. He pushes us into a climb, and I add a roll to the left, and the second missile sails under us.

"This is cool," I say, feeling simple excitement for the first time in who knows how long. No worries, just the calm of action and reaction, doing the thing I love.

"They're coming back around," says Kael.

The missiles draw fiery curves in the dark.

Lük and I share a glance. "Down," he says.

He pitches the craft and the earth comes into view. We angle toward it, the foggy blue of the atmosphere getting closer.

I check out the window and see the first missile closing. "And . . . ," I say, and roll us sideways. The earth appears above us as the missile sails beneath. Before it can turn, it skims the atmosphere, lighting up bright red and disintegrating in a trail of embers.

"Where's the other one?" Lük cranes his neck as we right.

"If we can't see it . . . ," I say, rolling us back over and trying to look behind us.

Lük yanks the lever and we spring upward.

Too late. There is a hideous explosion and a twisting of metal that all too quickly becomes silent, sucked away by the vacuum of space.

I look back and see the ship contorting, little moments of fire bursting and sucking out.

"The hull is breached," says Lük matter-of-factly. Maybe that's not an issue for someone who can't die, but for me, it's a problem. He works at the controls but we begin to arc downward, the earth rising to meet us and filling our entire view.

"At this steep an angle," Lük adds, "we'll burn."

More twisting and contorting behind us. Out front, the hull starts to glow red. Ahead of us, clouds and blue sea, but we'll be a shooting star long before that. I jam at the pedals, spin the wheel, but nothing happens.

"No use," says Lük. "Systems are wrecked."

"What do we do?" I shout.

The windshield begins to glow. Sparks shoot from the controls in front of us. Flames ignite in front of the ship and create a curtain of fire. I can feel the heat on my face.

Owen, to me.

"The Terra!" I flail to get the belt off. "Come on!" I grab Lilly's skull back from Rana and shoot out of the cabin, but now there is suction from the back of the craft. I see fissures opening in the metal, their edges melting. Everything is beginning to glow in a molten red, the craft disintegrating on all sides.

The suction makes my speed too great, and my hand glances off the Terra. Suddenly I am past it, careening toward the collapsing back of the ship.

"Owen!" Rana grabs my hand. She is holding on to the Terra. Kael helps to drag me back until I am against the side of the crystal cage, trying desperately to hold tight to its smooth edges with my fingertips, while still keeping Lilly's skull under my arm.

The question . . . says the Terra.

"I don't know it!" I shout.

That is because I must ask it, and you must do what the world has forgotten how to do . . . what was oldest must be new, and what was lost must be found. The secret remembered by the true.

Like the Terra's first words to me, beneath Lake Eden.

All that is required to free me is the power to resist all that you know I offer and to believe in what is right. The question is simple. As is the answer.

The ship is on fire around us. The heat all consuming. I feel my skin starting to blister.

"Hurry," Rana urges. Her grip on my arm is slipping.

Ask me, I say.

The Terra's ancient eyes meet mine. And she asks: *Will you let me go?*

It is a simple question, but when she asks it, I know why it has never been answered. If I let go of the Heart of the Terra, I must let go of life, eternal life, of the ultimate power. I must accept my own end, and the end of others, and of . . . I look down at the skull.

This is me, letting you go.

If I say yes, this will be good-bye for real.

Not just the Terra. Lilly. Elissa. The past. But also the future. The chance to have Lilly back. This is . . . letting go.

All of it.

And when I think of everything, the good and the bad, I wonder almost cruelly if all the suffering I've endured has actually made me ready for this. Because . . .

I am ready. I look into the Terra's blinding, ageless eyes.

Will you let—

"Yes."

There is so much heat and fire and wind already from the last breaths of air escaping our doomed ship and the light that bursts from the Terra blinds me completely.

The geometry of the crystal cage melts away, and the light shoots in all directions, and there, free, is the ancient girl who found me on a lake bottom, who called me through the depths. She opens her eyes, her old and new eyes, and smiles.

Thank you.

She is radiant and warm or maybe that is the heat of us burning, and I feel like I am light and she is light.

Come close, my children, and I will bring you home.

The Terra spreads her arms and somehow she is wrapping Rana and Lük and Kael and me within her light, and the heat of reentry recedes, and the need for oxygen recedes, and the black of space and the smell of melting leather and the feelings of emptiness and despair and loss and the orange of melting metal fade as we become a star falling to earth. . . .

I feel a weightlessness as my legs and arms seem to lose meaning, but this sets off a distant panic on the shores of my body and I gaze down to see that I am no longer holding the skull, Lilly's skull. My hands are still there, sketched in light, but the skull no longer inhabits them, it is weightless and dissolving, its polished surface ceasing to be, and inside, the complex alchemy of its circuitry is finally revealed in rainbow blooms of color, reds and blues and yellows with green and violet margins, blossoms connected and mingling, essence and intelligence, and it is bleeding into the white light that is now me, is now all of us.

I know that is Lilly, that energy, that color, but it is dissipating and I would panic if I had a heart or nerves or chemicals anymore, but I am just light and warmth, and it is peace.

Thank you, the Terra says again. *Now tell me, children, what do you wish?*

To linger no more, says Rana, and I feel Lük and Kael agree. The three, who have finally succeeded.

What do you wish? she asks me.

I can't. What I wish is impossible. All I do is look down at the colors, separating, the skull melted and gone. Lilly.

I wish . . .

And then all is a rush of air and light and a deafening sound like the wind from the dawn of the universe in my ears and there is light, light, and a whisper . . .

Good-bye . . .

Good-bye . . .

Good-bye.

26

WE ARE BREEZES, ROAMING THE EARTH, OVER SEAS and mountains and wastelands and jungles.

The Terra is no longer a girl. She is pollen made of light, riding the currents of wind around the planet, drifting down like snow, landing on every surface, skin, rock, and sea, and melting into it in tiny bursts of color. Blue, yellow, red, with lavender and green and orange margins.

In the parts of the world that are awake to see it, they name the passing cloud of light and its magical rain Tears of God, Rain of Souls, or solar magnetic anomaly.

In the wreckage of Heliad-7, they believe it is the Brocha de Dioses, and they hail the victory of the Three.

Everyone and everything is touched, and that day, we are silent, and we think. We wonder. We question.

A man has a conversation with a turtle and starts a religion.

Most people's reactions are more down-to-earth.

Life spins on. In the cells of infected humans, the latest pandemic continues to multiply and spread. In the milky Pacific, the nanoglobules of plastic continue to coalesce in a foggy sludge. In a severe concrete conference room in New Helsinki, politicians still bicker over the definition of "genocide." In a shadowy alleyway of the sunken Manhattan technopolis, a knife pierces a heart in a scuffle over a can of food.

But.

The wind keeps cycling, and the light keeps falling, the colors absorbed as the Terra returns, her song coming home to every cell; and in another place, a scientist sees the vaccine for the pandemic in the pattern of a leaf bud. In the silted depths of the Mariana Trench, a bacteria mutates and its offspring develop a random protein that allows them to metabolize plastic sludge. In the bloodstained palace of the warlord known as the Butcher of the Black Sea, a waking dream leads to a shed tear. In the alleyway in New Manhattan, the assailant still flees but calls for help before she does.

Around the spinning spheroid, its existence and qualities a coincidence of size, distance from a star, and galactic location, there is more silence and more knowing.

That we are the comet dust cryo patients of the big bang.

We are nature, someone said.

That we, each, are alive in this moment, together, not alone.

And I feel like I am a part of everyone and all things at once and forever.

Wind in our faces. Flying free.

27

FOR A WHILE.

Owen.

There is a small light in the distance, a pale blue, struggling through the murk.

Good-bye, it whispers.

I blink. Pressure against my eyes. A blur of green.

Water.

The view upward wobbles. There are blocky shapes and lines that vibrate in the waves like strings.

A dock.

Lane lines.

Above, there is light and a pattern of triangular lines, some enormous structure, like a curving ceiling or . . .

A dome.

Slippery plants coil around my legs, slide along my arms. The water is cold, but a fake kind of cold, perfectly controlled.

Something reflects in the water. That blue glow. I

move my head, and at the same time become suddenly aware of the pressure on my lungs.

A shape emerges from the greenish-brown water, swimming toward me. Large, globe-like eyes and a shimmering body.

A siren—

Or, a fish. A big, fat, fish.

They're just big dopes, she said. Or did she?

Zombie koi.

In Lake Eden.

But . . . how can I be here?

The fish regards me. I wave my arms, which feel so weak, so spent, and the movement startles the beast. It darts backward, its tail stirring up a cloud of brown particles, creating camouflage. After sizing me up for another moment, the fish decides I'm not worth the trouble and slips away into the gloom.

The pressure in my chest increases. Have to breathe. Need air. There has been no air for—*weeks*—too long and the body can only survive like four minutes without oxygen, I read it in a book, but my hernia—*cryo scar* . . . strange thoughts, memories or dreams, I can't tell, keep bleeding in—is cramping and I should never have taken that stupid swim test.

I scan the surface, looking for a streak of red on the dock. For Lilly. She needs to see me, needs to know I drowned. She's a lifeguard, the only one who can save me from this foolish choice.

But the dock is still. Little waves from the breeze make the lane lines shimmer, but that's all. No one swimming. No one splashing.

The need to breathe is overwhelming. *Go ahead, just use your gills*. But those are gone. Or were they ever there to begin with? But I have to breathe *now* or I'm going to drown—

No. I slam my hands down on the lake bottom and push myself up. I get my feet under me and thrust against the muck as hard as I can. I will not just lie down here and die, a pathetic turtle—*Ana*—on its back. I can save myself.

I shoot upward, through the brown and green and toward the mirror top of the lake, my chest ready to explode, kicking, cramp burning, and I burst free, my face into the air, sucking in a breath and slapping my arms against the surface to keep from dunking under again.

I squint in the light of the SafeSun lamps. It seems harsher than it had been, when we came down to the dock for the test. And where are my cabinmates? Leech? Beaker? Bunsen?

My ribs ache and I nearly slip back under, but ahead of me is the giant blue side of the trampoline raft. Just have to get there. I kick and thrash my arms, never the best swimmer to begin with. *I never should have taken this test!* but that still seems wrong. . . .

I grab the yellow ropes that stripe the sides, trying to pull myself up.

Just launch out of the water. The thought passes by but it makes no sense. More strange memories, or are they dreams? I can't tell. Right now I need to keep kicking, to drag myself up onto the rubber, but my cramp is killing me, and I'm starting to get that tingling in my legs, like I do when the pain is overwhelming and they shut down, and my fingers slip from the rough ropes. I'm sliding back in . . .

Hands lock on my wrists.

"Grab on to me."

I do and I pull and kick and am yanked up, belly whining against the rubber, and I'm on the raft, in a puddle of lake water.

I roll over on my back, gasping. And then bolt up to face my savior.

Lilly.

She is sitting back on her heels. Lilly Ishani, lifeguard and one of the CITs here at camp. "You okay?" she asks, breathless.

"Yeah," I say, "thanks for saving me." *Lilly saves me. I don't drown.*

Lilly dies in the ice.

Thoughts are lining up out of order, new, old, real, imagined. "I—" I start to say.

Lilly stares at me. Her eyes are huge, clear, seeing me. I realize now that she is soaking wet. And wearing jeans and a tank top and sweatshirt, all filthy, not her red life-guard bathing suit. I look down and see that I am in gray pants and an olive-green shirt.

Lilly nods over my shoulder. "We're here."

The docks are empty. So is the beach. The play fields of Camp Eden silent, no movement on the hilltop by the dining hall. No flag waving on the flagpole.

I turn and see a plume of gray smoke in the direction of the EdenWest city. Above, no TruSky or SimClouds, the SafeSun lamps naked and fake. There are cracks in the dome. Some burned-out panels have fallen away, revealing triangles of lethal blue sky.

As I gaze from one to the next, I notice the tiny square in my vision.

The eye I traded for a chance to bring Lilly back . . .

Okay. My thoughts quiet.

It all happened.

And this is real . . . unless . . . I stare hard at my hand, and poke it. Solid. We are not inside a skull.

Lilly coughs. I turn back to her. She's wringing out her hair. "Why did I wake up on the bottom of a lake?" she wonders.

"This is where the Terra left us," I say. "Given some of the places we've been, it's not so bad." As I say this, though, my brain finally starts to catch up to my racing heart. "We . . . but, Lilly, you . . ."

She gazes at me, and seems like she's about to speak, but tears fall instead.

Lilly is here. The Terra . . .

What do you wish?

I stumble toward her on my knees, the raft bouncing us awkwardly, and I almost fall over—

But I reach her.

I reach her and I grab her and hold her as tight as I can. I feel her breath on my neck and her wet hair against my face and it's Lilly, it's Lilly, it's Lilly.

Alive.

The wind seems to speak. *Thank you, Owen.*

And this is really me? I ask. And this is really Lilly . . .

Yes.

And why are we here?

This is the place where you chose to be true, to the Terra, to yourself. And you have been true, Owen. Now, live well.

And I know then that the Terra will never speak to me again. But she doesn't have to. I will hear her. Her music has returned to us all.

"You okay?" Lilly asks, as if she should be the one asking such a thing.

Except then I realize that I have hitched up, breath stuck, and that tears are spilling out, though only from my one eye.

"I love you," I say.

She breathes long and slow. "Tenth time," she says.

I will never know how she heard the seventh through the ninth.

"I love you, too."

We hug for a while. We kiss so hard we bang teeth, and we both taste like lake water.

"Also," Lilly says, "we kinda did it, didn't we?"

"Yeah," I say, looking around. "Somehow, we did." A flood of adrenaline washes through me, a mix of relief, happiness, guilt. "There's so much that happened. And the choices I made, things I want to say . . ." And these thoughts are just a door to so much more, the things I did, the people we lost . . . "If it hadn't been for you," I say, "I don't know if—"

Lilly puts a finger to my lips. "Later. Maybe."

"Okay."

We kiss again and I pull back just enough to glance toward shore. "Where are we going to go?" I remember the reports of this Eden having a revolt. Will the camp or the city be safe to get supplies? And where to after that? We could look for Nomads or head north. We could make for Yellowstone, try to find out if my parents are alive.

And who will we be in this new world? I feel different inside. Is everyone feeling this? This sense of *belonging*? And how will we all react? The wars, the devastation, even the selectees on *Egress* . . . what will happen now?

Lilly shrugs. "We'll go somewhere," she says. "Sometime." She takes my hand. "But later."

We lie back on the warm raft, and let our heads hang off the edge, our hands entwined, our shoulders and hips touching. We stare up at the ceiling of the dome, at the Eye, at the holes to the sky. Outside is the new world, but for now we are here.

The SafeSun dries our clothes and makes us shut our eyes, and we fall in and out of sleep, and kiss again later, and lie there some more.

"Now is what I want," I say.

We listen to the plunks of water beneath the raft and to the rustle of the leaves as desert breezes howl through the cracks in the walls. We listen to our breaths amplified by the raft, and smell the metallic brown of the lake, and feel the heat of the rubber, and we watch as a butterfly drops down and regards us with its camera eye, and all of it is music, and we feel like forever, and we never feel alone.

ACKNOWLEDGMENTS

IF YOU FIND YOURSELF ON THIS PAGE BECAUSE you read this whole series, thank you. If at any point during the journey you dropped me a line or wrote a review or took a moment to tell me what you thought, thank you five times more. You helped me to make this the best it could be. If I could charter a seaworthy vessel and take you all on a trip to Antarctica, believe me, done deal.

Also thanks to Katherine and Katie and everyone at Harper, to George and Caitlin and the team at Sterling Lord, to my friends and family and the librarians and booksellers and teachers who have been so generous. I had a blast. I hope you did, too.

FACT or FANTASY
in the Atlanteans series
By Kevin Emerson

I'm a big fan of science fiction and fantasy. How big? I can't make fish sticks without calling them fish fingers and custard, I refer to the night sky as "the black," and I always make time for second breakfast (well, technically more like elevenses). I was also a K–8 science teacher for many years, and a biology major in college. So, I love writing stories that blend both real science concepts and fantasy elements.

In the Atlanteans series, I got to explore so many cool ideas! While many parts of the series are pretty obviously fantasy, there are a number of interesting science concepts at work. So the question is: which ones are which? To find out, let's play FACT OR FANTASY! And any words that you see in **bold** are definitely worth looking up to learn more!

QUESTION #1:

In The Lost Code, *Owen and others at camp spontaneously grow gills. Is this possibility FACT or FANTASY?*

ANSWER: This is FANTASY, but there are four interesting concepts I was thinking about:

1. **Gill Slits:** Human embryos do have structures that look like gills, and these are called gill slits. These, of course, do not develop into gills, and so scientists are debating whether it is even accurate to call them this. Still, some people think these gill slits are a leftover echo of the long-ago animals we evolved from, kind of like how we have a **vestigial tail**.

2. **Junk DNA:** Later, Owen is told that the Atlantean skull activated parts of his "dormant" or "junk" DNA and is making his evolutionary clock spin out of control. This is what caused him to grow gills. Triggering such changes is fantasy, too, but we do have large areas of our DNA that seem to be inactive, and there is a lot of speculation as to what "dormant" genes do or did. I wanted to play with the concept that our DNA is our connection to the past, almost like a history book of how we evolved.

3. **Metamorphosis:** Later in the book, when Lilly thinks about how Owen's gills came and went so quickly, she refers to how some frogs can go through a metamorphosis from gill breathers to lung breathers in only twenty-four hours. This really happens! There are a number of other animals (notably insects) that perform such feats. This concept also served a theme in the book about how our bodies change without our control (you may have noticed that Owen's gill-growing happens right about the

time that teens experience many bodily changes). Those changes affect who we are, what role we play in a community (like the camp kids), and how we see ourselves.

4. **Selective Pressure:** Finally, there is a concept called selective pressure, which has to do with how the environment causes species to change. Since the world in the Atlanteans is changing so rapidly, I wanted to touch on this idea that after we change the environment, the environment might change us.

QUESTION #2:

In The Lost Code, *the earth has suffered from the Great Rise. Owen describes many facets of this: oceans rising, wars, plagues. Obviously the Great Rise is in the future, but is the possibility of such a thing based in FACT or FANTASY?*

ANSWER: Obviously the Great Rise that has destroyed the world in the Atlanteans is something I imagined happening in the future and is not real, but most of the concepts behind the Rise are FACT. (That said, it's extremely unlikely that they would all happen simultaneously over the next fifty years! The Great Rise is like a "perfect storm" of climate catastrophe.) Still, let's talk about the four main concepts behind the Great Rise:

1. **Sea Level Rise:** If all the ice in the world melted, it would raise the ocean level about two hundred feet. Even the most worried scientists don't think the Antarctic ice will melt anytime soon. But the Arctic ice and Greenland ice could definitely melt (and they have in *The Lost Code*). This would raise the sea level by about twenty feet. Doesn't sound like that much, but it's enough, when combined with severe storms, to wreak havoc on, if not ruin, the major coastal cities. And that's not all: over two hundred million people live along the world's coasts, and nearly 45 percent of the *world's* population live within about sixty miles of the coast. So think about what would happen if all these people needed to move . . . where would they go? The problem starts to get scary, especially if it happens faster than humans can respond with new places to live.

2. **Desertification:** The second huge problem with the planet warming is that warmer air can hold more water vapor (that's why it feels so humid in the summer). The warmer it gets, the more water will stay in the atmosphere, and the more places will dry out and become deserts. This is already happening in much of the southwest of the United States. So not only would there be fewer places to live because of ocean rise, there would be fewer places to live because large areas are becoming deserts. And

because rain has to fall somewhere, other areas are becoming tropics with dangerous monsoon and hurricane seasons, soil too wet to farm, not to mention new strains of disease.

3. **Ozone Depletion:** Not directly related to global warming (but related to humans' effect on the environment) the ozone layer is decreasing steadily over time. This is the part of the atmosphere that protects us from harmful sun rays like **UVB**, which you will see mentioned these days on sunscreen bottles. In *The Lost Code*, the ozone has been depleted so badly that being in the sun is dangerous, which is why everyone wears No Rad lotion.

4. **Pandemics:** So, if all these people have nowhere to live, things are going to get pretty crowded. And places with bad health conditions, like in refugee camps and crowded slums, are prime breeding grounds for diseases. In *The Dark Shore*, we learn that there have been at least six major pandemics, which are outbreaks of diseases that affect the whole world.

NOTE: Those last few paragraphs are pretty scary! So I just want to remind you: it's super unlikely that all these things will happen at once or that fast. This is a FICTIONAL world. So don't panic, but also learn what you can do to help keep our world safe for our future.

QUESTION #3:

In The Dark Shore, *much of the action later in the book revolves around the idea of the cryos, which is short for* **cryogenics.** *Is this idea based in FACT or FANTASY?*

ANSWER: This idea is based in FACT, and is one of the big ideas for how we might send humans out across space someday, but scientists have yet to successfully use cryogenics to freeze and reanimate a human (that process would technically be called **cryopreservation**). There are places where you can have your body (or just your head!) frozen, but those companies aren't entirely sure how to unfreeze you yet!

The biggest danger from freezing living tissue is the damage done when ice crystals form. Much of the research around cryopreservation involves finding chemicals that can be used to allow freezing without ice, but that also won't poison the tissue. So far, scientists have frozen things like human eggs, semen, embryos, and plant tissues.

Did you know there are animals in the world that successfully freeze and unfreeze during the winter? This is called **freeze tolerance.** There are a few amphibians, reptiles and single celled organisms that can do this. They pull this off by replacing the water in their cells with sugar.

QUESTION #4:

In The Dark Shore, *we encounter the second* **crystal skull**. *Are these crystals skulls FACT or FANTASY?*

ANSWER: Crystal skulls exist, but their origin and power are definitely FANTASY. The first crystal skull seems to have appeared in the late 1800s and was sold to the British Museum. This was during the age of adventurers looking for lost civilizations. The skull was rumored to be **Mesoamerican** in origin (likely Aztec). The most famous crystal skull is the **Mitchell-Hedges** skull, discovered in the 1940s.

Crystal skulls have been thought to be special talismans, alien in origin, and, you guessed it, relics from ancient Atlantis! In recent decades, these skulls have been examined and tested and determined fairly conclusively to be hoaxes that were created in modern times. All that said, I think they're spooky and cool, and I liked that idea that they could be objects that held Atlantean memory. Plus it would be creepy to find one glowing in a hidden temple!

QUESTION #5:

In The Far Dawn, *Paul says that our ancestors were microbes that traveled by comets, making the case that life on earth came from the stars. Is this idea based in FACT or FANTASY?*

ANSWER: This idea is based in FACT, or more

accurately, on as-of-yet unproven scientific theory, specifically the theory of **panspermia** or **exogenesis**. Some scientists have theorized that the first building blocks of life on earth, either organic molecules or primitive bacteria, arrived here on meteors or comets from older parts of the universe.

There are theories that the complexity of life may have taken longer than the age of the earth (which is about 4.5 billion years) to develop, while the **age of the universe** may be more like 13.8 billion years. Just based on those numbers, the idea seems possible (and fascinating!) to me, which is why I used it.

QUESTION #6:

In The Far Dawn, *the Paintbrush of the Gods uses fault lines to cause volcanic eruptions that will cool the planet down. Is this idea based in FACT or FANTASY?*

ANSWER: This is FANTASY, but again, I was thinking about a few fascinating concepts:

1. **The Ring of Fire:** The Atlanteans have placed the Paintbrush on a connected series of fault lines that is called the Ring of Fire. If you look at a map of the **tectonic plates** of the earth's crust, you will see this ring extending up along the western side of South America, North America, then around the southern coast of Alaska, and down the eastern coast of Asia.

These fault lines are areas of intense geologic activity (usually **subduction zones**). The Ring of Fire has over four hundred volcanoes—that's 75 percent of the active volcanoes in the entire world! If you could somehow set off all or many of those volcanoes at once, you could definitely change the planet. Unfortunately the Ring of Fire is also where 90 percent of the world's largest earthquakes occur, so you'd be likely to cause some other trouble as well (as the Atlanteans did).

2. **Terraforming:** Why would the Atlanteans want to make volcanoes erupt? They were trying to change the atmosphere to stop climate change. This was an ancient version of terraforming, which is the concept of altering a planet to make it better suited for life. Right now, scientists are trying to figure out how to terraform Mars, or other destinations in our solar system. Large volcanic eruptions could have the effect of cooling the atmosphere. You can probably guess why: the clouds of volcanic ash would block out the sun. The Atlanteans planned to harness the power of hundreds of volcanoes at once to blanket the earth in a cooling cloud, to stop their cities from flooding. The problem with volcanic eruptions is they can also have the opposite effect: by releasing carbon dioxide into the atmosphere, they can warm the planet. Or, by releasing lots of sulfur

dioxide, cause dangerous acid rains. I'm not sure the Atlanteans knew exactly what they were getting themselves into!

3. **Holocene Thermal Maximum**: But why were the ancient Atlantean cities flooding? Based on the reading I'd done about Atlantis, from Plato's ideas to newer books, it seemed like the Atlantean civilization would have most likely existed around ten thousand years ago, so roughly 8,000 B.C. This is an important date in the research I did about climate change, known as the Holocene Thermal Maximum. The Holocene is an epoch, or geologic time period, that spans from the last great ice ages until recently. (Some scientists argue that we should call our modern era the start of the **Anthropocene** epoch.) In the middle of the Holocene, there was a period of global warming not unlike ours, called the Holocene Thermal Maximum. During this time, it is theorized that great floods took place that very ancient humans witnessed. It is possible that global warming during this period was the cause of the many **flood myths** that exist in different cultures. This became the foundation idea for the entire Atlanteans trilogy: ancient people fighting against the same thing that we're fighting against now (and will be in the future, like Owen).

Thanks for playing FACT OR FANTASY! There are many other possible topics for this game throughout the Atlanteans trilogy. If you ever want to ask me about one, write to me on Facebook, Twitter, or by email: telegramforkevin@gmail.com.

And a special thank you to the following teen readers who gave me great feedback on this section: Abby, Samantha, Ethan, Ti'anna, Brendan, Colin, Max, Josh, and Annie. You rock!

Want more fantastic fiction from Kevin Emerson?
Read on for an excerpt from

EXILE

Formerly Orchid @catherinefornevr 5m
Former phenom band manager dines on nachos alone, or close enough.
Across town, other life proceeds without her. #pityparty #goingincircles

Just after dinner on the night before the start of senior year, Dad polishes off his guacamole garden burger, looks at me seriously, and asks, "So, now what, then?"

Tonight is also my eighteenth birthday, which means that I've known my dad for six thousand five hundred and seventy days, and so I probably should know that he means this question to sound supportive. Concerned, but supportive.

But my heart races, and all I can hear is *I told you so.*

"I don't know, yet," I reply, shoving the last chunk of burrito into my mouth.

"Honey, it's senior year," adds Mom, whom I've presumably known for about nine months longer, and who I know means to sound supportive, too. But Mom wears her worry on every word.

"I've heard," I say around food.

Now what. . . . Senior year is supposed to be the culmination, the big finale of an epic journey, but given our surroundings, I wonder if I'm going in circles instead.

We sit in a red-vinyl booth, hunched over a linoleum table decorated with a cliché painting of the Mexican desert. Around us blink the jalapeno-shaped lights and other assorted kitsch of La Burrita Feminista. Freshman year, I brought my five closest friends here for a birthday party, complete with poppers and present bags and personal piñatas, but invitations for this year's celebration went only to my parents and my aunt Jeanine. Maybe I'm not just going in circles. Maybe this is actually a downward spiral, like into a black hole.

My parents normally prefer something a little more sanitized than a radical feminist burrito bar, especially when it means driving all the way into Hollywood. And normally I'd prefer not to be spending my birthday with my parents. But I think they sensed that I had no other options, and found it in their hearts to make the effort, even if Dad defiantly ordered a garden burger at a Mexican joint.

Also, Aunt Jeanine loves this place. My parents think it's because she's secretly a lesbian. I'm more inclined to think it's because: a) she knows a good burrito and a fun atmosphere, two things my parents couldn't possibly comprehend, and because b) regardless of her orientation, she knows that men are vermin.

Dessert arrives before my parents' line of questioning can continue. Feminista has this crazy cake that you're supposed to split called the *Orgasmo de Cacao*. Any other night, I'd share one, but anticipation about tomorrow and a series of tweets I've been getting all evening have me wolfing down a whole one myself. Mom and Jeanine are sharing one, and Dad got, for dessert—I kid you not—a side salad.

As we dig in, I read tweets on my phone from all the people over at the Hatch, the best all-ages club in Silver Lake. They're seeing a band called Postcards from Ariel. Tonight's show is their North American tour kickoff. Thirty dates, coast to coast, celebrating the release of their new album, *Dispatch*. Postcards is from my high school. They graduated last year.

And they used to be mine.

I was planning to spend tonight at that show. Back when it was just the next show on the calendar. Back before Postcards got signed by Candy Shell Records, who subsequently rerecorded the album we'd been working on all spring, booked them a nationwide tour and, oh, fired their former management company, Orchid Productions, aka me.

One could argue, if one wasn't busy eating a two-pound skillet of chocolate cake, that I was the reason Postcards got that record deal, the reason there was big interest in them even after only one EP last fall. Those awesome rocket-ship mailbox T-shirts? Yours truly.

One could also argue that their lead singer, Ethan Myers, and I had something special.